A Sweet, Nerdy Romantic Comedy

LOVE IN THE STACKS

JULIE MILO

www.juliemilo.com

Cover Design and Illustrations by Sydney Christensen Creations

ISBN: 9798991947107

To myself. You did it! Fourteen-year-old you is jumping for joy right now. You wrote and published a book. Even if only three people ever read it, your book is out there in the world. I'm so, so proud of you.

Also, for Andy - ours is my favorite love story.

Author's Note

This novel is light, sweet, and funny—it's a romcom after all—but the characters deal with tough things in their lives just like real people. Here are some topics that are a part of this book:

Sudden death of a parent (in the past)

Emotional abuse in a relationship (in the past)

Depressive episodes (in the past)

Anxiety-fueled spiraling thoughts

BUT no characters die in this book, including animals, and there is no sex or other graphic scenes.

Chapter One

Nicole

"**L**ook good, feel good," I say aloud to my reflection in the mirror.

I need today to go perfectly at work, so I'm starting with my outfit, hair, and makeup on point. I carefully picked out the wide-leg trousers with subtle blue and white plaid stripes with a light gray background and paired them with a bright red eyelet blouse over a black cami. Silver ballet flats finish the look. It may be overkill for my position as a librarian at a small-town college, but I'm dressing to impress today.

I smooth over my hair with one hand as I give my reflection a final once-over. My naturally blonde hair is straight and chin-length, but for the last three months, it's also been a soft purple color. I might change over to a new color before long, but so far, I really love the lavender. I know that colorful hair styles are at odds with what many people picture when they think of a librarian—most are still envisioning an older woman with gray hair pulled up in a bun, cat-eyeglasses on a beaded chain, and a scowling face all wrapped up in a cardigan sweater. But that's not me, nor is it most of the real-life librarians I've worked with.

Okay, I do love a nice cardigan.

Today at our all-staff library meeting, I'm going to suggest adding a graphic novel collection, hence the nerves I'm trying to shake. Not sure you can get much farther from a 1950s shushing librarian than that.

I've worked at Parker Library on the Harkness College campus for about a year now, and while my boss, Herb, has been supportive and open-minded, the library—and the college itself—tend to lag a bit behind the times. I've prepared my case for why a graphic novel collection would be beneficial, including citing examples of libraries at larger colleges and universities that have done the same, but I'm not sure what kind of reception to expect.

I glance around my apartment to make sure I'm not forgetting anything, then I lock the door and practically skip down the steps in my nervous energy. I rent an apartment on the second floor of a converted bungalow three blocks from the college campus, and so far, I haven't needed a car. It's a relief for my bank account which is already balancing student loans in addition to typical things like rent, utilities, and food.

Adulting is hard.

I intend to spend the ten-minute walk to work in downtown St. Anastasia going over the bullet points of my proposal, but as

I breathe the early morning air, my senses are distracted by the picturesque scenes around me. The historic, downtown area that's home to Harkness College is flooded with tourists, restaurants, art galleries and museums, and cultural and historical sites, all right on the water. It has narrow, brick streets more reminiscent of European towns than a city in Florida. A typical suburban business district with box stores, fast food restaurants, and businesses surrounds the downtown area in short driving distance, but the character and personality of St. Anastasia all reside within the approximately ten square miles encompassing the official "city" limits.

I fell in love with those ten square miles and with the beautiful campus of Harkness College when I traveled from Texas to interview a year and a half ago. Before that, I had been working as an outreach librarian at the Austin Public Library, where I landed my first job out of library school—that is, my master's degree program for library and information science. A mixture of wanting something new outside of the city where I'd lived my whole life and a pull to be part of a college campus again had my eyes wandering to job ads for librarian positions in academia. Getting away from my long-term college boyfriend—now ex—was also pretty appealing at the time.

I scan my badge to open the back employee entrance to the library. As I enter the staff break room, my eyes land on Tasha, one of our regular student workers, with her eyes closed, resting her head on the table.

"Rough night?" I ask, nudging her gently.

She grumbles and lifts her head, shaking out her black curls. A crease from the table edge marks the deep brown skin across her forehead. "I had a paper due today that I may have put off until the last minute. I was up way too late finishing it."

"What about?"

"The intersection of feminism and race in theater in the 1990s," she responds, her brown eyes crinkling.

"Oh, so nothing too heavy?" I tease.

Tasha is an English major in her junior year with a minor in theater. She's considering a career in libraries, so she's around a lot, even when she's not working. She smiles. "Nah, just a BS piece really."

She eyes me up and down before adding, "You're dressed up today. Any reason?"

"Yes," I say breathily as I sit down next to her. "At the team meeting today, I'm going to pitch my graphic novel idea. I'm nervous but like an excited nervous."

"Oh, is that the idea you were talking about a couple of weeks ago? Starting a graphic novel collection?"

"Yeah. I love graphic novels, and I just see so many ways they could tie into the curriculum for the English, art, and even history courses. Plus, it would be a fun way to get students excited about the library."

"Sounds cool." Tasha grins. "Let me know if you need a student testimonial."

"You're teasing. But actually, that would be pretty helpful. Can you email me a quote?"

Just then, the cataloging librarian walks in, making a beeline for the coffeemaker with his mug.

"Good morning," he nods.

"Good morning, Alex," I respond. He cocks his head at me but doesn't say anything else.

As he leaves the room again, I can feel Tasha watching me. "What?" I ask.

"You know his name is Adam, right?" Her eyebrows rise as she puts a hand on her hip.

I groan and drop my forehead into my hands. "I do know that. What did I say?"

"Alex."

Great. Not only did I likely insult my colleague, but I will also now be replaying that interaction in my head for the rest of the day, reliving the embarrassment. I shake my head to clear my thoughts and change the subject. "How'd your paper turn out?" I ask Tasha.

She brightens. "Really good, I think. This was a pretty short one, and I wrote it pretty quick, but it's definitely a steppingstone to what I want to write for my senior thesis next year."

"Cool. Let me know how I can help as you work up to your senior thesis. Research, proofreading, whatever."

"I will." Tasha glances at the screen of her phone. "Ah, I need to get out to the circulation desk. My shift starts right now."

I nod as she sweeps her backpack off the table and we both stand. As she leaves the room, I open the refrigerator and set my lunchbox on the top shelf. I am scheduled to work the reference desk later this morning, but I can spend a few hours checking my email and polishing my pitch for the meeting first.

The Parker Library is a stand-alone, three-story building on the Harkness campus. Right now, I'm in the main staff work area, which has the back door out to the parking lot I used this morning, as well as an entrance leading in from the library itself. The staff area is just big enough to hold six offices, a break room, and a meeting room that can seat about fifteen people. As the newest librarian on staff, the office assigned to me is not along the exterior wall of the library, so I have no windows, except for the small rectangular one on the door that looks out onto the hallway. No natural light.

An hour or so later, I emerge out of the staff door and into the public area of the first floor and walk toward the reference desk. This part of the first floor is mainly a collaborative study space with tables and armchairs. The first floor also houses the circulation desk—a long, curved desk that contains a work area where some staff and student workers are situated. Here, students and faculty stop to check out or return materials, pick up holds, or even ask questions.

Diagonally across from the circulation desk is the reference desk. Though many libraries have done away with any kind of permanent reference desk, the Parker Library has yet to make that leap. We keep a desk just large enough to seat two people, with a large sign hanging from the ceiling above it saying ASK QUESTIONS HERE! During the weekdays, we switch off so that each librarian is on reference duty only about three hours each day.

Ingrid, one of the reference and instruction librarians, and I are scheduled on the desk this morning. Ingrid is a librarian in her fifties who has been working at Parker Library for twenty years. She's already seated when I arrive.

"It's quite busy here today," she notes as I pull out the chair to sit down.

"Yeah?"

She nods. "The second floor is nearly full."

I glance sideways at her. Her eyes are focused on the computer screen. "Should one of us do roving today so the second floor is covered?"

"That's probably a good idea," she answers. "Things always get busy the closer we get to lunchtime."

"What's your preference?" I always try to defer to the more tenured librarians on staff. After all, I'm happy to stay put at the desk or walk around upstairs.

She sighs. "My back has been a bit achy…"

"Okay, no problem. I can go upstairs," I offer.

"That would be great," she says, looking at me directly for the first time since I approached the desk. "Thank you."

"My pleasure." I mean it. While it is fun to sit in the main thoroughfare of the library watching everyone as they come in and disperse, it's even more fun to walk around upstairs in the midst of the students working. I get good insight into their general mood—are they panicky? Exhausted? Jovial?—and into their study patterns.

"Don't forget to log any reference questions for our statistics," Ingrid says.

"I won't," I respond as I prop my open laptop against my forearm and start toward the stairs. I haven't forgotten to log reference questions once in the year I've been here, so it's not likely I'll forget today. Not sure why Ingrid feels the need to remind me.

The second floor is the "stacks" part of the library—aisles of tall shelving filled with the library's print collection of circulating books. Along the perimeter of the second floor are group study rooms, individual study carrels, and one small classroom-type space that library staff use to host in-person library instruction sessions, or that students can schedule to use to practice presentations or meet in larger groups.

Once upstairs, I find the rolling media cart and set my laptop on it. I walk the perimeter of the library first, pushing the cart in front of me and keeping an eye out for anyone who might look like they're struggling. It really is nearly at capacity up here, mostly individual students cordoned off in study carrels, headphones on and staring into their laptop screens.

As I round the first corner, I see a couple at a table in a group study room, their chairs pulled out so they're facing each other without the table between them. A young man is holding up index cards, one at a time, while the young woman says something in response to each one. He shakes his head after a response, and she scrunches up her forehead, thinking before she tries again. This time, he smiles, and leans forward, placing a quick kiss on her lips as she grins. He instantly straightens and holds up a new card. She gets this one right away.

Well, that's adorable.

As I continue my path around the library, my mind's eye lights up, projector-style, with flashing memories of my own college boyfriend, Steven. We were together for three years while I was earning my bachelor's degree back in Austin. My first love. My only love so far. I was so much more serious about schoolwork than he was; I'm honestly not sure he ever stepped foot in the library, while I practically lived there. He never helped me study, but rather complained whenever I said I couldn't go out because of schoolwork. I guess I should have recognized that as a red flag.

"Excuse me..." I hear a tentative voice say on my right. I turn to smile at a student with long, wispy brown hair.

"Hi! How can I help you?" I ask.

"Well, sorry to bother you, but I'm working on a paper and the teacher is really strict about citations. Can you look at my reference list to see if they're right?"

"It's not a bother at all! Let's take a look." I follow her back to her computer. While I do scan her reference list as she asked, I also have her open the webpage for the library's citation guide, showing her how to match up the type of source she's citing with the template examples on the page.

After finishing up with this student and resuming my walk (after notating the reference question on the tracking log, of course), I'm stopped again by another student. The three hours pass quickly. Before I know it, I'm heading back downstairs for my lunch break, thinking ahead to the staff meeting that afternoon where I'll finally bring up my graphic novel idea.

Chapter Two

Adam

An internet trend a while back had women asking their male partners how often they think about the Roman Empire and finding out it was often, like multiple times a day often. My Roman Empire is, well, the Roman Empire for sure, but also Nicole Delaney. I groan, thinking of this morning in the break room. Does she really not even know my name?

The first time I saw Nicole was over a year ago when she came to Parker Library for her on-campus interview. The library director, Herb Wallen, brought her around and introduced her to everyone on staff—about ten of us total between librarians and support staff, not including student workers. I was focused on my computer screen when a knock on my open office door had me looking up, my eyes catching on the muted red color of long, straight hair first, and then the bright pink floral blouse peeking out from under a dark gray blazer. In the doorway, my boss cleared his throat.

"Adam, sorry to interrupt, but I'd like you to meet Nicole Delaney. She's one of our final candidates for the open reference and instruction librarian position. Nicole, this is Adam Burgess, our cataloging librarian. He's been with Parker Library for about a year now."

Nicole gave me a little wave, the smile stretching across her face brightly. "Hi, Adam! Nice to meet you."

Swallowing to moisten my suddenly dry throat, I stuttered out, "Likewise." I adjusted the frames of my glasses in an effort to do something with my hands other than awkwardly mimic her cute wave.

Nicole looked at me as if she expected me to say something else, and when I didn't, she smiled again and said, "Hopefully we'll be working together soon."

"Yeah," I managed to croak before Herb led her away down the hall. Though I hadn't planned to attend, I ended up lurking in the back row for the presentation that was part of Nicole's interview later that afternoon. All library staff were invited to attend, though only the official search committee members were allowed to ask questions and provide feedback after the fact.

She had been asked to present ideas to help first-year undergraduates engage with the library. Through the twenty minutes it took her to share her ideas, she radiated an energy I had never felt before. Optimistic. Passionate. Confident. I couldn't take my eyes off her. Though physically small, Nicole filled the room up completely. She scanned the audience as she talked, and we made eye contact several times. I mean, she made eye contact with everyone at least once, but my stomach buzzed each time our eyes met. She pulled me in, and I was captivated.

A little while later, I walked out the front door of the library for a quick break. I paused when I saw Nicole leaning back against the brick wall of the library building, her eyes closed, and shoulders hunched. Her interview was over, and presumably she was leaving campus to go back to her hotel, or maybe straight to the airport. Was she waiting for her ride? The difference between the Nicole of the interview presentation and the Nicole slumped against the wall struck me. She reminded me of a flashlight in need of new batteries, her light dimmed and flickering. Her eyes opened then as she glanced at the phone in her hands. I quickly turned and kept walking.

Since she was hired, I've seen her just about every day, at least in passing. Closer contact every other week when the whole team meets together. She's bubbly, often confidently contributing ideas and feedback. Not always waiting her turn to talk, as if what she needs to say is so life-altering that it bursts out of her mouth, exploding into the room like water breaking through a dam. I often wonder about the quiet, private moment I witnessed outside the library on her interview day. Wonder how she acts when her guard is down, when she's alone or with the people she trusts most.

I gauge the passing time by the guidepost of her hair—she never keeps the same style for more than a few months. After the long, brick-colored red hair, she showed up to work one morning with a short haircut the color of pink cotton candy, only slightly darker than her pale skin. When her hair was about shoulder length, the color changed to a bluish green, like a mermaid. Lately, she's kept her hair at about chin length, lavender, with the edges curling around her jawline. Her deep, emerald-green eyes should clash with the delicate purple surrounding her face, but instead the combination is mesmerizing. Add to that the dresses and blouses bright with color and patterns that she wears unironically all year long, she is radiant.

Objectively, have I seen prettier women than Nicole? Sure. Actresses and models are made up by professionals every day to reflect modern standards of beauty. But Nicole just ... sparkles. I'm not even sure how to describe it. It's like there's this glow around her and I'm drawn toward her inexorably. Anyway. She's clearly outside of my orbit. We're coworkers. Coworkers who don't even work together very often since we have totally different responsibilities. I'm not sure we've even spoken more than a few sentences at a time to each other.

I'm terrible at small talk; I never know what to say. And workwise, there's no need. She's a reference and instruction librarian, so her job is to be out in front of the students and faculty, teaching and conversing and helping them directly. She plans and hosts programs and events, answers drop-in questions, and presents in front of groups of students. I'm the cataloging librarian, so my job is to sit alone in my back office and develop metadata for new resources, making things easier to find electronically through the catalog and discovery system.

That afternoon, I enter the staff meeting room and sit in my normal spot in the corner for the team meeting. Herb sits in a seat near the head of the large conference table. Herb, the director of Parker Library for the last ten years, is a cheerful, unassuming man in his sixties. He has a mop of gray hair and eyeglasses that can only be described as "spectacles"—round with a wiry frame. The corners of his mouth perpetually tip up, as if he is prepared at all times to break into a grin. There's a rumor among the library staff that Herb spent the better part of his career working as a librarian for the CIA. I mean, it makes sense that an agency specializing in intelligence might need information specialists to help them organize it all, but I don't know if Herb was their guy. I've never asked him, but one time, I overheard Samantha, one of the reference and instruction librarians, mention it to him and ask if it was true.

He gave her a small smile and responded, "If I told you, I'd have to kill you." Then he laughed. But I noticed he never answered the question.

Herb starts the meeting, giving us updates on ongoing projects and reviewing what needs to be done before the December semester break which is about a month and a half away. Finally, he opens the floor to anyone on staff who has something to discuss. Nicole raises her hand.

"I'd like to pilot a small graphic novel collection for the library," she says, her voice confident. "My thought is to start with about fifty titles, tying the exact choices into the curricula for programs like English, history, art, possibly even education if we include some kids' titles."

"Interesting," says Herb. "Tell us more."

"I think it would be a great way to get students to engage with the library. We can plan some programming around the collection, track circulation stats, and hopefully, if the pilot is successful, add to those initial titles later."

"Are you anticipating this being a distinct collection? All together on their own shelf rather than mixed in with the other circulating books?" Herb asks.

"Yes, that's what I was picturing."

A few of the other reference and instruction librarians ask questions or give feedback, especially the ones who are subject liaisons for the departments Nicole named. Most of the faces in the room look interested or at most indifferent.

Finally, Herb ends the conversation by saying, "Okay, Nicole. Your idea has potential. Write up a short proposal that lists the titles and estimates what this would cost." He raps his knuckles on the table. "You should team up with Adam on this."

My head pops up from where I'm doodling in my notebook. I look at Herb with confusion and then at Nicole, who is looking at Herb with a matching expression. Then, she slowly turns her head and looks straight at me.

I gulp.

Huh. I guess she does know my name.

"Team up with Adam? Herb—" Nicole starts, but he puts up his hand to stop her.

"You'll need to coordinate with the subject librarians, of course, but you and Adam will run point. Come see me in my office in about an hour," he says. "We'll talk more about it then."

He wraps up the meeting, and as everyone files out, he claps me on the shoulder and says, "Walk with me to my office."

I follow him down the hall and as we step into his office, he closes the door. "Have a seat." He gestures to me with a smile. I do. He sits across the small, round table from me. "I'm sure you have questions about me asking Nicole to work with you on her graphic novel project."

"Well, just one," I replied. "Why?"

Herb grins. "Not something you're enthused about, huh?" Enthused is maybe not the word I'd use, no. Terrified maybe. Overwhelmed. Nervous. But also ... excited?

"Well, it's not that. I just don't really know anything about graphic novels," is what I say out loud.

"Maybe not, but you do know ... campus expectations. Rules. Even though you've only been here a couple of years, you understand the more ... political dynamics of Harkness and how to get things done delicately."

"I guess that's true." I shrug, thinking of a year ago when I created a communication plan around the library dropping all print journal subscriptions in lieu of electronic only. A lot of faculty members had a lot of strong opinions, but the bottom line was that the print journal issues didn't get used and took up space. We just didn't need them anymore. "Is Nicole's project one that needs a delicate touch?"

He sighs. "I hope not, but I suspect so. I'm concerned about a growing ... inclination of college leadership to micromanage our collections. The provost asked me recently for a title list of all the new books we added to the collection so far this year. I told him it would take me time to pull that together and he wasn't in a rush, but I don't know."

"Micromanage?" I ask. "Do you mean like censoring? Like if there was something on the list he didn't like, he'd tell us to get rid of it?"

Herb looks uncomfortable. "I just don't know. There's been nothing overt, it's just a gut feeling I have. I don't want to set Nicole's project up for failure, especially because graphic novels will be more difficult to defend from an academic necessity standpoint."

"So, you want me to ... what?"

"Just keep her reined in. Make sure that the titles she has in mind are ones we could defend to the provost, if need be. Ones that can be explicitly tied to the curriculum."

"Like behind her back?" I shift in my seat.

"No. Oh, no. I'll give her the same explanation I'm giving you. I'll let her know that you're good with rules and keeping things above board, for lack of a better term, and that's why I want you involved."

"Okay," I agree, my arms folded across my chest.

"We just need to color inside the lines here. Try not to push the envelope..." When Herb starts talking in clichés, I know the meeting is over. I stand to leave.

I close myself back in my office and pull up the cataloging system on my computer screen, intending to make some progress on a batch of e-books we just purchased. Of course, that's a bit ambitious given the events of the last hour and soon I'm totally up in my own head.

Not only will I now be working closely with Nicole on a project that she's passionate about and that I know nothing about, but I'm also supposed to play the role of what, the enforcer? I can't see how she won't resent me for it, and resentment is the last thing I want from her. This should be my chance to get to know her, to let her get to know me.

Finally. I chuckle to myself as I think, *She doesn't know me from Adam*. Heh. But now she could. I reach up and rub the back of my neck as I think about that possibility. I'll be honest, I know I don't make the best first impression. I come across as quiet and serious, probably nerdy. Usually, I'm totally content being who I am. I own my stoic personality, my quirky interests, and my less-than-hip wardrobe. My small inner circle of family and friends don't mind either, but it's been a while since I've even wanted anyone new to join that circle. So, the thought of opening myself up, especially to someone like Nicole, who might very well be the coolest woman on the planet as far as I'm concerned, is really freaking scary.

Chapter Three

Nicole

I return to my office after meeting with Herb. I'm feeling ... slightly discouraged. While technically I got the green light for my project, or at least to officially propose my project, Herb's concerns around it make me uneasy. It feels like he assigned Adam to babysit me. His explanation about college leadership breathing down our necks doesn't make me feel better. Herb doesn't trust me to do this project in a responsible way.

And I hardly know Adam. We've spoken maybe a handful of times. He's usually so quiet and serious. Given our profession, I assume he's also a bit nerdy, which is certainly not a negative. It's not like I'm the coolest woman on the planet. Frankly, I've never given Adam much thought until now. We've rarely interacted in the year I've been working here. I'm just not sure how well we'll work together and that makes me anxious. Not that I need a specific reason to be anxious. It's pretty much my default setting.

I pull out my phone to text my sisters in our group chat.

Nicole:

> Pitched the graphic novel idea, and Herb gave the okay, but assigned me a babysitter [eye roll emoji]

Olivia:

> yay but babysitter?

Nicole:

> Yeah, the cataloging librarian Adam. Herb pretty much said Adam is supposed to keep me from picking any titles the college leadership will find offensive

Olivia:

> offensive? you? [Laughing with tears emoji]

Olivia:

> they're on to you

Okay, point taken—I've never been one to shy away from controversy.

Nicole:

> Thanks so much.

Olivia:

> i'm just saying a babysitter isn't the worst idea

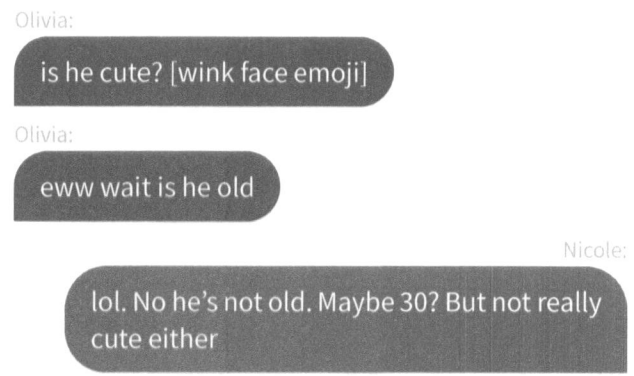

Olivia:

is he cute? [wink face emoji]

Olivia:

eww wait is he old

Nicole:

lol. No he's not old. Maybe 30? But not really cute either

I pause. Is Adam cute? I shrug. Not so much that it's caught my attention up to now anyway.

Nicole:

Where's Molly? I need her to weigh in here

Olivia:

[shrugging] locked in her lab testing samples or whatever it is she does?

Nicole:

Fine. Molly text me laterrrrr

Molly:

Sorry. I'm here

Molly:

Maybe he'll be helpful?

Molly:

Keep an open mind

Molly:

And congrats!

Nicole:

Thanks!

Molly is my older sister—she tends to keep me balanced with her calm, measured advice. She's three years older than me at twenty-eight, and an environmental scientist, focused on coastal research. She's pretty single-minded about her work. Olivia, who everyone except our family calls by our last name, Delaney, is our younger sister. She's twenty-one and in her senior year of college. She lives in Austin with our parents as she finishes her degree in ... I think exercise science? She's changed majors a couple of times, so I've honestly lost track.

I take Molly's advice to "keep an open mind" with me into my first meeting with Adam the next day. We agree to meet in my office at two o'clock. I'm shuffling through some papers in my top desk drawer when I hear someone clear their throat. I look up and see Adam standing in the doorway. I check the clock on my computer screen. Two o'clock on the dot.

"Come on in," I tell him, gesturing to a chair by my desk. I realize too late that there's a stack of books, graphic novels in fact, on the chair. "Oh," I say. "Sorry. You can just move those anywhere."

As Adam scoops up the books, I study him. He has thick, brown hair that's short and neat, the longer strands in the front combed to one side. He looks to be average height, taller than my five feet five inches by at least four inches. He's wearing khaki chinos and a hunter green pullover cardigan, the collar of his black, plaid, button-down shirt folded neatly over the sweater on the back of his neck and around to the lapels. He's lean but not overly skinny. As he sits, his eyes catch mine—light brown with long lashes behind square, black-rimmed glasses. His face is clean-shaven.

Adam looks at me expectantly, and despite my commitment to keep an open mind, I feel irritated and on edge.

"Hi," I say, not smiling.

"Hi," he answers hesitantly.

"I don't need a babysitter," I blurt.

The corners of Adam's mouth tip up slightly, but he answers seriously. "I didn't think you did."

"Apparently Herb does," I grumble, now regretting this approach.

"Nicole," he starts, and something in the way he says my name catches my attention. I can't put my finger on it, but it sounds ... practiced, maybe? "I don't think you need a babysitter. I'm positive you could do this all on your own. That being said, Herb assigned me to work with you, so," he shrugs, "put me to work. As far as I'm concerned, you're in charge, but I hope I can still be useful."

"I think that's the most words I've heard you say at once." I realize with a gasp that I've said this out loud and quickly backpedal. "I mean, we just haven't worked together much before this..." I trail off, feeling the heat in my face.

"I'm usually quiet," he says softly, his cheeks reddening slightly.

I instantly feel guilty for embarrassing him. I take a deep breath, recommitting to the whole "open mind" thing.

"How familiar are you with graphic novels?"

"Not very," he admits. "I don't read them personally and I've never cataloged any. But I've been looking at the online catalogs of other academic libraries with graphic novel collections. There aren't a ton, but enough that I got a sense of some best practices."

"Oh." Maybe Adam will be helpful after all. He certainly has done his homework. "What *do* you read?" I can't help but ask, even though it's taking us slightly off topic.

He cocks his head a bit as he answers. "History mostly. Nonfiction. Especially World War II."

Well, that seems to be on brand. I nod. "I can recommend some graphic novels that are related to history," I offer. "Actually, there's a massively popular comic called *Maus* that's about World War II, specifically the Holocaust."

"Are comics and graphic novels the same thing?"

"Well, yes and no. Technically, comics are shorter, serialized stories and graphic novels are longer and more stand-alone. But often we use the word *comics* to talk about the story itself rather than the medium. So graphic novels are comics, but comics aren't necessarily graphic novels."

He nods, looking at me seriously. I can really get going when I'm talking about this, and I've often seen a distinct glazed look on the faces of others when they're listening politely but aren't really interested. That's not how Adam is looking at me now. I get the impression that I have his full attention, so I continue, leaning in and making eye contact.

"There are, of course, graphic novel series, where each individual novel stands alone but also connects into the other stories in the series. There are several well-known kids' series, like *Diary of a Wimpy Kid* and *Dog Man*. But there are series written for adults, too."

"Are there nonfiction graphic novels, too, or mostly fiction?" Adam asks.

"Both. I've seen quite a few memoirs and biographies. There's some discussion about the use of the term novel to describe nonfiction in comics, but it's mostly from people who are outside the genre, not writers, illustrators, or fans. And if Truman Capote could call *In Cold Blood* a nonfiction novel back in the sixties, I don't see why graphic novels can't be nonfiction..." I trail off, realizing that I'm maybe getting carried away. "Anyway," I blush. "I'll step off my soapbox now."

"No," Adam protests. "I don't mind. I'm interested in learning about it, and I can tell you're not only an expert, but have a passion too. I like hearing interesting people talk about their interests."

He smiles then. A genuine smile that shows his teeth and crinkles the corners of his eyes. It transforms his face, and I find myself staring at the way the corners of his lips push the apples of his cheeks higher, his eyes creasing with enjoyment.

"In that case..." I laugh but don't continue. He laughs, too. I find that I'm not feeling irritated anymore. I'm almost at ease. Maybe this will work out after all.

"Would our graphic novel collection be mostly nonfiction?" he asks.

"Well," I answer, "mostly, I think, but it will depend on why we're selecting each particular title. Titles for the history department should be nonfiction, or close to it, but titles for the art department could be anything as long as the illustrations are particularly noteworthy."

"That makes sense," he says. Then, more unsure, "Can I make a suggestion?"

"Okay," I answer, bracing myself.

"I've been looking at graphic novel collections at other libraries, especially academic, and I see that there's no clear convention for classification. Some libraries are using author last name, especially for fiction collections, and some academic libraries are using Library of Congress." He pauses here and focuses his eyes on me, as if watching for my reaction. "We should use Library of Congress, so it matches the bulk of our collection upstairs and makes it clear how the graphic novels fit into our collection academically."

"But not shelve them with the rest of the collection, right?" I ask carefully.

"No. No, they can still be their own collection on their own shelf but ordered on the shelf and with call numbers that align with the larger collection. So, like, the Holocaust book you mentioned would be D 804 whatever."

He's talking about organizing the books by subject, rather than author or something else, using the Library of Congress classification system, which is the system most academic libraries use for their nonfiction collections. Almost everyone knows, at least by name, the Dewey Decimal system, which assigns numerical numbers to books based on subject and determines where they are placed on the shelf, but many don't know that Dewey Decimal is mostly used by public libraries and doesn't work as well for the deeper, scholarly collections at college and university libraries. I have to admit, I'm impressed that he pulled that classification number out of the air, matching it seamlessly to books about the Holocaust. I mean, I haven't fact-checked him, and *I* certainly don't have categories memorized, but I'm assuming he's right.

I haven't yet responded to his idea, and he's still watching my face closely. I wonder what it's telling him. I don't want to be overly enthusiastic—I'm still a little bitter about the situation as a whole—but it isn't really Adam's fault that Herb assigned him to babysit me. He's just trying to help.

"That works for me," I finally say.

Another smile, smaller this time. "Okay, good."

We coordinate schedules to set our next meeting. We need to start making a list of specific titles for the pilot, and the liaison librarians will need a chance to look at those title suggestions before we finalize the proposal.

The next couple of hours pass quickly, and soon I'm walking home. It's a cool November evening. Cool for Florida in the fall, anyway, a brisk sixty-five degrees as the sun starts waning. I pull out my keys as I walk up the short flight of stairs to my apartment. Opening the front door, I dump my purse on the entry table and head to my bedroom to change.

Now in joggers and an oversized Harkness T-shirt, I collapse onto the couch, letting myself relax for a few minutes before I figure out dinner.

Without prompting or permission, my brain starts replaying the interactions I had at work that day, like the brief run-in I had with Samantha, another librarian, in the breakroom. Making small talk, she said something about the cinnamon raisin bagel she was eating, and I told her I didn't like raisins. I consider how the tone of my voice sounded when I said that. Hopefully friendly and not argumentative or dismissive. I mean, I don't like raisins, but I don't know why I said so. Why not just make a noncommittal comment about my lunch or the deliciousness of cream cheese or anything that would invite connection instead of being off-putting? Ugh. Why am I like this?

I wonder what Samantha thought of the interaction.

I take a breath then—deeply in through my nose and then out through my mouth. I remind myself, or rather I hear the voice of my old therapist from Texas inside my head reminding me, that the people around me do not spend time dissecting their interactions with me. I am not important enough in their lives for them to even remember the conversations more than a few days later. I understand that on a cerebral level, I do, but on an emotional level, I'm still left spiraling a little. Maybe they don't remember the words or the tone of voice or give it much thought, but surely each interaction gives them a subconscious sense of me that combines to form their overall impression. Like, "Oh, Nicole? Yeah, she's that awkward woman who's always talking too much in meetings." And they don't even know how they arrived at that estimation of who I am, but it was built up over many small, forgettable moments of me saying or doing something weird.

Anyway. Yay, anxiety. The medication I take helps a bit with the spiraling thoughts, especially early in the day, but mostly it helps keep the serotonin and dopamine levels in my brain to a decent level. When I'm particularly stressed, I try to proactively do more things that bring me joy, like eating certain foods, being outside in nature, or reading. My body will actually start craving these things. The eating thing can get me into trouble though. I've never had a very fast metabolism, and my "little treats" add up. I am what would be considered "slightly overweight" for my height, but I'm trying to eat more like an adult and less like a teenager, even though I don't have much self-control when it comes to the food that makes me happy.

Speaking of—I force myself off the couch and make my way to the small galley kitchen. Dinner. I really should plan my meals better, but with just myself to worry about, I can't seem to find the motivation. Taking stock of the pantry and refrigerator, I pull out a box of pasta, a jar of fancy tomato sauce, and some steam-in-the-bag frozen vegetables. Easy. And a much better option than ordering take-out. Good job, Nicole at the grocery store three days ago!

When everything is ready, I carry my plate out to the small balcony just off the living room and set it on the table. I don't have a dining room or space in the kitchen for a table, so I mostly eat my meals outside. If it's raining, I eat on the couch or stand at the kitchen counter.

I step back inside to grab my tablet. Settling into a chair in the cool, evening air, I pull up an e-book on the tablet, setting it on the table next to my dinner plate.

I like graphic novels in print form, but for my other reading, I love e-books. They're convenient, don't take up space in my small apartment, and have the added bonus of being discreet. Truth be told, I'm a closet romance reader. I'm not sure exactly why I feel I need to hide it. I don't even read too much of the "spicier" stuff, though I do read some. My college boyfriend knew and teased me about it. Looking back, it may have been more mocking than teasing, really. We were both English majors, and he felt that genre fiction was beneath us, somehow. Like the only books worth reading are the literary ones; the ones that say something profound about people, about life. I do like literary fiction and appreciate how the words come together in beautiful ways, but nothing matches the joy I feel from reading a book with a guaranteed happily ever after. It's almost freeing that instead of eschewing the cliché, romance writers proudly advertise what tropes readers will find in each book. And readers love it, seeking out recommendations for books with their favorite situations and plot lines. I certainly gobble them up, that's for sure.

I sigh contentedly, enjoying the evening, my simple dinner, and my book.

Chapter Four

Adam

I pull into the driveway, big enough for a single car, in the back of my two-bedroom townhome that evening. The entry I use most often, leading into my living room, is technically the back door. After unlocking it and going inside, my first move, as always, is to greet my dog, Joan. Or rather, stay put while she greets me, rubbing against my legs and wagging her tail. She's a three-year-old pit bull mix who I adopted from a local rescue when she was a puppy. Joan, short for Joan of Arc, weighs about sixty pounds and has dark brown fur with white markings.

Dropping my computer bag on the couch, I grab Joan's leash from the side table and hook it onto her collar. We walk the same route we take every morning and every evening, winding through my small subdivision of townhouses, and then the small subdivision across the street. It's about a mile, but usually takes us thirty minutes to complete because Joan likes to stop and smell pretty much everything along the way.

When we get back to the house, I head upstairs to my bedroom to change clothes, trading my chinos and polo for athletic shorts and a T-shirt. Then, it's time to eat. I pour some kibble in Joan's bowl. She sniffs the food, and then, tail wagging, comes over to me, pushing her head into the side of my thigh. I bend down and scratch behind her ears.

"You're welcome, Joanie," I croon. Once I straighten again, she goes back to her food bowl and starts eating.

Wednesday nights, I have pan-seared salmon for dinner. I line up the ingredients on the kitchen counter: a salmon filet, extra virgin olive oil, salt, and pepper. I also make wild rice, microwavable in a pouch—not that I can't make it myself, but it just feels like there's not much point when it's just me. Finally, I have some fresh green beans I'll steam on the stove. Within thirty minutes, I'm sitting at my dining room table with my plate of food in front of me and my laptop opened to a *Civilization VI* live stream on YouTube.

After dinner, I relax on the couch with a book. I told Nicole I read nonfiction history, and I absolutely do, but I also devour dystopian fiction novels. As a lover of rules in real life, I find the inversion of order in dystopian fiction titillating, albeit a bit stressful. I can't abide such a reinvention of rules in ordinary life, but in books I find it cathartic and thrilling.

I like my routines, and I like the comfort of well-defined rules and boundaries. I've always been this way. At this point, I figure it's just part of my personality. I grew up in Naples, a small city in southwest Florida known for retirement communities, an only child to older parents—my mother was forty when I was born, and my father forty-five. They'd pretty much given up on the idea of having kids until I surprised them. They were kind and doting parents, but also pretty set in their ways by the time I came around. I didn't spend a lot of time with other kids, except at school—no siblings or cousins, or even really neighborhood children.

My father liked to tell a story about how, when I was nine and he took me fishing from a pier near our house, I brought a little booklet of fishing regulations and a measuring tape with me. Anything we caught, which wasn't much, I would identify and measure, looking up the regulation for that type of fish in my booklet. We were doing catch and release anyway, but I found the process of measuring and the clarity of knowing the rules to be soothing.

My dad got a real kick out of that story. Loved to tease me about how strict I was about following rules. He passed away about five years ago, now, when he was seventy. My mother still lives in the house I grew up in. Being a good five hours away from her means that I worry about her, but she's healthy and active and would personally kill me if I moved back home just to keep an eye on her.

Before it gets too late—I do have to work tomorrow—I put down my book and start my nighttime routine. In the kitchen, I pack my lunch for the next day and stash it in the refrigerator. I wash the dinner dishes and wipe down the counters. I take Joan out for one last short walk, checking the locks on both the front and back doors when we return. Then, we head upstairs. In the bathroom, I brush and floss my teeth. After climbing under the covers, I double check that my alarm for the next morning is turned on.

It's a typical evening for me—quiet and predictable, which doesn't bother me at all—but also lonely, except for Joan, of course. I've built this life—a job I enjoy, a cozy home in an interesting city, hobbies that keep my brain occupied, a dog I'm devoted to—and I'm content with my choices, but sometimes I wonder if I'm happy. Like maybe I've focused too much on comfort and not enough on growth and now I'm stalled out in life, plateaued in a day-to-day that's pleasant, but not extraordinary. I've always been one to stay inside my comfort zone, and since my comfort zone does not include talking to women, my dating history is light—a couple of short-term girlfriends in college and graduate school, dates here and there. Not blank, but sparse. I've been pining for Nicole for over a year but have never taken any steps to get to know her better.

I think about an old movie called *Stranger Than Fiction* where a man discovers that he's the protagonist in a novel when he starts hearing the omniscient narrator chronicling his thoughts and actions. Then, the narrator foreshadows the man's death, and he frantically tries to prevent it. One tactic is to just do nothing. He literally just sits in his apartment, going nowhere in order to avoid anything that might kill him. But that's a boring story, so the narrator has a construction crane crash through the apartment wall to get the plot moving again. In a smaller, less dramatic way, maybe Herb putting me on this project with Nicole is my crane, forcing me to break out of normal routines and habits. It's an opportunity. I can harness the momentum to be the protagonist in my own life—acting for myself to make things happen instead of waiting to be acted upon. Specifically, I can talk to Nicole. About more than just the project. I can show her I'm interested in her. Maybe even ... ask her out.

They're brave thoughts as I lie in my bed in the dark, but what I'll do with them in the light of day is another story.

A week later, I'm sitting at my desk in the library cataloging what seems like an endless list of new e-books. The morning dragged on, but now I'm back from my lunch break and getting antsy. Nicole and I have another meeting scheduled this afternoon about the graphic novel project, and once again, I'm both dreading it and counting down the hours. In the week or so since Herb paired us up, Nicole and I have emailed back and forth a lot, but I've barely seen her around the library. I mean, I know she's likely to either be in her office or at the reference desk, but I haven't yet thought of an excuse believable enough for why I would emerge from my cave to seek her out in either of those places.

I shake my head, checking the time on my computer screen. 1:30. I'm meeting with her at three. And it's Wednesday. Dr. Parker should be in his office.

I push my rolling chair away from the desk and stand. I make my way to the front of the library and when I turn toward the stairs, I may or may not glance over my shoulder at the reference desk. No luck. Looks like Samantha and Ben are on duty right now. I take the stairs two at a time and quickly arrive on the third floor, just around the corner from Dr. Parker's office.

Dr. Henry Parker was one of the founders of Harkness back when it opened in the 1980s. He was the first president—a position he held for twenty years—while also being a faculty member in the history department. In deference to his years of service, Harkness has since awarded him the honorary title of chancellor. He keeps a permanent office space on the third floor of the Parker Library building, which was named for him. He's kind of a fixture in the library, known for walking through the main lobby from the front door to the elevator with his dog, Beans, at his heels. Students go crazy for a Beans sighting.

It was Beans that brought about my unusual friendship with Dr. Parker. One day I was on the elevator, heading up from the first floor, when I heard "Hold the elevator!" and Dr. Parker and Beans joined me. It was pretty intimidating, to be honest. But then Beans nudged my hand with his nose, and of course, I scratched his head.

"He likes you." Dr. Parker smiled over at me.

"He's probably smelling my dog, Joan," I said.

"What kind of dog is Joan?"

"She's a pit-mix."

And then we talked about pit bulls, then dogs in general, then American history and World War II and books and restaurants and life. Not all on the elevator that first day, of course. But over time, we formed a friendship. An odd one, I'll give you that. He's seventy-five and I'm twenty-nine, so in many ways, he's more of a mentor to me than a friend. Actually, now that I think about it, Dr. Parker (as much as he insists I call him Hank, or at least Henry, I am really not capable of calling him anything other than Dr. Parker) is the same age that my dad would have been now.

Huh. Maybe I'll save that nugget to dwell on later.

The third floor is not really a library-controlled space but holds several classrooms, a technology lab, and a writing center, plus a few scattered faculty offices, including Dr. Parker's. When I get upstairs, his door is open, and I knock lightly to announce my presence. Beans lifts his head and pants in greeting. He's a large dog with fluffy white fur. Dr. Parker says Beans is a Great Pyrenees, but it looks like he's mixed with something else too. His ears aren't as floppy and folded over as most Great Pyrenees I've seen. As usual, Beans is lying on his own doggie couch, which given his size, is only slightly smaller than a loveseat for humans.

"Adam!" Dr. Parker booms. "Come on in."

"Thanks," I say, coming through the door. "Can I close it?"

He cocks his head at me. "Sure. Something important on your mind?"

"Kind of." I take a deep breath and sit down across from him, scratching Beans behind the ears as I talk. "I got assigned to work on this project with a colleague I haven't spent much time with. It's a passion project for her, and she kind of resents me working with her."

"That's tough," he says after a minute. "What's the project?"

"Graphic novels. They're—"

"I know what graphic novels are, Adam," Dr. Parker interrupts. "I have grandchildren."

I smile. "Of course you do. Anyway, Herb is worried the project might be a bit controversial and I guess he wants me to keep things reined in."

"That's a tough spot." He whistles. "Who's the colleague?"

I feel my face and neck turn warm when I answer. "Nicole Delaney. She's fairly new. Purple hair?"

Dr. Parker studies me. "Mmhmm. I know the girl. She's about your age, isn't she?"

"Uhh, give or take."

"Single?"

"I mean, that's not really relevant," I sputter. The warmth goes all the way up to my ears and down to my chest now.

"No? Alright then. I thought it might be relevant seeing how you're red as a lobster right now."

I sigh, giving in. "I might be hoping it becomes relevant. Hoping, but not expecting." I try to smile, but it feels more like a grimace.

"Uh huh." Dr. Parker is quiet for a few minutes. Then he asks, "Would you like to know what I think?"

"Definitely," I answer.

"For the project, focus on supporting her ideas and her vision. Make sure she knows you want to help, not take over."

"That makes sense."

"And as for the girl, take advantage of the opportunity you have here to get to know her, and for her to get to know you. You're a nice young man. Show her that."

Now it's my turn to sit quietly, absorbing Dr. Parker's words.

"Oh," he adds, "and if possible, introduce her to Joan. Dogs can tell what's what about people. If Joan likes her, you can feel good about taking the next step." He winks.

I laugh. "Duly noted. But, if she's at my house meeting Joan, I'm guessing we're already taking the next step."

Chapter Five

Adam

This time, Nicole is coming to me for our meeting. I fidget back and forth in my chair while I wait for her, watching the door but trying to make it look like I'm not watching the door. I'm twisted around in my chair, my face toward the wall when I hear her upbeat "Hi!" from the doorway. I spin back around, and my chair almost tips over. I place my hands on the desk to steady myself.

"Hi," I echo. My eyes are drawn to her outfit—a black dress with red flowers on it. The top part molds to her back and chest, hugging her curves. At the waist, the skirt flares out with layers of ruffles down to her knees. My eyes travel lower, to her smooth calves and down to the flat red shoes she's wearing that come to an uncomfort-able-looking point at the toes. I notice some sort of mark or smudge on the bare skin on the top of her foot, but I snap my eyes back to her face quickly when I realize I've been ogling. She notices, based on the annoyed look on her face. Not a great start. I try to recover.

"Come in." I gesture with my hand. "Your, uh, dress is nice." I mentally slap my hand against my forehead. Way to be even creepier, Adam.

Nicole sits in the chair on the other side of my desk and crosses her legs. I force my eyes to stay on her face and not dip back down to her legs. She doesn't look annoyed anymore, so I might have imagined it.

"Thank you," she says. "It's one of my favorites. And it has pockets."

I wait for her to get us started. Like I told her last time we met, I consider this her project.

"Have you had a chance to look through the list of potential titles I sent you?"

"Yes," I answer. "But honestly, they mean little to me. I looked up reviews for some of them, and they were solid for sure. I'm not a graphic novel or subject specialist."

"I know. I had the other liaison librarians take a look too, and they all picked out their top ten. That helped me narrow it down to the fifty titles we'll want to pilot. The list is pretty evenly divided between art, history, literature, and education."

"Sounds great."

"If I send you the list of fifty titles, can you look up pricing so we can include that in our proposal?"

"Yes, of course," I reply. Then, I hesitate to add, "Look, again, I don't want to overstep, but you know Herb gave me pretty specific instructions for my role on this project..." I trail off. Nicole's mouth is set in a firm line and her eyes glint as if she's poised to argue with whatever I say next. I choose my words carefully.

"How do you feel about me checking for ... red flags in the final list of titles? Like I'll just look up each one to see if other academic libraries own them, if the content or subject matter might raise alarms—"

"Sometimes the content that 'raises alarms' for certain closed-minded people is exactly the content that a particular person might need for catharsis or a sense of belonging or—"

"No, I know ... I'm sorry, I shouldn't have interrupted, but listen, it's not me you're battling here. Really, we don't know if you're ... we're ... battling anyone. I'm not saying we don't include the more controversial titles, but we should know that's what we're buying so we can be prepared. And if other academic libraries own them, too, it strengthens our case to the administration, if we ever need to make a case to them."

I hate this—my designated role as the voice of reason. And it's always been my role in nearly all the interactions I've had with other people my entire life. I've never really minded before—it's a responsibility that comes naturally to me—but it's never felt as ... I don't know, dream-crushy as it does right now on this project with this woman.

"I don't want to veto anything," I continue as she glares at me. "I just want to make sure we have a solid, academic case for the books on the list, because that's what will appease the administration more so than a touchy-feely…" I hold up my hands to ward off her protest, "what *they* would consider a touchy-feely argument."

Nicole continues to stare at me, not kindly. Ugh. I really hope she doesn't think I agree with the "touchy-feely" thing, that *I* would feel that way. But I know, I *absolutely know* that the majority of the leadership at this college would feel that way. From experience. From actually hearing the provost use the word "soft" and the phrase "they need to get over it and act like adults" when he was complaining to Dr. Parker about students requesting more gluten-free and vegan options in the dining hall. To his credit, Dr. Parker responded with some stats—apparently right off the top of his head—about the increasing prevalence of gluten sensitivity and how impressed he is with young people these days being willing to act on their convictions. The point is that there are politics at play here, always in everything, and you have to play the game a bit to get things done. Even if it's not ideal. Isn't it better to have a slightly toned-down graphic novel collection than no graphic novel collection at all?

"Fine," she finally grumbles. "In the meantime, I'll get started writing the proposal and we should be able to submit … what do you think? In the next week or two? How long will your," she holds up two fingers on each hand and flexes them quickly to indicate quotation marks, "red flag check take?"

"Submitting in two weeks sounds reasonable. Just after Thanksgiving?"

She nods.

I try to shift us back into a more agreeable topic. So far, this project feels like an impossible tightrope walk. I'm balancing between my desire to be a good employee and please my boss and my desire to give Nicole absolutely anything she wants. Not to mention that I actually agree with her. "Tell me more about the titles on the list," I encourage. "Which ones are you most excited about?"

Nicole eyes me warily as if this might be a trick, but soon she's practically gushing about the gouache artwork in *Kingdom Come*, the photograph reproductions and devastating details about the Dust Bowl in *Days of Sand*, and the engaging storytelling in *Lore Olympus*. The tension between my shoulders eases and I settle into listening, mesmerized once again by her energy and passion.

"You know what would be great?" she asks, almost bouncing in her seat now. "If we can, when we get to this point, highlight the graphic novel collection on library social media. Those accounts are super active because the content is always fun. Do you know who manages the library's social media?"

I clear my throat. "I do."

"You know who manages them?"

"Uh, no. Well, yes. But I'm saying that I manage the library's social media."

Nicole stares at me. "You do?" she asks. "But the posts are so funny!" Once again, she blurts out her thoughts before checking them, and her face turns bright red. "I mean ... sorry. I didn't mean it like that. It's just that you're always so serious."

Yeah, that stings. At the same time, though, I get it. I do cultivate a serious and quiet persona at work. I'm good at compartmentalizing—at work I focus on work stuff and outside of work I focus on everything else. I don't mix the two very often. I think of Dr. Parker's advice and my own commitment to break out of my comfort zone. If I want Nicole to see me as anything other than a colleague, I have to let her know who I am, including outside of work.

"Actually," I say, "internet trends and memes are kind of a passion of mine. In my free time, I run a meme library social media account where I try to capture memes from all over the web."

"Really?" Nicole looks intrigued.

"Yeah," I shrug. "Curating and collecting memes and gifs is one of my hobbies." I pronounce gif like the peanut butter because that's the only correct way to say it and I will die on this hill. If it's good enough for Steve Wilhite who freaking invented the format, it's good enough for me.

"That's pretty cool," she says, her eyes a little wide as she assesses me.

I smile. Maybe this is progress.

"Yeah. I'll send you the link if you'd like," I offer. Internally, I'm pumping my fist. She thinks something I do is cool!

After I go home that night, I sit on the couch with my laptop, scrolling through the hundreds, if not thousands, of memes and gifs I've collected so far. I'm looking for something specific. A meme that is funny, but not too personal. One that will make her smile. To say I spend an embarrassing amount of time on this is an understatement, but finally I find what I'm after. I send the image to my work email account and snap my computer lid closed with a satisfied sigh.

Chapter Six

Nicole

The day after Adam and I meet to discuss the title list for the graphic novel proposal, a new message pops up on my work account almost as soon as I open the program on my computer screen that morning. It's from Adam. It's a square meme with a few lines of text against a solid background:

"I've started investing in stocks. Beef, Chicken, and Vegetable. One day I hope to be a bouillonaire."

I can't hold back a laugh, even though the joke is hella corny. I shake my head, smiling. Another message pings.

Adam Burgess: Morning. Here's a link to my meme library if you're still interested

I click the "laughing face" reaction to the meme message and then type my reply.

Nicole Delaney: Definitely interested. Thanks for the laugh this morning!

Adam Burgess: [smile emoji]

The timing of his meme delivery is so precise, I wonder if he was waiting for my account to switch to available so he could send it right away. The day before in his office, he was ... awkward. Although I get the sense that's par for the course with him. I thought for a minute he was checking me out, but quickly pushed the thought away. It didn't feel creepy, and I didn't feel uncomfortable, but I don't know, it was weird. Then it was my turn to be awkward when I found out he manages the library's social media accounts. I was shocked, and I probably should have done a better job hiding it. I didn't miss the glint of hurt in his eyes at my reaction.

I sigh loudly. I'm obsessing about past conversations again. I take a deep breath in and refocus, using a technique my therapist told me about: the five-four-three-two-one method. I look around my office and name five things I can see: my desk, my computer, the hallway out the open door, the bookcase, the glaring blank walls. Now, four things I can touch: the cold from my water bottle, the softness of my gray trousers, the solid armrest of my chair, my phone in my hand. Three things I can hear: the voices of my colleagues down the hall, a chime from my computer as an email arrives, the rumble of the air conditioner as it turns on. Two things I can smell: the pear hand sanitizer I rubbed on my hands a few minutes earlier, the mustiness of the library air. One thing I can taste: the toothpaste still lingering on my tongue from getting ready for work that morning. Another breath and I shake the tension from my shoulders. Time to start the day.

Friday morning, I come into work to find another meme waiting for me. It's a photo of an older man with a thick white beard and an old-fashioned straw hat. He's standing in what looks like a grassy field, a farmhouse in view behind him. The text says:

"Be careful where you shop online. We ordered a german shepherd and now this guy lives with us."

There's no message this time, just the meme. And yes, I chuckle. And groan. So cheesy.

On the Monday before Thanksgiving, Adam and I are ready to put the finishing touches on our proposal. Adam has combed through the list of titles, and as promised, didn't veto a single one. He said they are all owned by at least one other academic library, and most have awards and professional recommendations we can use to cite their legitimacy. I shake my head thinking about it. I'm finding Adam difficult to read. On the one hand, I know Herb assigned him to this project—it's not like he chose to come in and be a buzzkill. But on the other hand, when he uses dismissive words like "touchy-feely", I have to wonder where his personal beliefs fall. Is he really that committed to keeping the peace at Harkness College? And at what cost?

Because of the holiday, work time is limited this week, so we squeeze in a quick meeting during lunch. We're the only ones in the break room, and we sit across from each other at the small table, our knees nearly touching. Once we iron out the final points of our project—I'll get it cleaned up and send it to Herb before I leave for the holiday—we sit in silence for a few minutes, eating our lunches.

"Thanks for this morning's meme." I smile at Adam. It was super silly: a picture of sticks of butter arranged to look like Stonehenge. The text shows a conversation between two people. The first asking, "is that butter?", to which the second replies, "no, it's stonehenge." And finally, the first person quips, "I can't believe it's not butter." At the top is the caption, "This is just margarinally funny." I didn't laugh this time, but I did roll my eyes so hard I almost got dizzy.

Adam smiles back. "You're welcome," he says. "I've got hundreds more where that came from. Literally."

"And you're going to send them to me one by one?" I ask, hoping he realizes I'm teasing.

"That's the plan." He smiles again.

He takes another bite of his salad, and I can't help but compare it to the peanut butter and jelly sandwich I have in front of me. And chips. And Dr. Pepper (because, of course, I am a Texas girl). The salad does look good. It's colorful with at least three kinds of vegetables in addition to the lettuce. Looks like shredded chicken mixed in there too.

This is the sort of lunch I ought to be eating. But the planning it takes to buy the fresh vegetables at the store, and then cut them up and put them all together before work each morning sounds exhausting. Plus, I'd get tired of it quickly. I'm a little jealous of Adam's willpower. I just know that by the third day of packing salad lunches, I'd leave that thing sitting in the refrigerator and be walking down the street to buy something yummy at a nearby café.

"Your salad looks good," I comment. "Do you always eat so healthy?"

Adam shifts a bit uncomfortably. "I try to," he answers. I think he's going to change the subject or just go back to eating in silence, but he continues. "My dad passed away a few years ago from a heart attack. He wasn't the unhealthiest guy ever, but he didn't really take care of himself either. He was only seventy." He sees my expression and adds, "Yes, my parents were older. He was forty-five when I was born. Anyway, my mom and I were devastated to lose him so soon. I decided then to do my best to take care of my health."

I'm stunned into silence. I'm … not sure why he just told me all that. I'm not sure what to say. Finally, a thought, though not a very sensitive one, stumbles out of my mouth, "Seventy years is a good, long life." Do I mean that to be reassuring? I'm honestly not sure.

Adam considers me for a few moments, watching my quickly reddening face. "How long until your parents are seventy?"

I do the calculation in my head. "About fifteen years."

"In fifteen years, will you be ready to let them go?"

Of course not. I mean, fifteen years sounds like a lot, but considering that I'm not even dating someone now, that would mean my parents wouldn't be around for my kids' graduations or weddings. My chest aches thinking about it.

"No," I answer.

"I wasn't ready to let my dad go either. And I don't want my wife and kids to go through what my mom and I did. So, I do everything I can to live a healthy life."

My eyes flick to his left hand. "You're married?"

His eyes widen in surprise, and he shakes his head. "No. No." He laughs uncomfortably. "I should have said my *future* wife and kids. Whoever they may be. No. I'm single." He meets my eyes briefly as he says this, then they dip back down to his hands.

"My parents married young," I share. "They were in their mid-twenties when my older sister was born. You're right. I can't imagine being without either of them. I'm sorry you went through that."

Adam nods slightly in acknowledgement. "Where did you grow up?" he asks.

"Austin, Texas. The rest of my family are still there, except my older sister. She lives in New Orleans. Where does your mom live, or any siblings?"

"My mom's in Naples, and I'm an only child."

"Are you heading home for Thanksgiving? How far is that?"

The library closes after noon on Wednesday until Monday morning. I'm not looking forward to it.

"I am. It's about five hours to drive from here, so not too bad. How about you? Going to Texas for Thanksgiving?"

I make a face. "No. I decided to save money and just buy the flight home for Christmas and not Thanksgiving. My sister Molly—the one who lives in New Orleans—isn't going either. I'm bummed, but since we get so much time off around Christmas, I'll be able to have a nice long visit then."

Adam has a strange look on his face. He starts to say something and then stops. He clears his throat. Finally, he says, "Well, Christmas will be fun. I'm sorry you don't have plans for Thanksgiving though."

I shrug. "I can catch up on my reading."

Chapter Seven

Nicole

The campus closes early on Wednesday afternoon, so I spend the morning shoring up my courage to hit send on the email to Herb, copying Adam, that contains the graphic novel pilot proposal. I am confident that this is a good project, that it makes sense for our students and will help them. But Herb's concerns, and Adam's diligence, have me questioning the whole thing. Finally, I hold my breath and send the email.

Within seconds, I get Adam's out of office reply in response: "I'm away from the office for the Thanksgiving holiday...", blah, blah, blah. I haven't even thought about setting up an out of office message. Thanksgiving is tomorrow. Won't everyone just assume I'm not in the office? And why would *they* be? This is an academic library, for crying out loud, not some sort of high-pressure corporate office. Adam, though, is fastidious. I think back on the collection of information I've gathered about him since we started working closely a few weeks ago. He reads history nonfiction. He's punctual and quiet, unless he has something to say. He's polite and eats healthily. He can tend toward oversharing—he told me about his dad's death, and he barely knows me. He's not married but wants to be someday. Well. Not sure why that matters, but anyway. Also, I think somewhat begrudgingly, he's smart and has good ideas. He's curious and a good listener. And he's closet funny. Like, you wouldn't think he's funny since he looks so serious all the time, but based on the memes he sends me, he definitely has a sense of humor.

I text my sisters on my walk home.

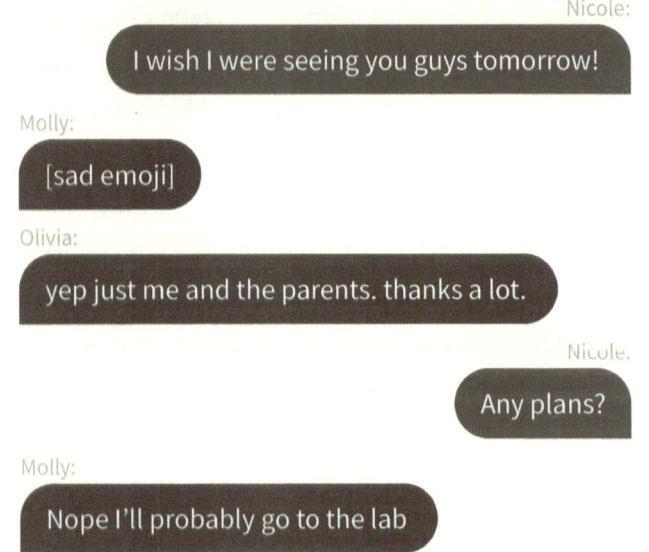

Nicole:
I wish I were seeing you guys tomorrow!

Molly:
[sad emoji]

Olivia:
yep just me and the parents. thanks a lot.

Nicole:
Any plans?

Molly:
Nope I'll probably go to the lab

Olivia:
i'm doing that turkey trot thing by ladybird lake

Nicole:
Eww. I'm not sorry to be missing that

Olivia:
haha

Olivia:
mom wants to do a video call after dinner

Molly:
I'll be around

Nicole:
Me too

When I get home, I realize I haven't been grocery shopping and have almost nothing to eat. *Come on, Nicole*, I think to myself. *You can do it; stores are still open, if crowded, at this hour on the day before Thanksgiving.*

After changing my clothes, I order a rideshare. I have the car wait out front at the grocery store, so I shop quickly. I'm definitely not cooking a big feast for just myself, but I do try to get somewhat festive foods: sliced turkey for turkey sandwiches, frozen sweet potato fries, and a Marie Callender's pumpkin pie.

Back home, as I'm putting the groceries away, I can't help but sigh. This is just pathetic. Alone for Thanksgiving. I take my pity party into the living room and binge watch every fall-related episode of the *Gilmore Girls*. When I first started watching this show, I was obsessed with Rory's boyfriends. I'm somewhat reluctantly team Jess, but really, I wish we could create a mixture of Jess's bookishness and Logan's charisma. That guy would be unstoppable. Anyway, these days I'm more drawn to Lorelai's love interest, Luke. If only I could find a man as supportive and committed as Luke. Cooking skills wouldn't hurt either. Sure, he's a little rough around the edges, a little antisocial, but so what? But I don't know when I'll be ready to date real men again anyway, so for now I'll settle for watching fictional Luke Danes in Stars Hollow.

On Thanksgiving Day, I watch the Macy's Parade alone and then the dog show that comes on right after it, because why not? I make myself a turkey sandwich and heat up some sweet potato fries in the air fryer. We try to do a three-way video call between my family in Austin, Molly, and me, but it's glitchy and frustrating.

I'm homesick. It seriously sucks to be away from my family during a holiday. Next time, I'll buy the airfare knowing it's well worth the money.

The next day, I try calling Molly, but she's keeping herself busy working in the lab. I try to call Olivia, but she's Black Friday shopping with her friend, Annie.

I start mindlessly scrolling social media and realize I miss Adam's daily memes. They've become such a part of my routine over the last couple of weeks. So, I sneak over to his meme library account and spend an embarrassingly long time exploring. He tries to capture everything, whether they're to his own taste or not, but I notice that he uses the hashtag #adamspick to denote his favorites. I go down the rabbit hole of everything with that tag and see quite a few I recognize from his messages. Without thinking, I "like" the ones that make me laugh. I like at least twenty posts before I realize with horror that Adam is probably getting notifications about my likes. My screen name is definitely recognizable—it's just NikkiDee (nobody calls me Nikki in real life though)—and I use my real picture for the profile.

I could go back and unlike each post one by one, but if Adam has already seen the notifications, he'll know that I unliked them and that will look weird. If he hasn't seen the notifications, will they disappear when I unlike the post? Or will they still be there, and he'll still see them and wonder why he's getting the notification when NikkiDee is not showing as a like on the post? I could change the profile picture and screen name of my account and lock it down so when he sees it, he doesn't know it's me. I could completely delete the account altogether. My finger hovers over the delete button when I realize I'm spiraling.

I set the phone down and do my deep breathing exercise instead. Then I put on shoes and go for a walk to guide my brain through the logic of reality. Fact: Adam will see that I liked a bunch of posts on his public meme social media feed. Question: So what? Answer: It's not a big deal. The feed is made for the public to view. Adam himself shared the link with me, so he knows I have it. He'll probably feel happy that I'm enjoying the content.

Once I talk myself down, I get out of my head and focus on the sights around me as I walk. St. Anastasia is a tourist destination, so there are plenty of people around for the holiday weekend. In fact, I would say it's busier than normal. Bunches of people are crowding together in the town square, looking like they're waiting for something. I wander over and settle myself inside the throng. I listen in on the buzzing conversation around me and discover that the city's lighting ceremony for their holiday light display is tonight. In about twenty minutes, in fact.

The holiday lights are a big deal in St. Anastasia. The city is often on travel lists of the "Best holiday light displays" and "Best places to visit at Christmas". I saw the lights last year, of course. Each of the tall oak trees in the city square drips with strands of warm white lights. The lights extend along the sidewalk by the water and over the bridge to a nearby barrier island. It's breathtaking! Businesses in the downtown area participate and compete for who has the best decorations. In the spirit of commercialism, the trolley companies that run historical tours during the day turn into rolling holiday parties at night, blasting festive music and ferrying tourists to see the lights around the city.

The annual lighting ceremony is a notable event, but I didn't go last year. The festivities start with a choir from the local high school singing carols. Then, the mayor gets up and speaks for a few minutes. Finally, it's the big countdown. "Ten! ... Nine! ... Eight! ... Seven! ... Six!" I chant along, in unison with the crowd. "Five! ... Four! ... Three! ... Two! ... One!"

In a flash of light, the switch is flipped and the branches above our heads sparkle in the November night sky. The collective energy around the square is one of excitement and awe. Around me, families with children point and clap at the bulbs. Couples steal kisses in the dim glow. And I'm by myself, but for the first time all week,

I don't feel alone. I feel like I'm part of something here, a shared experience amidst a community of people.

It gives me hope, for the first time in a long time—before Steven probably—that I belong. That despite my mental health struggles, and my loud hair, and my penchant for confrontation, it could be me out here one day, sharing this moment with a family of my own. And that I am deserving of that future, if I want it.

Adam's face swims to the front of my consciousness. I quickly swipe it away. To preserve the feeling of hope, a nebulous face on my future love is all I can handle at the moment. I'll admit an openness to the possibility of connecting with a man again, but nothing more. Without specifics, it stays a beautiful, hazy dream that will carry me through the rest of the weekend.

Chapter Eight

Nicole

I squeal as soon as I open the email from Herb. It's been two weeks since Thanksgiving. This is the last week of the semester, and the library is shutting down after next Wednesday for the winter break. I was afraid Herb would keep us waiting on the graphic novel pilot proposal until January.

But here it is! The email saying that he approves of the pilot project, and we can move forward.

I jump up from my desk and dart down the hall to Adam's office. The door is open, so I poke my head inside. He's focused on his computer screen, his eyebrows pinched together and his mouth in a serious line. For the first year I knew Adam, this is exactly the face I most associated with him—serious and grumpy. But, in these last few weeks where I've worked with him more closely, I've realized that the frowning, serious Adam is actually the exception rather than the rule. As if that thought has heralded my presence, Adam looks up just then. When he sees me, his whole demeanor changes. His brown eyes brighten, appearing almost amber in color, and his lips curve into an immediately pleased smile. His brows unfurrow as he removes his glasses and rubs his eyes before regarding me again.

"Hey!" he says.

"Hi," I answer, suddenly feeling shy about standing here at his office door uninvited. My face heats with his eyes on me, my stomach flipping in a way that feels almost like butterflies. Still standing in the doorway, I push my words forward into the room.

"Did you see Herb's email?"

"No." He frowns, and his eyes return to his computer screen as he clicks into the email program. "What did he say?"

"He said yes!" I step forward until I'm just in front of his desk. My hands are clasped together where I'm holding them just below my chin.

"What!" Adam jumps up. "That's amazing!" Suddenly, he's right next to me, wrapping his arms around my shoulders until my clasped hands are wedged between our chests. I freeze, then slowly relax into the brief hug. Coworkers hug, right? Coworkers can hug.

A warm feeling settles inside of me. *A hug from a coworker shouldn't feel like that*, a pesky voice inside me says. I push the thought away.

"Congratulations," he says into my forehead before releasing me and stepping away.

I clear my throat. "Thanks," I say. And then, "Hey, you too!"

He shakes his head. "It's your project, Nicole. This is your win."

I grin. "I'll take it!"

"Is there anything we can get done before the break?"

"Not really." I shrug. "The next step is to order the books, and I don't want them to come in while the campus is closed. We can regroup in January."

Adam watches me carefully, his serious face back in place. "Why don't we have lunch together next week," he suggests. "Just to review next steps so we can dive right in when we're back in January?"

"Sure. That could work," I answer.

It's Wednesday before we can make lunch happen—the last day before the long break. I have a suitcase sitting in my office since an airport shuttle is picking me up right from Parker Library for my flight tonight.

Adam and I walk to a local café for lunch. It's a small place that's open at breakfast for bagels and at lunch for sandwiches and cookies. The variety isn't huge, but what they do have is excellent. The bagels are freshly made every day. A small line snakes back from the order counter, but we don't have to wait long. When we reach the front, I order a turkey sandwich on an everything bagel. I skip the Swiss cheese, thinking about all the Christmas treats my mom undoubtedly already has piling up in the kitchen back home, but I can't pass up their signature herb cream cheese spread. *Mmmm.*

Adam insists on paying for my sandwich as a celebration of Herb approving the graphic novel project, and I'm only a little reluctant about letting him. He orders some sort of veggie sandwich on a whole wheat bagel.

The inside of the café only fits about three small tables and two of those are full during the lunch rush. The weather is gorgeous—seventy degrees with a cloudless blue sky and plenty of sunshine—so we opt to sit on the patio outside. Well, I opt to sit outside, and Adam follows me. Out here, ten two-top tables are interspersed with short trees all contained within a hip-high picket fence supporting a network of vines. I settle at a table near a part of the fence that overlooks the sidewalk. Adam sits across from me and without talking, we both dig in.

I'm thinking about the long evening of travel in store for me—the shuttle to the airport an hour away and then by some miracle I managed to find a nonstop flight to Austin. The flight's about three hours long, but I'll be switching into central time, so it won't be too much past my dad's bedtime when he picks me up.

Adam clears his throat. As if he's reading my mind, he asks, "When do you fly home?"

I'm just about to answer when a ping from my phone distracts me. I glance at it and see a message from the airport shuttle company, so I pick the phone up from the table and squint at it through the glare from the sun.

"No! Oh no!" I wail, as the words in the message sink into my brain.

"What's wrong?" I look up at Adam, and his forehead is creased with worry.

"Ugh. The airport shuttle I booked a month ago to take me to the airport after work tonight just canceled! One of their vans broke down, apparently the one I was supposed to be on." I rub my fingers across my forehead as I think. "I don't have a car, and, ugh, a rideshare will be so expensive, but I don't see any way around it—"

"I'll take you," Adam says quickly, interrupting my spiraling thoughts.

I freeze. "What?"

"I'll take you," he says again, surer this time.

"Adam, the closest airport is an hour away. You don't want to drive two hours after work tonight."

"For you, I do," he says. "I'm happy to."

"But," I hedge, "don't you have plans?"

He shrugs. "Not really. I was just going to pack. I leave tomorrow to drive to Naples."

It's really too kind and I shouldn't accept, but ... oof, I really don't want to spend the money for a rideshare.

"I'll give you gas money," I promise. Adam looks like he's about to protest, so I repeat in a firm voice, "I'll give you gas money."

He laughs and holds up his hands in surrender. "Deal."

Around four that afternoon, Adam appears in my office doorway. "You about ready?" he asks.

"Perfect timing." I smile at him from my desk chair. My laptop has just finished shutting down, so I snap the lid closed and slide it into my tote bag. I sling the tote over my shoulder as I stand and then retrieve my rolling suitcase from the corner, scanning my desk for anything I might have forgotten.

Adam steps into my office and reaches out his hand, taking hold of the suitcase handle. "I can take that," he says.

"Such a gentleman," I tease.

His car is a practical four-door sedan, white and wide, and I notice as I slide into the front seat, immaculately clean. Pretty on brand.

As soon as we hit the highway, traffic is slow. I check the maps app on my phone and it's still saying I'll get to the airport about an hour and half before the flight leaves, so that's good. Sure enough, the traffic thins, and our pace picks up.

Adam and I chat about our Christmas plans, the graphic novel project, and other odds and ends. It's comfortable, which is strange seeing how we've only been working closely with each other for a few weeks. Before I know it, we're pulling into the departures section of the airport and I'm directing Adam to my airline. He pulls up alongside the walkway and puts the car in park.

I hesitate before opening the car door. "You know," I say, "I won't be checking my work messages during the break, but I'd hate to miss any memes…"

Adam's ears turn pink. "Oh?" he says, keeping his eyes steady on mine.

"What if I give you my phone number and if you find any good ones, you can text me?"

He shrugs, picking up his phone. "I could do that."

I grin, rattling off my number as I fling the door open. "Thanks again, Adam. See you in a few weeks."

"Have a safe trip, Nicole."

The way he says my name, a little growly, makes me turn around and look at him again, but his face is impassive, so I push it out of my mind. The trunk pops open when I reach the back of the car, and I pull out my suitcase. I slam the lid down and step onto the sidewalk. With one last wave to Adam, I turn to walk through the automatic doors. I glance back over my shoulder; Adam doesn't pull away until I'm fully inside the airport. It's not until the plane is halfway to Austin that I realize I never gave him gas money.

Chapter Nine

Nicole

Dad meets me at the baggage claim and I throw my arms around him. When he squeezes me, my whole body stills, and my chest expands more fully than it has in months. My parents have always been a sanctuary. Peaceful and secure, I always feel centered in the midst of their love. Not that they've never lost their cool, but when they did, I always knew they loved me unconditionally.

"You should have waited in the cell phone lot," I chide. "You didn't have to pay for parking."

"Eh, I didn't know how much you brought, and I wanted to help with your luggage." He squeezes me again. "I'm glad you're home, baby girl."

As we wait by the luggage carousel for my roller bag to come through, I study my father. He's just under six feet tall with long legs and a round middle. His head of hair is full, but graying, combed back in the same hairstyle he's maintained all his adult life. I notice a few more lines across his forehead and around his gray-blue eyes since the last time I saw him. He doesn't look weathered by any means, but he looks his age, fifty-five years of life and laughter and experiences written across his features. He's wearing jeans and a bright red and green sweater.

I grin and nod at his chest. "Still a week until Christmas," I tell him.

"Your mother made me wear it," he grumbles. "Molly got in yesterday, so everyone's staying up late to decorate the tree tonight."

I hold up my hand. "I didn't say I didn't like it. It's very festive."

He shakes his head. "Uh huh," he says.

"Oh, there's my bag," I exclaim.

Dad insists on pulling it from the conveyer belt for me and rolls it out the airport doors toward the parking garage. When I step outside, I'm glad for my sweatshirt. St. Anastasia hasn't cooled off much yet, but here in Austin, it feels ten degrees colder.

My childhood home is in the southwest suburbs of Austin. The two-story brown and gray brick house was a beautiful refuge growing up. I had my own bedroom, which is still furnished how it was in my teens, and a large backyard that backs up against a protected green space—twenty acres of woods to explore. My sisters and I had secret hideouts throughout the wilds of that space, and I had a few hideouts for just myself, where I would go to read or think, especially during my tumultuous high school years.

My mom and sisters greet me when we get to the house, and then we dive right into decorating. Though my parents have already hung decorations in the grand entryway of the house and around the exterior, the Christmas tree is traditionally tucked in the back, in our family room overlooking the backyard, just for us. Dad has already set up the artificial tree next to the gas-powered fireplace. Stacked on the couch and the floor are plastic bins holding our family's hodgepodge collection of Christmas ornaments.

As predicted, Mom puts out plates of Christmas cookies and hands us each a mug of hot chocolate. We dim the family room lights so we're awash in only the glow of the twinkle lights on the tree. Olivia sets up her Bluetooth speaker and blasts Christmas music as Dad unpacks ornaments wrapped in old newspaper and tissue paper. Many are homemade—disfigured foam reindeer or Santas with cotton ball beards that me or my sisters crafted when we were children, name and age written on the back with permanent marker in my mom's handwriting. When Dad unwraps one of these treasures, he hands it to its artist, who hangs it on the tree.

Mom is in her element. Her hazel eyes dance with merriment as she tugs a hair tie off her wrist and loops it around her long, straight hair—gray for years now since she stopped coloring it in protest of unrealistic beauty standards for aging women. She's petite—several inches shorter than me—and plump in the way giving birth to three babies will do to a woman who has always liked sweets too much. Her red and green Christmas sweater matches my dad's, and her jingle bell earrings jangle with her every step.

We're finishing up the last few baubles when I check my phone. I have a text from an unknown 239 area code. I open it and see an image of a one-panel cartoon. In it, a woman sits in the center seat on an airplane reading a book with the title *Stabbing Strangers Who Talk to You* while her seatmates stare forward with wide eyes. The caption says:

"Wendy gets privacy by creating her own book covers."

The message attached reads:

"Hope you had a quiet flight! -Adam"

I laugh to myself, shaking my head. Then, still holding my phone, I tune back in to my family's chatter in time to catch the tail end of my mom's comment as I type a quick reply and save the number in my contacts.

"...pack up your ornaments for your own households," she's saying. "Before long, we might have some new young men and maybe even grandchildren in the family."

Olivia scoffs. "Don't get too excited, Mom," she says. "Molly hasn't been on a date in years, or even talked to anyone outside of her lab—"

"Hey!" protests Molly, but she's laughing.

"...I'm not even out of college yet, and Nicole—"

Molly cuts in again, smirking at me from across the room. "Nicole," she intercepts, "is smiling dreamily at something on her phone, so maybe there's hope after all, Mom."

I drop my phone onto the table. "What!" I sputter. "I'm not staring dreamily at anything. It was just a funny text, that's all."

"From who?" asks Olivia.

"Just a coworker."

Dad clears his throat. "A male coworker?" he asks.

The traitor. I feel my cheeks flush.

"Yes, this coworker happens to be a man," I say.

"A young man?" Mom asks, her eyes gleaming.

"Youngish," I hedge.

"Texting you at," Molly checks her watch, "eleven at night when the library is closed for the break?"

I don't correct her that it's actually already midnight in Florida.

I sigh heavily and frown. "You are all being ridiculous. Adam is my coworker, and he gave me a ride to the airport today after—" I ignore the clamor of voices *that* revelation elicits and talk louder, "AFTER my airport shuttle canceled last minute. I paid him gas money." No, I didn't. "And he was simply texting to make sure my flight went smoothly. As polite coworkers do."

I survey the faces of my family members. My mom looks gleeful, with Molly's expression only a slightly toned-down copy. Dad's eyebrows are raised in interest, a smile playing at the corners of his lips. Olivia looks smug.

Mom speaks first. "Well," she clucks. "Adam sounds like a gentleman. How old did you say he is?"

I send a syrupy smile in her direction. "I didn't," I say sweetly. "And I've had a long day of work and travel and decorating, so I'm going to bed."

"Okay, okay," Mom relents. "We'll leave you alone." She envelopes me in a hug. "Goodnight, my darling. Welcome home."

The next morning my parents are out playing pickleball with some friends. Olivia and I are eating breakfast when Molly walks into the kitchen. She's still in her pajamas, her brown hair mussed and her blue eyes blinking sleepily behind her round-rimmed glasses. Of the three of us, Molly is the one who looks most like Mom—petite like her with the same oval face.

As Molly sits to join us, my phone pings. It's Adam. Hiding my phone under the table, I open the message. Another meme. This one is a picture of hamburgers and hotdogs cooking on a charcoal grill with the caption:

"Eating two burgers in a restaurant: greedy, people are shocked. Eating two burgers at a BBQ: 'Is that all you're having?! Here, have a sausage!"

I swallow my laugh and settle for pressing the "laugh" reaction button on the message.

Nicole:

> As a Texas girl, I can't let this meme get away with calling hamburgers and hotdogs on a grill a "BBQ". That's a cookout

He texts back right away.

Adam:

> Noted. What's a BBQ then?

Nicole:

> A BBQ is barbecue. Smoked meats, BBQ sauce ... You didn't know this??

Adam:

I do now

Adam:

About to get on the road to Naples. Have a great day

Nicole:

Safe travels

I look up from my phone to see both my sisters smirking at me. "What?"

"The dreamy smile is back. What were you looking at on your phone?" Molly demands.

"Cute puppies," I lie.

Olivia blinks at me. "Looked like you were texting."

"Huh. Weird," I deflect.

"Was it Adam?" Molly asks.

"Guys, stop. I'm not interested in Adam. He's just a coworker." I roll my eyes and shift my feet under the table.

Molly holds up a hand. "Okay, okay," she placates. "After everything with Steven, we all just think it would be nice to see you in a happy relationship, that's all."

I sigh. "I'm not hung up on Steven, and I'm not interested in Adam."

"Good," Molly says.

After a few beats of silence, Olivia speaks up. "That *is* good," she says. "Because that means you are free and clear to come on a double date tonight with me, Brent, and Brent's cousin."

"Uh." I stare at her. "Who's Brent?"

She shrugs. "This guy I've been dating. His cousin is in town for Christmas and he's around your age."

"A blind date? That sounds truly awful," I gag.

"If you're not hung up on Steven or interested in Adam, I would think you'd be open to meeting new men," Olivia reasons.

"But I don't live here. Why meet a man in Texas when I live in Florida? I need a man who lives in Florida," I argue.

"Like Adam?" she asks innocently.

I growl. "No. No, not like Adam," I say through my teeth. "Fine. I'll go on the double date, if only so you will both stop badgering me!"

"Great."

Molly glances between us and clears her throat. "By the way, Olivia. You're heading into your last semester of college. Have you given any thought to your future?"

"Yes," Olivia responds.

"You have?" Molly raises her eyebrows. "What are your plans?"

Olivia smiles sweetly. "Tonight, I plan to go on a double date." She jumps up from the table. "And right now, I plan to take a shower."

Molly rolls her eyes. "We're not done talking about this!" she calls after a retreating Olivia.

Chapter Ten

Nicole

I hadn't expected to be dating on this trip, so I did the best I could for my outfit with what I packed. I'm wearing dark wash jeans with a silver tank top under a red cardigan. Olivia scoffs when I come out to the living room in my outfit.

"You look like a librarian," she says.

"I am a librarian," I counter. "But what about this outfit says librarian?"

She appraises my clothes for a few minutes, then says, "The sweater."

I sigh. "Well, it's too cold to go without it, so you and what's his name will have to deal."

Of course, my outfit looks dowdy next to Olivia. Though the youngest, she's the tallest of the three of us at five feet seven inches, most of that made up of her legs. Her body is athletic and muscular—the kind that looks amazing in any outfit. She's wearing a black, sparkly romper with a deep V-neck, and a cropped denim jacket over top. Her long, platinum blonde hair is pulled sleekly into a high ponytail. Though she doesn't often wear heavy makeup, I can tell she had fun with it tonight—her eyes have a shimmery red shadow around them, with lipstick to match. She's the very definition of glam.

Olivia drives us in her jeep to meet the guys at the restaurant.

"What's my date's name again?" I ask.

"Dylan."

I nod. "And your boyfriend is Brent?"

She laughs. "Brent is not my boyfriend. We're just dating."

Got it. "How long have you and Brent been dating?"

She shrugs. "Not very long. I don't date during the season." Olivia plays division one soccer at her university, and their season just ended a few weeks ago. She's a dedicated and talented player —probably one of the only things she takes seriously in her life.

The restaurant is an upscale, trendy place in the heart of downtown Austin. They have valet parking, but between a college student and a librarian, we opt to find our own cheap street parking a block away and walk in.

"Have you been here before?" I ask as we approach the restaurant. The sign on the building reads, "Molecule & Morsel: House of Molecular Gastronomy." My younger sister definitely tries to stay on trend, but still, this place doesn't seem to be her style.

"No," Olivia answers, looking warily at the sign. "Dylan picked it, I think."

"Molecule," I nudge. "Maybe you should have invited Molly instead."

She cracks a smile as we pass through the front doors. I gaze around at the interior of the restaurant. Against the back wall is a sleek bar with garish gold accents. The walls are wallpapered with a green and white floral pattern, large enough to give the appearance of being inside a jungle. The tables have a simple, rectangular, single pedestal design with white marble tabletops. The chairs are bow back and made of metal painted bright turquoise. The lights are turned low with recessed can lights strategically placed as spotlights on the gold accenting.

We approach the host stand, but before the model-esque hostess can ask us pretentiously whether we have a reservation, we hear an authoritative voice call, "Delaney!"

Olivia lifts a hand in recognition, and we make our way toward our dates. When we reach the table, Brent stands, giving Olivia a kiss on each cheek before pulling out a chair for her. He is tall—well over six feet—with raven hair, beige skin, and eyes so dark, that in the dim lighting of the restaurant, they look almost black. He's wearing a tailored suit and looks so much like one of those suave city businessmen you see in Hallmark movies that I have to wonder where my baby sister met him. At school? Seems unlikely.

The other man, who I assume is Brent's cousin and my date, Dylan, stays leaned back in his chair at the table, making no efforts to hide his leering gaze on Olivia's legs and chest.

"Hi!" I wave. "I'm Nicole. You must be Dylan?"

Dylan lolls his eyes in my direction, where he proceeds to scan my body up and down for an uncomfortable amount of time before saying, "I dig the hair."

"Uh, thanks," I say, shaking off the cringey feeling as I sit. Dylan is also wearing a suit, but where Brent's looks too slick, Dylan's looks too sloppy. It hangs on his thin frame, the untucked shirt spilling onto his lap like a dinner napkin. He has brown hair, buzzed low against his scalp, and brown, bloodshot eyes.

Olivia and Brent make introductions all around. The guys have already ordered a bottle of wine for the table, and we each have a glass of water as well. I sip mine, grateful to have an excuse not to talk. After twenty awkward minutes of small talk, during which I learn that Brent works for a tech company—"schmoozing" is how he describes it—and Dylan says nothing at all, a server approaches our table.

"Have you been to Molecule & Morsel before?" he asks. Olivia and I shake our heads. "We are a molecular gastronomy restaurant that serves only the most experimental and avant-garde dishes. Our menu changes daily and is limited to three options. Here are tonight's listings."

He hands us each a wrinkled piece of what looks like notebook paper that has been crumpled and then smoothed out again. Hand-written in pencil are three lines: foam-infused risotto, molecular ravioli, and Lancashire hotpot with beer-braised cockles.

A smile pasted to my lips, I slide my eyes to Olivia, who looks every bit as uncomfortable as I feel, but is probably doing a better job hiding it.

She raises her eyebrows but politely orders the risotto. That seems safe, so I do the same. Brent opts for the ravioli, and Dylan asks for the "hotpot" with a smarmy wink.

When the server brings our plates, I look down to see a tablespoon of risotto suspended in what looks like green sea foam with a single kernel of roasted corn perched on top. I look over at Olivia's plate—same as mine—then back to mine, then back to Olivia's again.

"Enjoy," the server warns before walking away.

"Is this food?" I whisper across the table to Olivia.

"Uhhh," she equivocates, scratching her forehead, "so it would seem."

Just then, Dylan erupts from beside me. "Of course it's food, you bumpkin!" he bellows, swaying alarmingly far into my space. "It's science food!"

People at the tables around us turn to stare. One guy even pulls his phone out and holds it up like he's preparing to record the scene.

Dylan's close enough now that I can smell alcohol on his breath. Instinctively, I lean away. Olivia narrows her eyes and hisses, "Brent, is your cousin *drunk*?"

Dylan leans toward her across the table, his chest pressing down against his plate, smearing food across the front of his jacket. He whispers loudly, "I was pregaming. Brent said not to say anything and just stay quiet."

"Dude!" Brent protests. "I told you not to be a cockblock!"

Olivia and I exchange a look and simultaneously stand up from the table.

"Don't worry, you didn't need his help." Olivia's nostrils flare as she glares at Brent. "Lose my number!" she bites out before storming away.

I hurry to catch up, and we burst through the front doors together, flooding onto the sidewalk outside.

Olivia looks at me, wide-eyed and flushed. "Oh my gosh," she whispers.

I try to stifle my laugh, but a small burst escapes. Olivia snorts, then quickly covers her mouth. My shoulders shake from the effort of holding it in, my eyes watering. Olivia grabs the arm of my sweater, pulling me out of the doorway and down the sidewalk until we collapse against a brick wall, both wailing with laughter.

Choking on the words, I exclaim in faux offense, "He called me a bumpkin!"

Olivia howls. "I didn't know people still used that word!"

When we finally compose ourselves, Olivia says, "At least we didn't have to eat that weird food!"

"Science food!" I shriek and we fall apart again.

Walking back to the car, I bump Olivia's shoulder. "Sorry about Brent."

She shrugs. "No big loss."

"How did you meet him anyway?"

"Dating app. It was only our third date. The first two were decent enough."

I scrunch my nose. "Really?"

She shrugs again. "I'm not looking for 'the one', Nicole. I'm just having fun. But, hey," she adds, "I'm sorry for making you come out, and about Dylan. What a Dyl-hole."

I bark out a laugh. "Don't worry about it. I'm focused on work right now anyway. I'm not interested in dating."

She's quiet for a few steps. "Liv?" I question.

"If you say so," she acquiesces.

When we reach the car, I grin at her. "In-N-Out on the way home?"

"Yes, definitely. I'm starving."

Lying in bed later that night, I think, if nothing else, at least this experience got me through the seemingly insurmountable hurdle—and least in my brain—of my first date since Steven. It also reminded me what I definitely *don't* want in a date. I text Adam.

Nicole:

> Any good memes for bad dates?

Adam:

The dots disappear and reappear for a while, before he finally sends me a meme featuring Anna Kendrick with a wide grin on her face. It says:

"I hadn't had a date in a while, so I went to the grocery store and bought some."

I groan.

Nicole:

I can actually hear the rimshot on that one

Nicole:

But I meant the other kind of date

Adam:

I was afraid of that. Are you okay?

Nicole:

Yeah, just need a funny meme to cheer me up?

Adam:

At your service

He sends a second meme, this one is a view of a woman's face with a man's shoulder in the foreground, showing that she's sitting across from somebody. Her eyes are wide. The caption reads:

"When he asks me to repeat the fake phone number that I gave him again."

Nicole:

[smiley face emoji] Thanks, Adam. Night

Adam:

Good night, Nicole

Chapter Eleven

Adam

B ecause I don't know what else to say, I text Nicole a funny meme every day during the winter break. It's easier than texting anything real; the coward's way forward. But while sometimes she receives the memes and just reacts to them, other times, she responds, telling me about her day and what she and her family are doing.

So now I know that there are bats that live under a bridge in downtown Austin and at dusk, they all fly out en masse. I know her family always drives around their neighborhood to look at Christmas lights, and one house goes all out with music and toy trains weaving across the yard. I know that Nicole and her sisters went out and bought corny, matching Christmas pajamas and all wore them Christmas morning as a surprise for their mom, who may or may not have cried. I know that on New Year's Eve, they all stayed home, even Olivia, and ate fondue and ice cream together on the couch as they watched the ball drop.

And in turn, Nicole now knows about the lighted boat parade I watched with my mom and Joan and a picnic of Publix subs. She knows we visited my dad's grave and left a sprig of holly berry on the top of his headstone, and my mom definitely cried. She knows I got together with my high school best friend, who is now married and has an adorable three-year-old, with another baby on the way. She knows that I went to bed early on New Year's Eve, because when she texted me "Happy New Year" at midnight, I didn't reply until the next morning.

I also know that she went on dates, or at least one that she mentioned, a bad one. Perhaps she went on other dates, too, but they were good, so she didn't text me about them. I wanted so badly to fish for information about that date, but of course, I couldn't. Why would I care? I'm only her coworker and now text buddy, I guess.

On the first day back at work in January, I'm on edge wondering how our texting over break will translate into real life, or if it even will at all. Before I leave my house to head to the library, I text her a meme featuring Jim from the show *The Office*. In the first panel, he's pointing to a chart that says "Always give 100% at work." In the second panel, the chart clarifies "Mon - 14%, Tues - 26%, Wed 42%, Thu - 15%, Fri - 3%".

I add my own message: "What percentage for the first day after a long break?"

She texts back: "Ready for 100% on the graphic novel project!"

Okay, very work focused, but to be fair, so was the meme I sent.

❦ ❦ ❦

At the library, I don't run into Nicole until mid-morning in the break room. Susan, who is Herb's administrative assistant, and Ben, another of the librarians, are discussing their grandchildren while getting coffee. Ben's daughter had a baby right before Christmas, and Susan is gushing about the photo. The refrigerator door closes to reveal Nicole, holding a container of yogurt.

She startles a little when she notices me. "Hi," she manages to say.

I smile, drinking her in. Her hair is a little longer, with blonde showing at the roots. She's wearing black dress pants with a light blue sweater. She looks tired around her eyes, but otherwise her face is the same as the one that's been popping up in my thoughts since I dropped her off at the airport weeks ago.

"Hey," I finally answer.

I let the pause stretch on too long, and Susan and Ben are watching us now. Nicole notices.

"How was your break?" she asks quickly.

I frown and rub my chin. "Um," I brilliantly verbalize. She pretty much knows how my break was. My eyes dart to Susan and Ben. Does she not want our coworkers to know that? Nicole looks at me expectantly, but with an air of detachment. "Uh, good," I answer vaguely. "How was yours?"

"It was great," she replies. "But I'm ready to get back to work. Let's set up a time to discuss the graphic novel collection more."

I tilt my head to the side. "Discuss the graphic novel collection?" I repeat, shuffling a step closer to her.

She steps back. "Yes. We're ready to order the books and start cataloging them, aren't we?"

I nod. "Mm-hmm."

"Good. I'll look at your calendar and send you a meeting invite for later in the week."

Susan and Ben have gone back to their conversation. Nicole glances at them and then gives me the smallest, abashed smile, her eyebrows wrinkling endearingly.

I sigh. "Sounds good."

"Thanks." Nicole sidesteps me and is out the door with her yogurt.

I shake my head to unbind my thoughts, but I can't remember now why I came into the break room to begin with.

When I get back to my desk, I text Nicole.

Adam:

> That was weird

Nicole:

> I know. Sorry [frowny face emoji]

But no explanation. I try to get it out of my head and focus on sifting through the dozens of emails, mostly junk, which came into my inbox during the time off.

True to her word, Nicole emails me that afternoon with an invite to meet on Wednesday in her office.

The next morning, I text her a meme of a woman sitting by the water reading a book. The image says:

"Oh yeah, I'm outdoorsy ... if outdoorsy means I read outside."

She marks it with the laughing reaction but doesn't text back.

While I was in Naples during the break, my mom tried to get me out of the house more.

"Adam," she scolded, "you can't just sit around with an old lady your whole vacation. Why don't you go do something fun?"

But I didn't really have anywhere to go. Other than my high school best friend, Mark, who was busy with his own family, I don't know anyone in Naples anymore. Mom and I watched Hallmark Christmas movies together, I went with her on her errands, and I played my computer games or read. I went on runs with Joan in the mornings or evenings when the air was cooler. My mom has an active social life, so a couple of times I found myself sitting at home alone on a weekend night while she was out with friends.

One day, in the week after Christmas, we decided to change things up and went to the beach. Regardless of the calendar, it was close to eighty degrees in south Florida, and while that is not warm enough in my mind to get in the water, it is a pleasant temperature for enjoying the sound of the waves crashing against the sand and watching seagulls dive bomb tourists with their picnic lunches.

"Your dad loved the beach," Mom sighed as we sat side by side in our beach chairs.

I turned my head to see her face in profile. Her long, straight white hair was pulled back in a loose ponytail. Her brown eyes glistened, and her lips turned up in a soft smile. "I remember," I said.

"He was a quiet man, didn't like crowds, so in our younger days, we would often head to the beach after dinner. Most of the tourists and families and sunbathers had gone back to their hotels or homes by then, and we would sit together and talk as the sun went down."

I smiled, picturing them on the beach together at sunset. "That sounds romantic."

"Sometimes," she began and then paused, "sometimes I wonder how life would have gone if circumstances were different."

"What do you mean?"

"If I had passed before your father, I mean. What would his life have been like without me? I miss him every day, but my brain is just programmed to need people. I have my book club, and my committees at church, and the volunteering I do. I rarely feel lonely. Your father, though. Most of the time, I had to force him out of the house. He would go anywhere I asked him to but would never be the one to suggest it. He would have been terribly lonely, I think. I'm not sure he would have tried not to be."

She turned to face me, then, her forehead creased together in between her eyebrows. "You remind me a lot of him," she said.

And while it's a comparison I loved to hear, I knew she didn't mean her words as a compliment.

I sighed. "I know."

"What do you know?"

I shrugged. "That I'm lonely. That as comfortable and orderly as my life is, I'm missing out."

She nodded. "And what are you doing about it?"

Nicole's face came to mind. "There's a woman I'm interested in," I admitted.

Mom's eyebrows rose halfway up her forehead. "And?"

"And it's complicated. She's a coworker, and I don't want to bother her."

"Do you know that she would think your interest is a nuisance?"

"No. Honestly, she seems lonely, too. I've been trying to be a friend."

Mom nodded. "Friends is a great place to start." She grinned at me. "What's her name?"

I laughed. "Oh, no. I'm not telling you anything else. Until," I allowed, "there's anything more to tell."

She chuckled and took my hand. "Okay, fine. Just tell me this. Is she the type that will get you out of the house? Who won't let you miss out on life?"

"Yes," I murmured, the word tumbling up in the breeze floating out to sea.

I meet Nicole in her office on Wednesday, the order list for the graphic novels in hand. I tell her that I placed the order already and the costs were pretty close to what we estimated in our original proposal.

"That's good," she says absently, focusing on her computer screen. She's gotten her hair done in the last couple of days, I note. Still lavender, but the color is refreshed in stark contrast to the area around her eyes, which looks more fatigued than before.

"Yeah," I continue. "The books should start coming in next week and then I'll be able to catalog them."

Nicole's quiet, the usual light in her eyes dimmed. She droops in her office chair, her neck bent and shoulders sagging.

"Hey," I prod. "Is anything wrong?"

Her eyes snap to mine. "No, of course not."

"Are you sure?" If she deflects again, I'll let it go.

"Okay," she admits, her eyes trained on her computer screen. "I guess I'm a little down, a little lonely, after spending the long break with my family."

"That's hard," I say gently. "It sounded like you all had a lot of fun."

"We did." She sighs wistfully. "My sisters can be a pain, but they're my best friends. It's hard being so far from them all the time."

I stay quiet, hoping she'll continue opening up. But instead, she shakes her head, her hair swishing back and forth, and affixes a fake smile to her face.

"Anyway," she says. "How long will the books take to get here?"

Barriers back up. I let it go and answer her question.

"I placed the order today, so they should start trickling in next week. None were backordered, so they shouldn't take long to arrive."

"Great!" she says. "As they come in and you work on the cataloging, I'll continue talking to faculty members about plans to incorporate the graphic novels into their courses, and work on plans for marketing and programming around the collection."

"For faculty members, does anything seem promising so far?" I ask.

"Yes, actually. I've talked to two different instructors who are pretty excited. Dr. Calder in the art department wants to do a whole unit in one of her courses about comic art, having the students look at examples from published works before they try it for themselves." Nicole's eyes sparkle as she talks, and I'm relieved to see the light returning to her face.

"That sounds amazing," I say. "We could see if any of the students in her course are interested in displaying their finished comic art in the library—sort of an exhibit to go along with the collection."

"Yeah, great idea. I'll talk to Dr. Calder." Nicole jots down a few words on the notepad in front of her. "I think that's it for today, then," she finishes, looking up at me.

I stand to leave, and to my surprise, she stands too, walking with me toward her office door. At the doorway, she places a hand tentatively on my arm.

"Adam?" she starts. She's quiet for a moment and I wait for her to gather her thoughts. Finally, in an earnest voice, she quietly says, "Thank you."

I meet her eyes. "Anytime," I promise.

That afternoon, I check upstairs for Dr. Parker. His office door is open, and as usual, Beans is lounging near the desk.

I rap out a knock as I stick my head through the doorway. "I wasn't sure you'd be here today."

"Well, I try to get here every Wednesday, if I can," he answers. "How was your Christmas?"

"Quiet," I reply, taking a seat. "I visited my mom in Naples. How was yours?"

He chuckles. "Not quiet. All three kids came with their spouses and the grandchildren. We had a full house. Christmas morning was glorious! Toys and wrapping paper and chaos everywhere."

His eyes are shining, and I feel a pang of longing in my chest.

"How many grandchildren do you have?"

"Six now," he counts. "My oldest daughter has three little ones. My son has two. And my younger daughter and her husband had their first in November."

I smile and nod.

"I'm glad you came by," Dr. Parker adds. "I was thinking of starting a project to organize my personal papers going back as far as the founding of Harkness. That's something the library might be interested in, yes?"

I clear my throat. "Yes, absolutely. We don't have an archivist or any archival collections at the moment, but I can't think of a better starting point than your personal papers."

He nods. "I'll talk to Herb. I'm sure there's something I can do to lobby the board for funds to hire an archivist."

His statement, said nonchalantly, gives me pause. I've had inklings before that Dr. Parker, despite his "honorary" status, still wields a good amount of authority at Harkness, but this is the boldest statement he's made to that fact, at least in front of me. I wonder just how involved Dr. Parker still is in the college's decision making.

Dr. Parker eyes me knowingly. "Anything else I can do for you today, Adam? How are things with your girl?"

"I don't have a girl," I protest.

"Not yet, but you're trying to woo one, aren't you?"

"Uh, in a manner of speaking."

"And how's it going?"

"Not great," I admit. "She's reserved. I'm still trying to work my way from coworker to friend, but her walls are pretty high."

"Hmm," Dr. Parker muses. "Has she let you in at all?"

"Actually, yes," I concede. "A little bit here and there. But then it's like she realizes she's doing it and shuts down."

Dr. Parker's eyes flash. "One thing I've observed in life," he says, "is that often the people with the hardest defenses are the ones most worth knowing. For whatever reason, it sounds like this young lady has learned not to trust others with her vulnerabilities."

I nod. That sounds right. "So, what can I do?" I ask.

"Give her every reason to believe that you are in her corner; that you're trustworthy. But let her come to you." He nods thoughtfully.

"What do you mean?"

"Don't pressure her. Don't push her. Just be there, quietly and steadily. She'll notice. And you'll be the first person she thinks about when she's ready to open up."

Chapter Twelve

Adam

In mid-January, Nicole pops into the doorway of my office, her hands grabbing either side of the frame as she leans forward. Her eyes sparkle, and her mouth twists up in a bright grin. We've been back to work for just a couple of weeks.

"What are you doing tonight?" she asks, her eyebrows quirking upward. The neckline of her mint green shirt dips down into a V, teasing the slightest hint of cleavage. Her black pants cling to her hips before flowing down around her ankles. My stomach flips over as I slowly bring my gaze back up to her face. She's watching me, waiting for my response.

"Nothing," I shrug. Well, not nothing. I plan to sit on the couch with my dog's head on my lap as I play *Civilization*, but I know most people would not consider those "plans", and besides, I'm guessing she's asking for a reason, and I want to know what it is.

Anything with her or having to do with her would absolutely trump my current plans.

"Awesome. I'm going to this thing called Soapbox over at the amphitheater on the island. Do you want to come?" She looks eager and hopeful, and I want her to look at me like that always.

"Yes," I answer quickly, my head bobbing up and down.

She pauses, her eyebrows pulling together. "Don't you want to know what it is first?"

Oh, yeah. I guess the social convention here would be to find out more before agreeing. "What is it?" I ask, knowing that even if she says it's a seminar about the history of clowns, my answer won't change.

Nicole leaves the doorway now and drops into the chair in front of my desk, folding one leg underneath her. She rests her forearms on the edge of my desk, gripping each of her elbows with the opposite hand. Leaning forward, she meets my eyes.

"It's this event where people get up and speak for like five minutes, each to share a story or information on a topic they're passionate about." She pauses, or maybe just stops for a breath.

"Yes," I say.

She gives me a puzzled look. "Don't you want to know the topics for tonight before you decide?"

No. Don't care. If Nicole's inviting me, I'm going.

"Ah, sure. Of course. What are the topics?"

She tells me a bit about some of the speakers and what they'll be talking about. No clowns, but one person will be talking about the art of mime through the ages, so pretty close.

"It starts at six, so we'll need to go pretty much right after work, but they have local food trucks so we can get dinner there," Nicole finishes explaining.

"Honestly," I say, "it sounds great." And it really does. This event sounds like something I'd go to on my own, if I had known about it. "I'm definitely in."

Nicole's face lights up, and my chest becomes a pinball machine. My heart pings wildly in every direction, and then, her beaming smile directed right at me causes a crescendo of flashes and clanging bells. It takes a minute or two for my body to regulate and my logical brain to click back into place.

"Oh, wait," I start.

"What?" she asks, her face falling. She sits back against the chair and crosses her arms over her chest. "You can't go after all?"

"I *can*," I say slowly, "but I'll need to stop home first to let my dog outside. And it's not exactly on the way."

"You have a dog?" Her eyes flash with interest, and she leans forward again.

"I do. Her name is Joan. Maybe I can meet you there?"

"Well..." she hesitates.

"It's just that it's already a long day for her while I'm at work, and I don't want to make her wait longer," I clarify.

"No, I get it. That's important. And responsible. It's just..." she trails off again. Her cheeks turn pink as her eyes search my face beseechingly. Oh. Disappointment rolls through me when I realize what she's trying to say, but I play it off.

"Ohhh," I force my tone to be as light as possible. "I understand. You need a ride. You invited me for my car." I force a smile so that she sees I'm teasing.

Her entire face is red now, and she winces at my words. Her chin dips down. "No," she starts. "Well, a ride would make things easier for me, but..." Her jaw sets, and she lifts her face back up to mine. When she speaks again, her voice is firm. "I would like a ride, but I want it to be with you. It's not about your car; it's about you, Adam. I heard about Soapbox, and it reminded me of when we were talking in my office about graphic novels, and you said you like hearing people talk about things that interest them. I thought you'd enjoy it and that we could go together."

I'm quiet for a moment as my breath bottles up in my chest, stuck as I consider Nicole's words. She thought of me. She remembers my words from months ago. She wants to go with *me*. Finally, I nod and lick my lips, the tips quirking up slightly. Holding her gaze, I offer a solution.

"I *would* enjoy it, more so if we go together. How do you feel about riding with me to my house? I'll walk Joan real quick and then we can head out?"

Nicole exhales a quiet breath and nods. She swallows before saying, "That works for me if you're sure it's okay." She laughs nervously. "You might not want a random coworker at your house."

We lock eyes. "You're not a random coworker," I tell her.

She tilts her head slightly, waiting for me to say more, but I don't explain. Another beat passes.

"Okay then," Nicole grits out, slapping her palms against her thighs and standing. "I'll meet you back here in a few hours?"

I give her an easy smile. "Sounds great. I'm looking forward to it, Nicole. Truly."

She dips her chin as she backs toward my office door, a shy smile playing at her lips. "Me too," she says, and then she's gone.

On the ride to my house after work, Nicole's quiet. I don't say much either, but my mind is spinning. Tonight will be the first time that Nicole and I will spend real time together outside of work. Driving her to the airport in December doesn't count. I know what this means to me—letting her see more of who I am and hopefully breaking down her walls a bit more so I can know her better. She's guarded—with me, but also with other colleagues at the library. She projects confidence in meetings, but I'm starting to get the sense that her confidence doesn't extend to personal relationships. She holds back. I see snippets of her unfiltered personality from time to time, and I crave more. What I wouldn't give to be someone she trusts enough to be vulnerable with, to be wholly herself around.

It's a slow process. I'm deliberately holding back; spoon feeding her flashes of my feelings, my attraction. If she knew the depths of this crush, I'm certain it would overwhelm her. I feel a twinge of guilt. Am I lying to her? Manipulating her? I don't pressure her though; this is at her speed. And the thing is, I *know* she enjoys the time we spend together. She sought me out for this event tonight.

She invited me. Yes, she needed a ride, but I believe that it mattered to her who provided that ride. And she chose me. If we get to the friendship zone and never pass it, fine. I'll find a way to deal with that. For now, though, she's still seeing me as just a coworker, and I know we can be more to each other than that.

I pull into the driveway, and Nicole sighs happily. I turn in my seat to look at her. She's staring up at my townhome.

"It's so cute," she breathes. "I've always wanted to live in a townhome. My family took a trip to Baltimore when I was a kid, and I just fell in love with the beautiful red brick rowhouses. I imagined this whole future for myself where I lived in one and worked for a publishing house in the city."

Another snippet of the full Nicole. I tuck this knowledge into my memory, like a delicate piece of parchment sliding into an acid-free folder.

"So, what happened?" I ask.

She looks at me, as if only just remembering that I'm here. She studies my face, her eyes ticking back and forth as if calculating how much to reveal. Finally, she smiles.

"I realized that I don't like the cold. And also, book publishing is probably not the right fit for me. Too competitive." She shrugs and reaches for the door handle.

We get out of the car and step toward the door to my place just as a chilly breeze gusts through.

"It feels cooler out now than this morning," I comment. "Must be a cold front."

Before Nicole can respond, I open the door and Joan's right there, blocking our path with her tail wagging. I back Joan up enough for us to get through the door, and then she's bumping her head against Nicole's thighs in greeting. Nicole drops to her knees, scratching behind Joan's ears and cooing to her in baby talk. Joan eats it up, angling closer until she's practically on top of Nicole.

Laughing, I introduce them unnecessarily. "Nicole, this is my dog, Joan."

Nicole lifts her face to mine for a moment, a wide grin on her lips. "Well, I hope so. Otherwise, what's she doing here?" She immediately returns her attention to the wriggling pup.

I watch for a few moments, my heart squeezing in my chest. Nicole's face is shining. She's radiant. Her soft purple hair falls in front of her face as she bends her head toward Joan. Her lips are pursed as she sweetly croons praises, and her nose wrinkles adorably. I've never seen her look so beautiful.

Shaking my head to clear my thoughts, I walk through the dining room space to the open kitchen to set my lunchbox on the counter. I deposit my computer bag onto the dining room table on my way back to the living room. When I pick up Joan's leash from the side table, the metal jingles, finally wrenching her attention away from our guest. Joan bounds toward me. Nicole takes the opportunity to rise to her feet, clasping her hands together in front of her as she looks around the room.

"I'm going to walk Joan real quick," I tell her as I snap the leash onto Joan's collar. "Feel free to look around or have a seat or whatever. It shouldn't take long." Nicole looks nervous, so I offer her what I hope is a reassuring smile.

Joanie and I don't do our typical thirty-minute walk, of course. I just take her around the block, giving her enough time to do her business before heading back to the house. The air has cooled even more, and I'm shivering as we step inside. January and February are typically our coldest months in north Florida, and by cold, I mean cold to me—with average highs in the sixties and lows in the forties. Occasionally a cold front will come through that drops us down an additional ten degrees or so for a few days. Feels like we're heading into one of those now.

I dart my eyes around for Nicole and see her in the corner of the couch under a blue and gray buffalo check throw blanket. My heart almost stutters to a stop at the vision. She looks so cozy, so at home. Like I could slide under the blanket next to her and sweep her feet into my lap. Having her here, in my space, among my things, is messing with my head. I feel a yearning unlike anything I've felt before; a desire to hold her, care for her, protect her.

I'm not sure what she reads on my face, but Nicole smiles timidly as she moves the blanket and stands to walk toward me. She halts six feet away, hovering just out of reach.

"I got cold. Sorry if I overstepped at all." Her chin dips toward the floor and my eyes follow. She's barefoot, her shoes next to my spare flip-flops by the door.

"You're fine," I say, my voice gravelly. I clear my throat. "It's actually getting pretty cold out there. You said the event is at the amphitheater? So outdoors?"

She lifts her head to meet my eyes, concern on her face. "Yeah."

"You can borrow one of my sweatshirts." I wince at my own tone. Though I mean it as a suggestion, it comes out sounding more like a command. Nicole starts to protest, but I level her with a determined glare. "You'll freeze. And you've already told me you don't like the cold. It's no trouble. Really." My voice is gentler this time, mollifying.

Nicole nods. "Thank you," she murmurs. "That would be really nice."

Joan whines to remind me that she's still on her leash. I let her loose and tell Nicole I'll be right back. I run upstairs and grab a sweatshirt for myself. I deliberate a little over which sweatshirt to lend Nicole before chiding myself to not overthink it. I pull out a plain, dark green zipper hoodie.

When she puts on the hoodie downstairs, I realize my mistake. The sweatshirt is too big on her, of course. The sleeves swallow her hands, and she shoves them up, the fabric bunching around her elbows. The bottom hem hits her about mid-thigh. The color, though. It's just a touch darker than her eyes, making them glow with an ethereal blaze. I literally cannot look away.

"Adam?" Nicole's voice brings me out of my stupor. The look on her face is half amused, half annoyed, and I know I've been caught staring.

"Yeah," I grit out.

"Ready to go?"

I shake my head to clear my thoughts. Dragging a friendly smile back to my face, I answer, "Yep! All set."

We both say goodbye to Joan, who is not thrilled we're leaving again so soon. In the car, I turn up the heat and activate the seat warmers. We'll be especially glad for those when we're trying to defrost after the event.

I glance at the passenger seat and my chest tightens. Nicole sitting there, in my sweatshirt, her smile lighting up the car, feels natural. Like she's always been by my side. Like she always should be.

Chapter Thirteen

Nicole

This is my second time attending Soapbox. The first time, Tasha told me about it, and I caught a ride with her and some of her friends. Considering I'm more than four years older than them and in a completely different stage of life, it was a bit awkward. I had a good time, but the evening didn't click. I just know Adam will appreciate the variety show of expertise as much as I do, so I'm hoping for a better experience tonight.

I glance over at Adam in the driver's seat. He's focused on the road, hands precisely at ten and two on the steering wheel. I snuggle down into the warmth of the heated passenger seat and pull Adam's sweatshirt tighter around me.

I'm not blind or clueless. I know Adam has a thing for me. But he's never overtly hit on me or made me uncomfortable in any way. I feel flattered and desirable when I catch his lingering looks. But it can't happen. I realized several years ago, with the help of my therapist, that every boyfriend I've had—all three of them—was interested in me first.

With my first boyfriend in high school, Ethan, I was crushing on a completely different guy when his best friend let it slip that Ethan liked me. I had hardly noticed Ethan up to that point, but now, suddenly I forgot all about my crush and instantly moved on to him. We dated for three months toward the end of sophomore year, but I often wondered if we even had anything in common. Would I have been interested in Ethan if he wasn't interested in me first?

Senior year, I dated Brandon from Halloween all the way through graduation. Again, I barely knew he existed until he asked me out. It felt nice being noticed. Being sought out. Personality-wise, I actually found Brandon kind of annoying, but it felt good to have a boyfriend. When we split before Brandon left for his out-of-state college, I wasn't heartbroken.

And then, of course, Steven. That was a whole trainwreck—so much so that even the thought of a new relationship starts my brain spiraling down the drain of worst-case scenarios. I will never again let anyone make me feel that broken.

My therapist suggested a lack of self-confidence might contribute to my apparent pattern of, essentially, taking what I think I can get in terms of dating. If low self-esteem was my problem in high school, my relationship with Steven definitely didn't help matters. Since him, I haven't had strong feelings of attraction to anyone, and if any man has been interested in me, I was oblivious to it. Until Adam. But I've recognized the pattern now, and I'm determined not to continue in it. So, if a man, like Adam, is interested in me when I don't feel the same, that man is not an option.

Adam and I are coworkers. Colleagues. Nothing more. Despite the cute way his lips pinch and his eyes twinkle when he's sharing a funny story. Despite the amazing way his hoodie smells wrapped around me. Despite his adorable dog. I just don't see him that way.

We arrive at the amphitheater with just enough time to hit up the food trucks and snag seats before the program starts. There are three trucks, including my favorite—a food truck that focuses solely on arepas. All kinds of fancy, complicated arepas with different fillings and even toppings. My usual is the black bean, sweet plantain, and cheese arepa. So good. Adam's in line at the grilled cheese truck when I get my food, so I grab us a table.

I watch as he orders and then waits to the side for his food to be ready. He didn't change after work—neither did I since I didn't go home first—so he's wearing khaki colored corduroy slacks and black loafers. Over the red and gray plaid button down shirt he wore to work, he's added a sporty navy pullover hoodie that fits snugly across his chest. As the window attendant hands Adam his food, he pulls his hands out of the front pocket of his sweatshirt. He turns and scans the crowd, so I wave to get his attention.

Adam carefully sets two paper boats of food on the table. Before he can sit, I grab the sleeve of his sweatshirt and shout, "Tater tots! They had tater tots?"

He settles into the chair next to me with an amused expression. "Nope," he deadpans.

I release his sleeve only to smack the same spot as he grins at me.

"Sorry. I just really love tater tots. I didn't know that food truck had them." I eye the ever-increasing line and check the time on my phone. "Maybe I have time to get some before the first speaker..."

Adam checks his phone as well. "I don't think so, Nicole. If they start on time, you won't make it." He peers at me through the glass of his lenses, his expression unreadable. "Just take these."

"No, I can't do that. They're yours. What else did you get?" I inspect his other plate. "A wrap?"

He shrugs. "Yeah. Chicken Caesar. But seriously, I won't eat all these. At least split them with me? Eat as many as you want."

I know it's a line. If I hadn't said anything, I'm sure he would have eaten all the tater tots he ordered and paid for. But for tater tots, I'm willing to play dumb a bit. "Okay, thanks," I say.

I pop one tot into my mouth, and it's perfect. Crisp on the outside, warm in the middle. Yum. This. This right here is why my weight is always a little higher than I'd prefer—I just enjoy food too much.

The Soapbox host calls the crowd to attention. Our seats are decent—to the left of the small stage and only a few rows back. Soapbox is held on the auxiliary stage, which is a more intimate venue than the amphitheater's main stage where they hold concerts and local high school graduations. The auxiliary stage is slightly raised—easy to hop onto without stairs, but high enough that I have no trouble seeing the host up there. Seating is mostly small bistro tables like the one Adam and I share, with some bench seating right in front of the stage.

The host is a Black man with long, curly hair, and who is, without explanation, dressed like a pirate. He explains the sequence of the program: there are ten presenters who will speak for five minutes each. A five-minute break in between each presentation will allow them to switch out the slide decks and the new speaker to get situated.

The first presenter is a high school student who talks about surfing as a metaphor for life. He tells a story about his first wave, and how his success required him to be present in the moment with focus and intent. I actually find myself tearing up a little as he describes his moment of triumph—that's what he calls it.

Following the surfer, a woman who looks to be in her forties talks about her path from writing fiction as a hobby to self-publishing online. She's published four romance novels in the last two years with plans for three more in the upcoming year. I send myself a text with her name so I can remember to look her up later. As if I need anything else on my TBR.

By the start of the second break, Adam and I are done eating. It doesn't escape me that he ate maybe three tater tots, and I polished off the rest. I feel guilty, so I scoop up the empty containers from both of us and take them to the trash. I'm not gone more than a few minutes, but when our table is in sight again, I see a woman with dark brown hair standing there talking to Adam. She looks to be about his age, maybe a few years older. She's pretty in a girl-next-door way and is dressed in a black pencil skirt with nude tights and a red cowl neck sweater.

I drop into my chair, and Adam shifts his attention to me before glancing back at the woman.

"Nicole, this is Ashley—Dr. Cartwright. She works at Harkness, too. She's presenting later tonight. We both started working at the college around the same time and were in new employee orientation together." Adam smiles at Ashley as he introduces her.

"Ashley, this is Nicole–"

"His coworker," I quickly interrupt. I'm cementing the boundary lines. We are coworkers. Period.

Adam's eyebrows furrow together. "Uh, yeah, Nicole and I both work in the library." See, he agrees. Coworkers.

I turn my attention to Ashley. "What are you presenting about tonight, Dr. Cartwright?"

She meets my eyes and smiles. "Call me Ashley," she insists. "I work in the coastal environmental science department at Harkness. My work right now is mainly focused on using constructed oyster reefs as living shorelines to protect salt marshes from erosion. I'm going to talk about that."

I feel the crankiness trickling out of my body as I take in her words. My brain is pinging, and I'm not sure which part of her statement to focus on first.

I start with: "My sister is a coastal environmental scientist. In New Orleans."

"Oh," Ashley exclaims. "You should try to recruit her over to Harkness. We're still growing our program and could use more faculty."

I consider that for a minute. "I'll definitely let her know, but she's more about laboratory work than teaching. She's a researcher more than anything." I shrug.

"Ah, I see. We're not really a research institution, as I'm sure you know. What's your sister's research focus?"

As we're talking, Adam pulls a chair over from a neighboring table and sets it between us. Ashley smiles at him and sits, her attention back on me.

"Good question. She recently switched research teams, but I think she's researching algal blooms in the Gulf? Does that sound like a thing?" I laugh. "Her name is Molly Delaney."

"Definitely a thing. I'll look up her work."

"Speaking of work, yours sounds so interesting! I guess I'll hear about it when you speak, but I'm dying to know more."

I feel Adam's eyes on me and when I turn my head, I meet his gaze. He's beaming as he watches Ashley and I talk. He has a gleam in his eye, gaze trained on my face, as if waiting for my reactions. I give him what I intend to be a questioning look.

Ashley notices the exchange and stands. "I better head back to my own table. They're about to start again, and it'll be my turn before long." She reaches her hand out to shake Adam's. "So nice to run into you here, Adam. And Nicole...." She smiles at me. "Really nice meeting you. Would you like to get together sometime for lunch or coffee? We can talk more."

I nod, smiling. "I'd like that. Email me?" I know she'll be able to find my contact information through Harkness' email system.

Ashley nods once before making her way to the other side of the stage where she's sitting with a few other people.

Adam is still beaming at me when I turn to glare at him. "What?" I ask, my cheeks heating up.

He shakes his head. "I'm just thinking that I may have something new to add to my list of skills." I raise my eyebrows at him in question and he smirks. "Friend matchmaker. You two seemed to hit it off."

I laugh. "As if you had anything to do with it!" I hit his shoulder playfully. "You didn't know Ashley would be here tonight, and besides, I dragged *you* out, so pretty sure this is a coincidence."

He grins. "Maybe so. But still, I'm glad. Ashley is a nice friend." He seems to emphasize the last word. "Her fiancé is a great guy, too. We've hung out a few times." He watches me out of the corner of his eye.

"Cool," I say nonchalantly. I know what he's doing. But it doesn't matter because Adam and I are just coworkers.

The rest of the evening is full of listening and talking and laughing. Between each speaker, Adam and I chat about the presentation topic and then off on tangents wherever that leads us. Ashley gives a phenomenal presentation. I text Molly throughout with my commentary, which she mostly ignores.

After the last presentation, we wait for the crowd to thin before heading back to the car. Adam nudges me with his elbow. "You should do this," he says.

The night has only gotten cooler. I have my hands balled up inside the front pockets of the hoodie I'm wearing. I'm ready to get back to those heated seats in Adam's car.

"Do what?" I ask, watching the bottleneck of people exiting through the gate.

"Present at Soapbox."

My head snaps toward Adam, and I laugh. "What would I even talk about?"

Adam shrugs. "Graphic novels. Comics. Tater tots." He grins slyly at that, and I blush thinking about how many of his tots I ate. "Whatever you want. You speak well, know how to hold the audience's attention. I think you'd be great."

I laugh again, but Adam's gaze is serious, earnest. "I don't know," I say. "Maybe." That actually might be fun. Turning the tables on him, I ask, "Why don't you present? You could talk about memes."

"I'm not super comfortable speaking in public," Adam admits. "Why do you think I'm in technical services instead of instruction?"

"That's valid," I allow. "But speaking in public more could help you feel more comfortable."

He blanches at the thought. "Yeah, I really don't think so."

As Adam drives me home, the car is dark and quiet. The silence is companionable; just right for two people who spent the last few hours talking about everything and nothing. Even though I gave so much of myself tonight, letting Adam know me in a way I haven't with anyone new in a while, I'm surprised that I feel full, not depleted. The warmth from the seats in Adam's car spreads into my core, my heart radiating the same heat.

He pulls up in front of my apartment and insists on walking me to the stairway leading up to my front door. We both stop at the bottom of the steps. There's electricity between us, an energy I can almost feel crackling in the air. I'm afraid if we touch, I'll feel the shock on my skin like an electrostatic discharge.

Adam reaches up as if to brush the hair off my face, but stops, leaving his hand hovering in the air near my shoulder. "Thanks for inviting me, Nicole. I had an amazing time with you," he says, his voice low and rough.

"Me too," I whisper. I clear my throat, the spell of the cold night air and Adam's proximity blurring the lines of my thoughts. My mouth is speaking again before my brain has time to process the words. "Do you want to come up for a few minutes?"

His hesitation, the split second of his eyes tracking my face with reluctance, is like a bucket of water on my head. It jerks me back into the real world, into my right mind.

Before Adam answers, I blurt, "Never mind!" I laugh robotically. "I mean, no, of course not. It's late. Why would you?"

There's regret written all over his face, an apology on his tongue. When he starts, "Nicole…"

I laugh again and dart up the stairs before he can say anything further.

"Wait, Nicole." He extends his arm, as if to pull me back down, then drops it helplessly to his side.

"Good night!" I call behind me, feigning a nonchalance that I hope covers my supreme embarrassment. I slam and lock the door behind me, sliding my back down until I'm on the floor with my head in my hands.

Annnnd … I'm still wearing his sweatshirt.

Chapter Fourteen

Adam

I consider texting Nicole after that debacle in front of her apartment last night, but then I think I'll give her some space and just talk to her when I see her at work tomorrow. But I don't see her at work. Her office door is closed most of the day. She's nowhere to be found during the lunch hour. And even her time on the reference desk, where I could have at least walked by to see her, even if we couldn't have talked, coincides with an online committee meeting I have to attend for a state library organization. She's elusive; I'm pretty sure intentionally so.

She's embarrassed. It's not like I didn't *want* to end the night in her apartment. Of course I did. Even now, my body aches to be close to her, to take up the same space. But her invitation was impulsive, and I don't want to be a regret. Even as she said it, I felt like she was as surprised to hear the words coming out of her mouth as I was.

How do I explain that I hesitated, and would have declined, out of respect for her? Out of the hope for something more between us than a moment of opportunity? It wasn't a rejection. And how do I explain all that without embarrassing her further, implying that I understood the shrouded intentions behind her invitation, that those intentions were there, as much as she'd like to deny it now?

When I get home, I text her.

Adam:

> I didn't see you around the library today. Everything okay?

Nicole:

> Of course. Sorry our paths didn't cross

Adam

> Can we talk about last night?

I wait a minute. Five minutes. Ten. No response. Sighing, I leave my phone on the kitchen counter as Joan and I take our evening walk.

When we return, she still hasn't responded. I don't hear back from her until after I've finished dinner and am washing the dishes.

Nicole:

> No need. Nothing to talk about

Okay, so we're pretending it didn't happen.

Adam:

> So we're okay?

Nicole:

Of course. See you around the library

Seems very *not* okay to me, but whatever. I groan in frustration. We made so much progress yesterday, just to have it all derailed in a moment. I *know* she's attracted to me. I know she feels the pull between us, or at least she did last night. So, she doesn't trust ... me? Herself?

If I can just get her to drop her walls again, maybe we can talk about all this. No games, no pretense. She'll have to talk to me tomorrow, anyway. We're meeting about the graphic novel project in the afternoon.

♡ ♡ ♡

I take it as a good sign the next morning when I don't find my sweatshirt washed and folded on my desk. She kept it. That has to mean something, doesn't it? Even if all it means is that she hasn't done laundry yet. I try to put Nicole out of my mind and instead work on cataloging the graphic novels that, you know, I ordered for Nicole. Ugh, I'm a mess.

I walk into Nicole's office that afternoon for our meeting and freeze in the doorway. I quickly catch myself, and pasting on a smile, continue into the room. Someone pulled an extra chair into this small space, and Tasha is sitting in it.

"Adam, hi." Nicole smiles politely, the light not reaching her eyes. "Tasha is going to join us today. I thought it would be a great opportunity for her to learn since she's considering getting her master's in library science after she graduates. Plus, we can have her help us with some of the more administrative parts of the project."

I sit in the remaining chair to the left of Tasha and with an entire desk between me and Nicole.

"Great idea," I lie. "Welcome, Tasha."

Tasha flashes me her usual confident smile but glances furtively at Nicole when she doesn't think I'll notice. Tasha is a buffer, plain and simple. She's here so Nicole doesn't have to be alone with me.

The meeting is short. I give an update on the cataloging. Nicole talks about the faculty members she's met with who are interested in incorporating graphic novels into their courses. She never meets my eyes. It's tense, and I'm tense and frenetic, and the quiver in Nicole's fingers as she writes her notes gives her away, even as she appears otherwise calm and collected.

I can't. I can't go back to this. At least let's be friends again.

When the painfully awkward meeting ends, I head upstairs to the third floor. I don't know if Dr. Parker is in his office, but I'm going to check.

"Adam, my boy!" Dr. Parker booms when I peek my head into his open office door. "Come in."

I do, closing the door behind me. Before taking a seat, I squat next to Beans and scratch his ears.

"Hi, Dr. Parker," I say as I sit in my usual chair.

Something in my tone must catch his attention, because his head snaps up and he studies my face.

"You look and sound miserable," he finally says. "What's going on?"

I feel miserable. I'd love Dr. Parker's advice, but I stop to think about how best to explain what's happening without saying anything that might embarrass Nicole further.

"The wooing is not going well, I take it?" he asks.

"You could say that," I answer. "We've been spending time together as friends."

"Well, that's good! Friendship is the foundation for any good romance."

"No, yeah. The friendship part is fine. But while we were spending time together, she said something that she now feels embarrassed about. She's been avoiding me ever since. And when she has to talk to me, she's super formal and professional." I run both hands down my face before setting my elbows on my knees, staring at the ground.

"Hmm, that's tricky," Dr. Parker muses. "We already know the lady can be a little prickly—any progress on finding out why that is?"

I shake my head.

"Hmm. If she's afraid to feel vulnerable, and then she lets down her walls a little only to embarrass herself in front of you, she would naturally want to put the walls right back up. How did you react when she said whatever it is she said?"

I straighten in the chair and look at him. "I tried to talk to her, but she ran off. And then I texted her about it a couple days later, but she just pretended it never happened."

"You ... texted her?" Dr. Parker shakes his head at me in disappointment.

"First of all, texting is a perfectly acceptable mode of communication for my generation, preferred even. Second of all, I didn't want to just text her, but she's been avoiding me, remember?"

Dr. Parker's eyes flash with amusement. "I'll pretend you didn't just call me old since I know what a precarious emotional state you're in right now."

"Sorry," I mumble, rubbing the back of my neck.

"You're forgiven," he says impatiently. "But I think I know what you need to do. You need to show her that you still respect her, still care about her. That her words didn't affect how you see her."

"Okay," I nod. "Yeah, that makes sense. Show her that it didn't change my opinion of her."

We sit quietly for a few beats. "Any ideas on how to do that?" I finally ask.

"Adam, I have been happily married for close to fifty years. *You're* the one who wants to woo the young lady, so *you* need to come up with your own grand gesture. I can't do everything for you." He shakes his head.

"Yeah, fair enough," I say.

As I think, my eyes drift to the view outside the window. Dr. Parker's office overlooks the west lawn and gardens of the college, with the main building and its stunning architecture in the background. Something nebulous niggles at the back of my mind, something I feel like I need to remember. I work at it, pulling it forward until it comes into focus.

Oh.

Oh. I've got it. I know what I need to do.

Eyes wide, I jump up from my chair and see Dr. Parker beaming at me from behind his desk, leaning back in his chair.

"Looks like you've got something," he says with a wink. "Come back and tell me about it next week."

"I will! Thanks, Dr. P." I call on my way out the door. Mentally, I'm already making a list of everything I'll need.

Chapter Fifteen

Nicole

It's another four days before I see Adam again. It makes sense. He's off Thursday and Friday since he's working the weekend. I want to avoid him. I want to pretend nothing happened. I pushed him away. It's what I want, so I shouldn't feel disappointed that it's working.

But, in truth, I'm walking around a little lost. I'm so used to talking to Adam now, joking around with him. I haven't even gotten a meme from him since before Soapbox. He doesn't send them every day anymore, but usually it's at least a couple of times a week.

I'm embarrassed, and I'm ashamed. I saw the hurt on Adam's face in our meeting the other day, and I know I caused it with how cold I was toward him. And he didn't even do anything. It was all me. By now, he's certainly given up. I would if I were him.

Monday morning, I run into Tasha in the break room, and she tags along with me to my office when I tell her I have a project for her. I unlock the office door and am stunned to see a large, framed poster hanging on the wall to the left of my desk. It's huge—like five feet wide and four feet tall. The image is a photograph of the gardens right outside the library—what would be my view if I had an office on the exterior side of the hallway. I stop so abruptly that Tasha bumps into me from behind.

"Sorry," I mumble as I move closer to the picture to examine it better.

It's lovely. The frame is nothing extravagant, just simple poster framing. The photo looks to have been taken with a high-quality camera—even blown-up this big, the image is crisp. Colorful flowers—pink hibiscus, white gardenias, and purple azaleas—frame a cement pathway shaded by four palm trees. Beyond that, the imposing architecture of Harkness's primary building stands tall. The primary building, which now houses the dining hall and some of the dorms, was a luxury hotel built in the 1880s by a well-known oil tycoon who spared no expense on the design or materials. The background is the unblemished blue of the sky. It's beautiful.

"Where did this come from?" I wonder aloud.

"Really?" Tasha answers, reminding me of her presence. "Where do you think it came from?"

I turn to stare at her. "No," I protest. "I'm sure it's something Herb had put in all the offices."

With impeccable timing, at that moment, Herb pops his head into the office. "Nicole," he says. "I'd like to see you and Adam in my office at 9:30 please. Does that work for you?"

"Yes," I answer. I start to ask about the poster. "Herb—"

"Hey, nice picture," Herb interrupts. "I hope you didn't put any holes in the wall hanging it."

He pops out again, and I turn to see Tasha with her arms folded across her chest giving me a smug smile.

"As I said," she smirks, "where do you think it came from?"

I shake my head, not wanting to jump to conclusions. Surely after the way I've been treating him, Adam wouldn't do something like this for me. Although, I remember, I did tell him a couple of months ago how I wish I had some natural light in my office. The poster isn't natural light, but it's definitely more welcoming than the blank wall.

Tasha fiddles with something on my desk and holds a folded piece of paper out to me. "Let's find out," she says. "This has your name on it."

Indeed, written in meticulous print in black ink on the front of the piece of paper, is simply *Nicole*.

I unfold it to find a printed-out meme. The image is of a super cute Pomeranian puppy's face. Around it are the words:

"Here's a cute puppy to brighten your day."

It's not signed, but there's no doubt who left it on my desk, and therefore who hung the poster in my office. The gesture floors me. My eyes start to sting, and I have to blink hard to keep the tears at bay.

Tasha, who I've forgotten again, puts a hand on my shoulder. Tilting her head, she catches my eyes and says softly, "Nicole, with all due respect, I know you are a full-grown adult, but what are you doing?"

I laugh and shake my head. I'm not sure myself. I murmur a goodbye as she leaves to take her spot at the front desk.

My phone pings. It's a text from Adam. Well, a meme in two comic strip-style panels. In the first panel, a goldfish says to another goldfish "You wanna hang out later?" The second panel zooms out to show the two goldfish alone in a small fishbowl. The second goldfish answers, "Yeah, probably."

I chuckle and shake my head. He's a little wrong though. I don't want to hang out with Adam because of a lack of options. I want to hang out with him because he's genuinely nice to be around.

I'm surprised by how much I enjoy hanging out with him. At the same time, I don't want to lead him on or give him any impression that I want to be more than colleagues. I cringe, thinking that inviting him into my apartment late at night is *not* the way to get that point across. But if there's a chance we can go back to our work relationship and how it was before Soapbox, I'm definitely on board.

I catch Adam outside Herb's closed office door just before 9:30. He watches me approach, apprehension written on his face and in the way he grips his hands together. I smile at him, a true, honest smile that I feel to the tips of my ears. His shoulders slump in relief. He smiles back, the warm, wide grin I've gotten used to. I stop in front of him, my hand finding his like a magnet.

"Thank you," I whisper. "I've been awful. I'm sorry."

"Let's forget about it," he says, squeezing my hand.

I hesitate for a moment, then ask shyly, "Can I hug you?"

Instead of answering, he pulls me in and wraps his arms around my back. My arms loop up and around his neck, my head resting ever so gently on his chest. Every part of me that's touching him feels hot, like I'm standing too close to a fire. My pulse quickens, and I lean into the embrace.

Herb's office door opens, and we quickly pull apart. "Oh," Herb squeaks, startled. "I was, um, just looking for you two. Come in, please."

He disappears into his office as Adam blushes and I chuckle. Adam thrusts out his arm gallantly, ushering me through the doorway.

We each take a seat in Herb's office. With everything that's happened already this morning, I haven't had a chance to obsess over this meeting. Herb hasn't given any clues as to what it's about.

With that thought, Herb clears his throat and asks, "How's the graphic novel project going?"

"Great!" I respond enthusiastically. "We should be ready to start circulating the books, in what?" I look to Adam. "About two weeks?"

Adam nods his agreement. "I just need to finish cataloging, and Nicole is working on the marketing plan."

Herb claps his hands together once and says, "Excellent. I've got to tell you, I've been seeing more and more buzz about graphic novels in the academic library chatter since you proposed this idea in the fall, Nicole. As a matter of fact," he pauses here as he pulls something up on his computer screen. "I think the two of you should submit to present about this project at the National Library Association Annual Conference."

"Really?" I ask, trying to veil my excitement. The NLA conference is the biggest library industry conference in the country. Presenting there would be huge on my résumé.

"Yes. The conference is in New Orleans in mid-April, but presentation proposals are due at the end of next week. You'd have to submit something right away if you're interested. We have some library budget dollars available to pay your way to the conference if your presentation is selected, if we scrimp a little."

I look at Adam, but his face is pale. I turn back to Herb.

"Sounds like a great opportunity," I say. "Adam and I will discuss it, and we'll let you know if we decide to submit."

As we step into the hallway, Adam starts, "Nicole—"

I cut him off quickly. "Let's talk in your office."

He nods and we walk down the hall.

When we're settled in with the door closed, I jump in before Adam can tell me all the reasons we shouldn't submit to do the presentation. "I think we should do it," I say. "I know you're not a fan of public speaking, but presenting at NLA would be so cool!"

Adam hesitates. "The last thing I want to do is disappoint you," he says. "But I'm not sure I could get through a whole presentation. When I say I don't like public speaking, I mean I get really bad nerves. My hands shake. I've even been known to, um," he pauses, his ears turning red, "vomit. Maybe you should just do it by yourself?"

"I don't want to present about the graphic novel collection by myself. We worked together on this, and you contributed a lot of good ideas that you should get credit for."

Adam shrugs helplessly. "I don't know, Nicole."

"Oh!" I exclaim. "What if I help you prepare? Like teach you some tricks and exercises you can use to calm your nerves before the presentation?"

"What, like picturing the audience in their underwear?" he asks doubtfully.

"No, that trick sucks," I scoff. "Other things. Breathing exercises. Visualization. That kind of thing."

Adam studies my face. I put my hands together in a supplicating gesture and mouth, "Please?"

He sighs. "Yeah, okay. Sure. Let's do it." I cheer and Adam hurriedly adds, "But, if our proposal is accepted, you have to meet with me one-on-one at least three times before the conference to practice and help me learn your techniques."

"Deal!" I say and put out my hand.

He grabs it and shakes, the concern on his face giving way to a quiet smile.

With the deadline looming, Adam and I meet for lunch almost every day over the next week to decide on a title, write our abstract, and finalize the proposal. I'm wildly happy with the result. On the final day before submissions close, we triple check everything and click "Submit."

"Now we wait," Adam says, arching his eyebrows dramatically.

"Now we wait," I agree.

Chapter Sixteen

Nicole

Turns out, I'm no good at waiting. The not knowing is what drives me crazy. If our proposal is not accepted, that's fine. I can move forward. If it is accepted, that's great. I can make plans for the conference. But not knowing either way? My brain can't handle all the possible outcomes.

I keep busy by planning the launch party for the graphic novel collection. We scheduled it for the middle of February and are going all out with food and activities as a fun way to introduce the Harkness community to the graphic novels. Herb gave me a conservative budget, but I've already found a few ways to save money on low priority costs and spend more on a couple of flashy ideas I have. Like I noticed that every time the library hosts an event, we buy paper plates, napkins, cups, and all that. But there are always leftovers that get shoved in a closet in the back hallway by my office. So instead of buying more paper products for the graphic novel event, I'm just going to use what we already have. Economical and more eco-friendly!

The week of the party is busy. Not only are students gearing up for midterms and starting to linger in the library more, but I let Ashley, the science professor I met at Soapbox, convince me to meet her for lunch.

I spend the morning before my lunch with Ashley at the reference desk. Around 11:30, an older woman with long, white hair walks into the library. She wears green slacks and a white cable knit sweater with a denim jacket over top. Around her neck is a black and white striped scarf—the fashionable kind, not the kind for warmth.

As she approaches me at the reference desk, I notice her deep brown eyes and the laugh lines around them.

"Hello," she says, smiling at me broadly.

"Hello," I respond.

She studies my name badge. "Nicole," she hums. Then, under her breath, "So pretty."

Um, what? I try to catch the eye of the security guard across the library. During business hours on the weekdays, the library doors are unlocked and open for anyone to come in. Evenings and weekends, we're more locked down, with students or employees required to scan their badge for entry. St. Anastasia gets a lot of tourists and sometimes groups of them will walk in just to see the building. We ask them to stay on the first floor, but they're normally quiet and respectful as they look around.

But this ... this is a new one. The woman is by herself which makes me think she's not a tourist.

"Is there something I can help you with?" I ask tentatively, still trying to telepathically call the security guard over.

"Now that you mention it—"

Just then I see Adam speed walking toward the desk, having just come out of the staff office area.

"Mom," he says breathlessly. "I thought you were going to wait for me outside?"

My mouth falls open. This is Adam's mom? I look her over again, and now I notice the resemblance. The slender frame. The brown eyes. The lilting smile.

"Well, honey, I was, but then I thought I'd pop in to see if I could meet any of the coworkers you've hinted about." Adam's face flushes red. "And now having done so, I can definitely see what you mean." She winks.

"Means about what?" I ask innocently. I can tell she's teasing him about something, and I give in to my urge to join her.

"Nothing," Adam says quickly.

Adam's mom places her hand on his arm. "Honey, aren't you going to introduce us?"

Adam rubs the back of his neck. Shoulders drooping in defeat, he announces, "Mom, this is Nicole. Nicole, this is my mother, Mary Burgess."

"Nice to meet you, Mrs. Burgess," I grin.

"It's Dr. Burgess, actually." She smiles back. "But you can call me Mary."

I nod. "Mary," I say, "are you a medical doctor, or...?"

She chuckles. "No. I have an education doctorate. After many years as a schoolteacher, I became a high school principal."

I raise my eyebrows. "Brave," I say.

She shrugs. "It had its moments."

Adam looks back and forth between me and his mother. He clears his throat. "Well, we should get going—"

"What brings you to Parker Library today, Mary?" I ask, ignoring Adam's obvious efforts to pull his mother away.

She beams. "Adam's taking me to lunch."

I put my hand to my heart. "Aww," I can't help but gush. "That's so sweet."

She grins slyly, glancing at Adam. "He's a very sweet man," she says. "And handsome. Don't you think he's handsome, Nicole?"

"Um..." My face feels warm as I decide how to respond.

Adam quickly jumps in. "You don't need to answer."

But I notice a glint of curiosity in his eyes. I throw him a bone.

"Of course he is," I answer Mary honestly. "A man with glasses always looks so distinguished."

I didn't think Adam's blush could go any deeper, but at my words, his face is literally crimson. Mary looks smug as she pats his arm. I feel a little smug, too, but I can't explain why.

"Well, dear, let's get going. We can talk to Nicole more later."

"Are you here all week?" I ask hastily.

"Yes," she replies. "I don't leave until Sunday."

"You should come to the graphic novel launch party on Thursday. It's a project Adam and I have been working on."

She eyes Adam questioningly. "I'd love to. Adam's mentioned the project, of course. He's quite excited about it. But he never mentioned who he was working on it with."

Adam grimaces, and I get the feeling they'll have a lot to talk about over lunch. I pause. Like me?

Finally, I grin. "See you Thursday, then."

"It was a pleasure meeting you, dear."

I echo her sentiment and let my mind drift for my last few minutes at the reference desk. On Monday, Adam texted me a meme with a picture of a loaded baked potato and the caption:

"If you're not happy single, you won't be happy married. Happiness comes from eating potatoes, not from relationships."

I texted him back: "Especially in tater tot form."

Our earlier ease is back, and I'm relieved that I didn't ruin our working relationship with my idiotic moment. Technically, I've known Adam since I started working here, I guess. But over the last four months of working together, I've seen another side of him. And he has seen other sides of me, too.

I inwardly cringe, remembering our embarrassing encounter after Soapbox a month ago. I don't even know what came over me. I don't want to kiss Adam. Do I? Yes, he's handsome. And funny. And sweet. But I don't want to date anyone. And if I did, I wouldn't date a coworker who so obviously has a crush on me. My heart skips a beat and my stomach flutters. Of course, it's silly to think about.

Just then, Samantha arrives to relieve me at the reference desk. I run to my office to grab my phone and then walk to the restaurant in time to meet Ashley.

We're eating at a kitschy pub about a block from the college, popular with both tourists and locals. The pub is housed in what was once a home built in the 1800s in the Florida cracker architectural style. It's supposedly haunted by the late owner who died of a broken heart when his wife, for whom he was building the house, left him for another man. At night, the pub is rowdy, but during the day, it's a decent place to get a burger.

I see Ashley waiting for me on the front porch of the pub, and she smiles. We hug awkwardly, and she says, "I'm glad we're finally doing this."

"Me too," I reply. When I met Ashley at Soapbox last month, she said she'd email me, but I hadn't really expected her to follow through. I've had trouble making friends since moving here. Most people, I've found, are already pretty happy with the friends they have and aren't eager to add more. I figured Ashley was just being polite.

But she did email, and we've been chatting back and forth for the last couple of weeks. She's the one who pushed for us to meet up in person, and I'm grateful.

After we order and start talking, I find that Ashley is also not a fan of small talk. We launch right into a fairly deep discussion of the history of the pub and other ghost stories from around St. Anastasia.

"Have you ever been on the ghost tour?" she asks. I shake my head. "It's fun! The tour guide is in character as a ghost, and the group walks all around downtown, learning about different spooky sightings and stories. We should go sometime! My fiancé, Paul, loves it."

"Oh, that's right!" I remember. "Adam said you were engaged. Tell me about Paul."

"He's dreamy," she says with a goofy smile on her face. "We moved here together after I got the job at Harkness. We met in D.C."

"And when's the wedding?" I ask.

"This summer." She grins. "I'm not teaching any classes, so lots of time for wedding prep."

"What does Paul do?"

"He works for a tech company. He can really work from any-where, which is nice. His job's really flexible." She pauses. "What about you and Adam?" she asks casually. "Are you together?"

"Oh no," I quickly protest, my pulse speeding up. "We're just friends. Well, coworkers. Friend-type coworker people." Ashley gives me a strange look. I sigh. "I had a bad breakup a while back," I explain, "so I don't really date."

"That's too bad." Ashley frowns. "Adam's a really great guy."

"Yeah, I know."

Ashley looks at me skeptically. "You wouldn't start dating again, even for a guy like Adam?"

"It's complicated." I shake my head.

She shrugs. "If you say so." Then, after a few minutes, she hints, "You know, Adam might like the ghost tour too."

"Maybe," I allow. "I mean, no, he would definitely love that. But we'll see."

Before I'm ready, it's time to head back to work. I still have a lot to do to get ready for the launch party in two days. Before parting ways, Ashley and I exchange phone numbers and promise to do this more often.

I run into Adam again on my way back into the library. He's alone, so his mom must have left already.

"Where'd you take your mom for lunch?" I ask him.

"The Seville Café," he responds. "Do you know it?" I shake my head. "You know the old hotel building a couple of blocks from here that they turned into a museum? When it was a hotel, it had this huge indoor pool. The bottom of that pool is now the café dining room. It's pretty cool."

I gape at him. "That sounds amazing."

Adam eyes me cautiously. "We should go sometime."

The flutter is back in my stomach, but I will it away. "Yeah, that would be fun," I say casually. "We can talk about the graphic novel project."

Adam smiles, but I see the disappointment in his eyes. "Sure," he says.

Thursday morning is a blur of activity as I run around getting all the pieces in place for the graphic novel collection launch party. Despite the emphasis I've been putting on it in my own brain, the "party" is actually a pretty casual affair. We scheduled two hours in the middle of the day when students, faculty, and staff can come into the library and enjoy light festivities in honor of the graphic novels.

We have a table of refreshments, including iced sugar cookies I had specially made with comic book action words in colorful designs: Wham! Zap! Ka-boom! Pow! The cookies used most of my event budget, but they look amazing.

And they match my dress. I ordered, using my own money of course, a comic pop print dress online. The dress has a black background covered with comic book action words and speech bubbles in bright red, yellow, blue, and orange. The skirt is semi-pleated and flares out over my hips, flowing down to my knees. It has a sweetheart neckline, and since it's a tank-top style and I'm at work, I wear a sunshine yellow cardigan over top of it. My red ballet flats add another bit of color. It's all ridiculous, and I love it. Will I ever wear this dress again? No, probably not, but I'm having fun wearing it today.

We set up a second table with drawing supplies so students can create their own comic-style artwork. Displayed above this table are sample pages from the graphic novels in our collection.

Then, of course, front and center, the focal point of the event, is the shelf of graphic novels, newly cataloged and ready to check out. We have fifty total to start with, so we'll see how well they circulate over the next few weeks and months. My hope is that we can justify buying more before the fall term.

The event goes well. Students flow through, munching on cookies, drawing, and flipping through the graphic novels. The most frequent question of the day is, "I can check this out?"

I repeat, "Yes, of course. Please do," over and over again and my cheeks start to ache from holding a friendly smile in place. I'll be exhausted after the event is over. I plan to shut the door to my office and just be alone for two hours this afternoon to recover.

My outfit gets lots of compliments, though I'm not sure if they actually like how it looks, or if they're just impressed with my bravery for wearing it in public. I know that despite my best intentions, I'll spend some time dissecting everyone's words and glances later, trying not to feel embarrassed after the fact.

In between smiling and answering questions, I keep glancing at the doors. My eyes frequently wander to the back door that connects the public area of the library to the staff offices, but I also watch the front door too often. I know what, or rather who, I'm looking for, but I don't see Adam or his mother until the last thirty minutes of the event.

Adam helped set up tables this morning, but that all happened while I was out picking up the cookies from a local bakery not too far from the college. Being that Adam is not an interacting-with-people type of librarian, we agreed that he should make an appearance at the event but doesn't have to be here the whole time. Even still, I'm surprised I haven't seen him at all yet today.

Finally, the back door opens, and Adam emerges, smiling back at his mother who's close behind. He turns and our eyes lock across the room. He gives me a once-over, the smile on his lips replaced with a look of awe. Eyes wide, he stalks toward me, Mary watching him closely with a smirk on her face.

"That's quite a dress," he says when he reaches me.

"I hope I don't look too ridiculous."

"Not at all. You look amazing." The heat in his eyes confirms his words.

I press my fingers to my warm cheeks to cool them down. "Thank you," I say carefully. "I thought it would be fun."

He surveys me again, his gaze lingering on the bodice of my dress. "It is," he affirms. "I like the pattern."

Mary approaches us, then, exclaiming, "Well, don't you look festive!"

I turn toward her and smile, though I can still feel Adam's eyes on me.

I end up chatting with Mary the rest of the event, in between answering questions from the last few guests trickling through. I really like her. She's funny and whip-smart, and maybe because she reminds me a bit of my own mother, I don't feel like I met her just this week, but like we've been good friends forever. Adam hovers on the periphery, interjecting comments from time to time, but otherwise listening quietly. At one point, he steps away to examine the artwork left behind on the drawing table, and Mary rests her hand on my arm.

"It's been so nice meeting you, Nicole," she sighs with a contented smile.

"You too, Mary, but listen, I don't want you to get the wrong impression. I'm not sure what Adam's told you—"

"He's told me nothing, dear."

"Okay," I continue, watching the top of Adam's head across a group of students walking past, "but you should know that Adam and I are just coworkers. He's lovely to work with, but that's all this is." Desperately, I reach for her hand and cling to it, willing her to understand.

She squeezes my hand gently, her eyes soft. "It will work out," she murmurs.

I want to shake her a little, make her realize I'm not a match for her son. I also have the unexplainable but frantic urge to pump her for information, ask her *what* will work out, and *how* exactly, and how can she know for sure?

But Adam returns, and we drop our hands while he gives us a quizzical look. I force a smile and finish out the event, thoughts swirling and counting down the minutes until I can escape to my office.

Chapter Seventeen

Adam

My mother's visits always set my world a little bit on fire. My routine is off-kilter, and my house has more activity, more noise, than normal. Joan loves the extra attention, and really, so do I, but it leaves me feeling drained.

And this visit, with Mom interacting with Nicole, has me particularly on edge. Clearly, based on the hints she dropped, my mom figured out that Nicole is the coworker I told her about at the beach back in December. At lunch, I asked her how she knew.

"I didn't," she said with a smile. "I simply saw a pretty young woman around your age and decided to investigate. When you came out and were so nervous, that confirmed it."

I groaned. If I could just act normal around people, especially Nicole, my crush would be less of a problem.

"She's delightful, though, Adam," Mom continued. "Radiant. I can see why you're drawn to her."

"Mom, can we please not talk about this?" I begged. But she wasn't wrong. Nicole is radiant.

And then at the graphic novel launch party, I never should have left them alone. Who knows what Mom said to Nicole. Afterward, I could tell Nicole felt overwhelmed. I don't know if the event drained her energy, or if my mother had something to do with it, but Nicole stayed in her office, door closed, the rest of the day. I had to email her the news that, already, ten of the fifty graphic novels had been checked out. Just on the first day! She didn't respond until the next morning, but when she did, she was excited. Well, as much as I could tell from the text of an email.

But ever since then, she's acted a little differently toward me. Not anything as dramatic as after Soapbox—she's still friendly—but her responses to my texts are slower, and I feel a distance forming, as if she's holding me at arm's length. It could be in my head. After all, we're not working as closely together now that the graphic novel collection is launched and circulating, so maybe the distance I'm feeling is a natural one.

Then one day, she appears in the open doorway of my office with a wide grin across her face. She's squealing and bouncing from foot to foot.

I regard her with raised eyebrows. "What's going on?"

I stand, and before I know it, her arms are around my neck, her body pressing into mine. My pulse skyrockets to the point that I worry I may have a heart attack. *It's just a hug*, I tell myself. Still, I slide my hands around to her back and pull her closer. I inhale the scent of roses and oranges in her hair. My eyes drop closed as every part of my body touching hers zings with pleasure. She pulls away slowly.

"Not that I mind," I joke, "but what was that for?"

Her eyes are shining. "We did it, Adam! NLA accepted our presentation proposal! We're going to present at NLA!"

"That's so great." I try to feign even an ounce of her excitement. "I'm happy for you."

"For us," she corrects.

Sure. I smile weakly. I'm buoyed by her excitement, but less than thrilled about the idea of presenting. Upside: more time with Nicole. Downside: speaking in front of people. But I can make that work for me, too.

"Don't forget," I remind her, "you promised to help me with public speaking. At least three sessions."

She rolls her eyes. "I know. We'll figure that out later. Let's go tell Herb!"

She drags me down the hallway, but Herb's door is closed, and Susan tells us he's in meetings the rest of the day.

Nicole emails Herb instead, copying me. He replies later in the evening, expressing his congratulations and adding:

"One caveat. While the library does have the budget to fund the trip to New Orleans for you both, we do need to be conscientious about the costs. So, you'll need to drive together instead of flying. Whoever owns the car you take will be reimbursed for mileage, but that will be far cheaper than two round-trip plane tickets. I'll be available in my office tomorrow if you have questions."

I immediately google the distance. It takes about nine hours to drive to New Orleans from St. Anastasia. We'll obviously need to take my car since Nicole doesn't have one, but I'm fine with driving. My heart thumps. A road trip with Nicole. And multiple opportunities over the next month to work with her as we prepare for the presentation. Sounds like the aloofness between us I was fearing won't be an issue again for a while.

Nicole calls an impromptu meeting the next day. We start by discussing the driving plans, which she's fine with. Then, we move on to planning the presentation itself. We decide to talk about the process of starting the graphic novel collection all the way through, from suggesting the idea to writing a formal proposal to ordering and cataloging, and finally launching. At the end, we'll include the little data we have for circulation so far. We split the sections. It makes sense for Nicole to be the one to talk about the initial idea and writing the proposal, including background information about what graphic novels are and their known benefits for education. She'll also talk about title selection, but I'll chime in there, too, with information about looking up reviews and comparing the titles to other academic library collections. Of course, I'll present on ordering and cataloging choices, while Nicole concludes with how we set up the launch party.

"It will be helpful for our public speaking lessons," Nicole begins, raising her eyebrows, "if you draft a sort of script for your parts of the presentation. It can be as detailed as you need, anywhere from bullet points to full sentences."

I laugh humorlessly. "Full sentences, and I'll stare at the paper the whole time and read too fast."

"O-kaay," she says. "So how do you see this going?"

"Badly," I answer.

She shakes her head and chuckles. "No, I mean logistically. Do we meet during work hours? Here in the library?"

I consider my list of demands, so to speak. "After work hours," I say. "I still have other work I need to get done, so I want to focus on that during the day. And maybe with Joan and everything, we would be more comfortable working at my place?" Plus, then she would be at my house, in my space, again. I could cook for her. We could sit together on the couch with the lights low, and maybe—

"After work is fine." Nicole's voice breaks through my train of thought. "But how hard would it be for us to meet here? I mean, with Joan and everything? I'm just thinking that it'll be best to practice in a more formal environment like the classroom upstairs."

My heart sinks. "Fair enough," I answer. "That makes sense." Though I've been accused of being *too* sensible at times, right now, I want to throw sense out the window. Who needs it? "And as far as Joan," I continue, "if I could go home and walk her, maybe eat some dinner in between, that could work."

"Yeah," she says with a nod. "That works. Maybe like seven o'clock? The library should be pretty quiet then, too."

I dip my head in agreement. "This Wednesday for our first session?"

She grins. "I'll be here. And cheer up. It'll be fun."

Well, if anyone can make public speaking fun, it will be Nicole.

At the first session on Wednesday, I haven't had time yet to draft my script, so we start with some basic techniques that are supposed to help me feel less nervous ahead of the presentation.

Nicole's right that the library is very quiet. Midterms have just finished up, but it's not time for finals just yet. Several students sit throughout the second floor in study carrels with laptops set up in front of them, but it's not crowded by any means.

We're meeting in the second-floor library classroom. It's a small room, intended to host sessions of twenty-five or fewer, with a presentation screen in the front of the room and a projector mounted to the ceiling. A podium sits to the right of the screen, equipped with various connector cables.

I'm still dressed in my clothes from work. Nicole suggested that wearing them would help since they are the type of clothes I'll wear during the presentation. So, when I went home to walk Joan and grab a quick dinner, I didn't change. Nicole, however, is now in navy blue joggers and a fitted pullover hoodie that says "Antisocial Book Club" across the front.

"It will be good if you can get to the presentation room early at the conference," Nicole is saying. "That way you can get a feel for the room and eliminate any nervousness from rushing around."

"Okay," I say, jotting down her words on a legal pad I brought with me for notes. "Get there early. Got it."

"Having a specific breathing pattern helps to calm nerves, too. One example is box breathing. Have you heard of it?"

I shake my head, so she continues. "It's where you breathe in for four counts, hold your breath for four counts, exhale for four counts, and then hold again for four more counts. Try it."

We box breathe together for a few rounds, and I have to admit that I do feel looser when we finish.

"Another tactic to use ahead of the presentation, but which might feel a little silly, is to, like, shake out your jitters."

I raise my eyebrows. "My jitters?"

"Yes. You know, like you could stretch your arms, roll your shoulders, even run in place. It helps loosen up the muscles that you've been holding your tension in."

"Ah," I say. "That actually makes sense." Not sure how I'll do that at the conference without looking ridiculous, but it does make sense.

"Of course it does," she retorts, looking mildly offended. "One of the bigger pieces of advice I've seen is to be prepared. As you write your script, and we practice it—that will be our next two sessions—you'll feel more confident. But," she shrugs and her eyes twinkle, "that's not necessary for everyone."

I eye her skeptically. "You don't need to prepare before a presentation?"

"Before a presentation like this, I definitely will," she says. "But I could also make a short speech about something I know a lot about without any preparation at all."

I laugh wryly. "Uh huh." I tilt my head at her. "I don't think so."

She gets up and walks around to stand at the podium. "Watch," she says. "Give me a topic. It's got to be something I know about."

"Hmm," I think. "How about which potato-based side is the best?"

She grins at me and then proceeds to talk for three minutes all about tater tots and how and why they're superior to mashed potatoes, fries, and my personal favorite, baked potatoes.

"Wow." I applaud when she's done. "How do you do that?"

"I don't know," she shrugs. "I've always been good at extemporaneous speeches. I don't get nervous when I'm speaking in front of people." Then she adds with a sardonic smile, almost under her breath, "It's just everything else that bothers me."

"What do you mean?" I ask, cocking my head at her.

She shakes her head. "I'm not so great with casual small talk."

"Who is?"

We look at each other and at the same time, we say, "Extroverts." We both chuckle softly.

"But yeah, that's me," she says dryly. "Nicole Delaney: good at presentations, bad at small talk." She rolls her eyes. "I'm a mess, Adam."

I catch her eye and hold it. "I don't think so," I say softly.

Her cheeks turn pink, but she doesn't respond.

The air turns heavy around us, the energy shifting. I take one step closer, and then another. She watches me, staring at my mouth. Electricity crackles between us, and Nicole shivers.

But then, as if coming out of a trance, Nicole tosses her hair and steps back. "That's probably enough for tonight, right?" she asks.

"Uh, sure," I agree hollowly, rubbing the back of my neck.

"Okay, great. I'll see you tomorrow." Then she gathers her things and she steps toward the door.

"Wait," I say. She tenses and turns back toward me. I can't read the expression on her face. Annoyance? Hope? Desire? Okay, that last one is probably wishful thinking. "It's dark," I finally say. "Let me give you a ride home."

She takes a breath. "Yeah, that should be fine. Thanks."

Chapter Eighteen

Adam

Our next session goes slightly better. I have my script ready this time, so Nicole has me up behind the podium.

"Okay," she directs. "Let's start by visualizing your presentation. Think through the whole thing in your mind. From the start when the moderator introduces us, all the way through to questions at the end. Visualize yourself commanding the room, speaking confidently–"

"Not puking?" I cut in.

She closes her eyes briefly and sighs. "Yes, Adam. It would be preferable if you don't vomit during our presentation."

"Okay, wait a second." I circle around the podium and pick up my legal pad and pen from the nearby table. I write, while saying the words aloud, "No vomiting. Got it."

I lift my head to see Nicole's reaction and am rewarded when a puff of laughter escapes her lips. She shakes her head, trying to hold it back. I grin. Making her laugh is everything.

"Behind the podium!" she chastises, and I quickly move back into place.

"Alright," I say. "I have visualized the presentation. What's next?"

"Now," she commands, "use the podium to your advantage. Think of it as a touchstone. Touch it or hold the edges to steady yourself. The rigidity of the podium is a reminder that you're safe. The ground is steady at your feet."

I press my hands against the podium and stomp my feet lightly against the floor. "Yeah," I say. "I can see that. It's a grounding technique, reminding my body that I'm safe and it doesn't need to go into a fight, flight, or freeze mode."

"Exactly. So, I think we're ready to run through your script now. Whenever you're ready."

I walk through a round of box breathing, grip the edge of the podium, and shuffle my feet against the ground. Then, I start reading from my script.

Nicole lets me go on for a few minutes before she stops me. "Overall, not bad, but I have some notes."

Pinching my lips together, I gesture for her to continue. "First, I know you're just reading through on this go-round, but during the real thing, you're going to want to be comfortable enough to look up at the audience and make eye contact every so often."

"Yes," I agree. "It would be fantastic if I were comfortable enough to do that."

"But you don't think you will be?"

I click my tongue and point at her. Nailed it.

"Fine, we'll see. But second, you're fidgeting too much up there."

I am? I don't remember fidgeting. But even here, in a room containing only Nicole, reading the script felt almost like an out-of-body experience. Who knows what I did.

"Start again," Nicole urges, "but this time focus on holding your hands and feet still."

I take a deep breath and start reading again from the beginning of my script. I don't get nearly as far as the first time before Nicole stops me.

"No, you're still ... you're still fidgeting." She blows out an exasperated breath. "Here, I have an idea."

She stands and circles around the podium to walk up behind me. Positioning her arm below mine, she takes the pen I'm still holding out of my hand. "First, we'll put this down. Actually, let's move it out of the way completely." She tosses it across the room.

"Hey!" I protest.

"It's for the best," she insists. "You were spinning it around and clicking it and it was distracting from your words. No pens around you during the presentation."

"Oh," I say, chagrined. Didn't realize I was doing all that. "Yeah, that's a good plan."

"Now," she says, reaching her other arm around and positioning it below my other arm. We're standing with my back to her front, with her arms underneath mine, her hands curled around my wrists. Because of the size difference, she's practically plastered against me, and I feel the weight of her on my back like pressure points. "I'll hold you steady while you talk so that you don't fidget. Start again."

I take another breath, but my heart is racing, and it has nothing to do with public speaking. I start reading. Her hands grip my wrists with more pressure, keeping them firm against the podium. I realize with a start that I had been trying to lift them. She's right about the fidgeting.

I continue, losing focus on the words I'm saying as the warmth from Nicole's body seeps into mine. I'm sure she can feel my pulse going crazy in my wrists. But tuning into my body for a moment while my eyes continue reading and my mouth continues saying words, I recognize a flutter on my wrist—Nicole's thumb skating almost imperceptibly across my skin. Back and forth in a very intentional-seeming path. Against my back, I feel her heartbeat drumming at a wild pace. Farther up, her cheek rests against the top of my spine.

I close my eyes; the words coming out of my mouth slow and then stop altogether. But Nicole doesn't say anything, doesn't seem to notice. My pulse slows, and her heartbeat matches the pace. And then we're quiet, hearts beating together in a steady rhythm. I hold still, reluctant to move and break this spell, knowing that at any second, Nicole could pull away, realize what we're doing and put a stop to it.

And then, as predicted, she does. Her arms drop, and she steps away. I immediately feel the absence of her heat against my back. I want to spin around and pull her to me, tuck her head under my chin and continue holding her. But I don't. Instead, I move to the side, giving her space.

I clear my throat and looking her in the eye, I ask, "Was that any better?"

She holds her arms, hands moving over the fabric of her sleeves as if she's trying to warm herself up, but her cheeks are flushed. She glances away and says into the distance, "Yeah, that should work."

The conference is next week. In between creating slides and public speaking practice and my normal job, I've registered for the conference, booked my hotel room, and reserved a spot for Joan at a local doggie resort. I told my mother about the conference, of course, and she's excited for me. More so after I told her the presentation topic, and she realized it was based on the project I had been working on with Nicole. Yes, I had explained to her, Nicole is also going to the conference. Yes, we're driving together.

For our final public speaking session, Nicole decides we should do a full run through of the presentation with our slide deck and both of us speaking. And an audience. Considering the first two sessions, I wonder if inviting the small audience has more to do with practice for me or protection for herself. Not protection against me, to be clear, but protection against herself since she, for some reason, feels like she needs to resist anything happening between us.

We meet during work hours to make things easier for our audience, which consists of Tasha, Herb, and Susan from the library, and

Ashley, who Nicole has apparently developed a friendship with since Soapbox. Definitely feeling smug about that one.

I treat the rehearsal as if it's the real presentation. I arrive in the classroom thirty minutes before we're supposed to start. I get the laptop connected and pull up the slide deck, making sure that the projector is working, and the screen is in place. Before anyone else arrives, I do the whole shaking-out-my-jitters thing, rolling my shoulders and jogging in place for a few minutes.

Nicole comes in with Ashley, the two of them laughing about something. Ashley takes a seat, and Nicole joins me at the front of the room.

"You doing okay?" she whispers.

"So far, so good," I answer. "I still need to do my breathing."

She fiddles with the slide deck to give me space. I do a couple rounds of box breathing as the rest of our audience trickles in. I even take a minute to visualize the presentation. Not sure how effective it is though, because while I imagine Nicole's portions going flawlessly, mine look a little shaky in my mind's eye.

After a few minutes, Nicole gets everyone's attention, and we start. She speaks first and when she transitions to me, she gives me an encouraging smile. I stand at the podium, my hands flat against the surface. I focus on keeping still and looking up from my script at the audience every so often. Nicole is in charge of advancing the slides, so I don't need to worry about how I'll fumble that. When I pass the figurative mic back to Nicole to finish the presentation, I breathe a sigh of relief. Nicole wraps up her last section and then calls for questions, signaling the end.

Our makeshift audience applauds, and Nicole bows theatrically. Turning to me, she says quietly, "We'll debrief in a few minutes." Then, she walks over to our colleagues in the room to talk to them.

Herb approaches me. "Excellent presentation!" he says as he pats me on the back. "You'll both make us proud at the conference next week."

"Thank you," I say, chagrined.

When the audience members have all filed out of the room, Nicole comes back up front where I'm still standing.

Palms up, I lift my hands in question. "How was it?" I ask, cringing to hear the answer.

But Nicole smiles. "Not bad at all," she says. "Your voice was a little shaky, but you didn't fidget, and you looked up enough. How did you feel?"

"Drained," I answer. "But I can see how this practice run will make it easier to present at the conference. I have a better idea of what to expect now. Thank you."

Nicole grins. "Don't thank me. It was all self-serving. This is my presentation, too, and I can't have someone puking in the middle of it."

I laugh and shake my head. "Maybe I won't eat that day, just in case."

Chapter Nineteen

Nicole

R oad trip time!

Adam meets me at my apartment early on Thursday morning. It's supposed to take about nine hours to drive to New Orleans from here and I'm hoping to get checked into my hotel room and freshen up before the conference welcome reception tonight. Adam texts that he's outside, and I peek out my window to see his white sedan. I navigate my roller suitcase and computer bag out the door onto the landing at the top of the stairs. As I fumble for my keys, Adam jogs up the stairs behind me and takes my suitcase.

"Thanks." I smile at him as I finish locking up.

His gaze travels from my face down to my body and then back up again, but he doesn't say anything. I'm dressed comfortably for the long car ride: yoga pants swirled with black, purple, and white color splotches, and a purple T-shirt.

I trail down the stairs behind Adam, and as he loads my suitcase in the trunk of the car, I take the opportunity to assess him. It's the first time I've seen him not in work clothes, I realize. Even though we've hung out after work a couple of times, he wore the same clothes he'd had on all day at the library. Honestly, I figured Adam's casual outfits would be pretty similar to his work attire—solid-colored chinos and polo shirts. But Adam stands in front of me this morning in cargo shorts and a graphic T-shirt, cheap flip-flops on his feet. I've only ever seen him in pants, and I look away quickly when I notice his calf muscles flexing as he moves the bags around in the trunk.

Huh. Impressive definition. Didn't expect that.

The black graphic T-shirt he's wearing is a reference to something, but I don't understand it. There are honeycomb type shapes all connected to each other, a dotted line connecting circles within two of the hexagons. Underneath, it says "…Just one more turn."

Slamming the trunk, Adam smiles at me and says, "Do you have everything?"

"Oh! I think so," I answer.

Instead of standing here ogling Adam, I should be getting in the car. I open the passenger side door and settle into my seat, setting my bag at my feet and moving my water bottle from my bag to one of the cup holders in the center console. The driver side door opens, and Adam climbs in. Resting his hands against the steering wheel, he turns his head to meet my eyes.

"Road trip rules," he says. "Passenger is in charge of music."

I match his grin and say, "Perfect, because it just so happens that I created a couple of playlists especially for this trip. Do you mind if I connect to your Bluetooth?"

"Go for it," he answers as he starts the car.

I pull out my phone and connect it to the car's stereo system. I scroll until I find the first playlist: eighties pop classics. Adam groans as Madonna's "Material Girl" starts blasting through the speakers.

"Maybe you can take a turn driving later and I'll take over the music," he offers. "Is this the kind of music you typically listen to?"

"No," I laugh. "But it seems appropriate for a road trip. Peppy. Nostalgic. Easy to sing along."

"Nostalgic?" he asks. "How old were you in 1984?"

"Um, negative fifteen..."

"That's what I thought."

"But that's beside the point. It can still be nostalgic. I listened to songs like these on the oldies station in my dad's car as a kid."

"Fair point." He laughs.

We're quiet for a while, listening to the playlist. I need a few more miles and a bunch more sugar in me to start singing.

Finally, Adam looks at me and says, "I've gotta ask. What's the story with the shirt?"

"My shirt?" I look down at it and laugh.

"Yeah. Fran?"

I laugh again. The purple T-shirt I'm wearing is a fitted crew neck with a set of two white buttons coming down the center chest area from the collar. On the right breast is embroidered the acronym

"SAB" in white thread in block letters. Underneath that, also embroidered in white, but in a fancy script, it says "Fran".

"It's a thrift store find," I explain. "From back in Austin. I'm pretty sure SAB is some kids' baseball league or something, and I'm guessing this was a coach or parent assistant's shirt."

"But your name isn't Fran," he says unnecessarily. "Why did you buy it?"

I shrug. "I thought it was funny. Fran's not a name you see every day, and I thought, I could be Fran. Plus, I like the color and fit of the shirt."

He shifts his eyes away from the road briefly to give me a curious look. "So, did Fran become your alter ego or something?"

I roll my eyes. "Or something. Nah, it's just a joke. No one really understands it, and I think that's why I like it. Gotta leave the people wondering."

"You like defying expectations." It's not a question, but it still feels like he's asking.

I consider a minute. "I like doing what feels right to me regardless of whether that fits into other people's expectations or not. Like, I'm not going to do something I don't actually want to do just because nobody expects it, or just because everyone expects it."

"Hmmm," Adam murmurs, encouraging me to continue.

"Like you know there are so many librarian stereotypes out there. And yeah, some of them are not me at all, but some are definitely me. I do like to read. I do like to drink tea. I do wear cardigans. And I'm not about to give those things up just to buck convention. But I dye my hair in all sorts of colors. I have tattoos. I don't–"

"You have tattoos?"

"Yes. The point is I'm just me. I'm not a mousy librarian. I'm not a sexy librarian."

Adam makes a choking noise, and he's conspicuously focusing on the road in front of us. His face turns red up to his hairline.

"What?" I ask.

"Nothing. Just ... I tend to disagree about that last part." Now I'm blushing, but before I can even think of how to respond, he quickly continues. "But I see what you're saying. The fact that I'm a male librarian throws people for a loop. Plus, I'm a dog person, not a cat person. I do wear glasses though. And I'm pretty awkward." He smiles.

"Hmm," I say. "I tend to disagree with that last one."

He looks over at me quickly, and I grin. Before he turns his head forward again, I see his small, pleased smile.

"Let's circle back to those tattoos," he teases.

I laugh. "I have a small one on the top of my foot. And a slightly larger one over my rib cage. How about you? Any ink?"

To my surprise, he nods. "I have one. It's a fishing rod that goes around my bicep. I got it in memory of my dad. Deep sea fishing was our favorite thing to do together."

"That's really sweet," I say quietly. "I didn't know you fished."

He shifts uncomfortably in his seat. "I haven't been since he died," he admits. "But I really loved it when I was younger." After a pause, he asks, "What are yours? If you don't mind sharing."

I shrug. "Nothing too exciting. My sisters and I got the foot one together. We each got the letters MNO in script. Our first initials.

My older sister is Molly, and my younger sister is Olivia. The one over my ribs is kind of embarrassing."

"Now I have to know," he says with a grin.

I hesitate. "It's just some song lyrics."

"Embarrassing song lyrics? Let me guess. Justin Bieber or something?" Adam teases.

I make a face. "Ugh, no. Never." I pause again. The real answer is not so much embarrassing as it is revealing, and I'm not sure I want to reveal that much yet.

Adam notices my hesitation. "What if I tell you something embarrassing about me?" he asks. "Tit for tat?" As he says it, his eyes light up. "Or should I say, tit for tattoo?"

I groan and roll my eyes. "That was bad, Adam."

He shrugs. "I liked it. So, what do you say? Want me to go first?"

I consider his offer. On the one hand, I'm dying to know Adam's embarrassing story. On the other hand, if I hear it, I'll be honor bound to share my own cringe-worthy past. Or at least a piece of it.

"Okay," I finally relent. "You first."

He takes a breath, and his ears are already turning red, so I know this will be good.

"When I was in graduate school," he begins, "the school of library and information science, also known as SLIS, had a yearly tradition of printing a 'Men of SLIS' pin-up calendar."

"Oh my gosh," I choke.

"It was funny on two levels, both related to the tradition of firefighter pin-up calendars to raise money for charity. First, it poked fun at the relatively low number of men in library science programs.

Second, because male librarians are maybe not as ... physically fit, let's say, as firefighters tend to be, positioning them in stereotypically sexy poses has a more comedic effect." The twitch at the corners of Adam's lips belies the smile he's holding back.

"I get why it's funny, but don't tell me..." I'm practically holding my breath now in anticipation.

"Yes," Adam nods solemnly. "I was Mr. July. On the beach."

"Nooooo!" I can't hold back my laughter. "That's too funny! Were you shirtless?"

"You'd like that, wouldn't you?"

I abruptly stop laughing and whip my head around at the uncharacteristically flirty comment. Judging by the deep red of his face and neck, Adam is just as surprised by his words as I am. An awkward silence fills the car, but by the power of suggestion, my brain is now inventing a picture of what a shirtless Adam might look like. No six-pack abs certainly, but the muscle definition I've seen in his arms and calves suggest a lithe runner's body. I mean, we know the man takes care of himself with his healthy eating and daily walks with Joan. I imagine a firm chest, with defined collar bones and strong shoulder muscles. My eyes glaze over as I stare out the front windshield.

Adam clears his throat. "To answer your question, no. I wore a tasteful sweater vest."

I bark out a laugh. "At the beach!"

He glances at me and grins.

"I *have* to see this," I tease. "Where can I find a copy?"

"I do have a copy," he admits. "But I've hidden it so well that hopefully no one will ever see it again."

"Boo! Such a killjoy." I laugh.

When the car is quiet again, Adam nudges me with his elbow. "Your turn."

"My story is not nearly as interesting," I say. "Do you know Chelsea Jordan?"

"No," Adam responds, a question in his voice.

"She's a musician whose songs are kind of dark and emotional. I was really into her music in high school. When I was in graduate school, I got a tattoo of lyrics from one of her songs." I've doled out just crumbs, but they may be an easy trail to track; I brace for his follow-up questions. I got the tattoo during my breakup with Steven.

"What's the lyric?" he asks.

I take a deep breath, using my finger to trace the letters underneath my shirt. "Love in force / Gunning for you."

Adam is quiet for a beat. "That's haunting," he finally says. "But not embarrassing."

Now it's my turn to sit wordlessly. I slowly shake my head. "Maybe not," I say in a low voice.

To my surprise, he doesn't ask anything else.

Chapter Twenty

Nicole

We've been driving for a few hours when I see a billboard and shoot up in my seat.

"Buc-ee's!" I shout. "We have to stop!"

"What?" Adam looks at me incredulously. "We have to stop *where*?"

"Buc-ee's," I say again. "I didn't realize they had them here!"

"What is Buc-ee's?"

"It's the best! It's got huge bathrooms and food and a cute store and cheap gas."

"So, like a gas station?"

"Well, technically, but it's so much more than that. They're from Texas. We used to stop at them all the time when we'd drive to visit my grandma in Houston. We could stop there for lunch!"

"A gas station for lunch?" Adam sounds doubtful.

"You'll see. Do you trust me?"

He glances sideways at me, and I try to look as earnest as possible. He sighs.

"Fine. Where is it?"

"The billboard said it's still about twenty miles up the highway. Oooh, I'm so excited! You won't regret it, Adam, I promise!"

Even as I say this and see Adam smiling and shaking his head at me, I start to second guess. *Will* Adam like Buc-ee's? It's very Texan—big and crowded and loud. It can be overwhelming. Does he like barbecue? I know he tries to eat healthy, so his options may be limited at a super travel center known for its brisket sandwiches, fudge, and sugary "beaver nugget" corn snacks. We're getting closer; I just saw another billboard advertising the Buc-ee's exit five miles away.

"Um, actually, Adam, we don't need to stop at Buc-ee's if you don't want to," I offer tentatively.

Adam's eyebrows pull together, and he glances over at me. "Why not? You were so excited."

"I was, but I don't know. I'm probably being silly. It's just a gas station." Even as I say it, I think about the gasps such a statement would elicit from my Texas family and friends. I silently apologize to Buc-ee the Beaver for disparaging his establishment.

Adam reaches over as if to place his hand on top of mine, but then hesitates and pulls back.

"No way," he says emphatically. "You got me all excited. I have to see this now. I need to experience this Buc-ee's place for myself. I'm intrigued."

I hesitate. "I think you're just being nice."

"Nicole, honestly, I've never seen someone get that excited about a gas station. I need to know why."

I smile, feeling the buildup of excitement again. "Okay!" I clap my hands. "But we have to take a picture with Buc-ee."

"Uh, okay, we can do that." Adam merges over to the far-right lane. "This is the exit up ahead. Hopefully there will be signs saying which way to turn."

"You won't need a sign," I say.

Adam follows the exit off the highway and before he can ask what I mean, he can see for himself. Sprawling off to the right is a large building surrounded by dozens of fuel pumps. A line of cars and trucks stretch from the parking lot, down the street, and out to the main road where vehicles, including ours, wait to turn left into the travel center.

His hands resting on the steering wheel, Adam looks at the gas station, then at me. "What *is* this place? Are we getting gas or going to Disney World?"

"It's the Disney World of gas stations," I answer with a laugh. Adam looks incredulous, and maybe a bit concerned, but I'm done worrying about it. I'm all-in now.

We finally park and make our way to the front entrance. I point to the gleaming bronze statue of a five-foot tall beaver wearing a T-shirt and ball cap, its cartoonish mouth wide open to reveal two buckteeth.

"Picture time!" I remind Adam.

Adam shakes his head and chuckles, still looking a bit stunned. He cooperatively moves to one side of Buc-ee while I stand on the other. I lift my phone and capture a selfie.

As we step away from the statue, a mom pushes four small children in our place and shouts "Smile!"

I walk through the automatic doors, Adam trailing close behind me, passing rows of fire pits and foldable lawn chairs. We enter the second set of doors, and I'm hit by several sensations all at once. I smell the barbecue and candied nuts right away. I hear the din of voices from the dozens of people walking around the huge store, and then, loudly, "Fresh brisket on the board!" Finally, I see shelves and racks lined with kitschy merchandise. Some of it features the cartoon face of Buc-ee the Beaver, while some are pieces of folksy home decor and accessories.

I feel a heavy hand on my shoulder and turn to see Adam's wide eyes taking it all in. "Seriously, Nicole," he says. "What is this place?"

I laugh but don't answer him. "Restrooms are that way," I say after spotting the sign. "I'll see you at the meat counter after."

A few minutes later, I find Adam watching the workers cut up the large slabs of beef brisket.

"Hey," I say as I sidle up next to him.

"Hey," he responds. "Those bathrooms were..."

I laugh. "I know. Not like other gas station bathrooms you've been to, huh?"

He shakes his head. "Actually, as a rule, I don't stop at gas station bathrooms. Don't trust them. But here ... it was so clean. So many stalls. So many people."

He shifts his focus back to the meat counter. "What do you recommend?"

"Sliced brisket sandwich, for sure. I mean, the chopped is fine, but I think the ratio of meat to sauce works better on the sliced."

"Sliced it is." Adam picks up two wrapped brisket sandwiches from the warming tray and hands one to me.

"Let's get a basket," I say.

We step around a few groups of people, and I see a stack of shopping baskets near a rack of chips. I take one for myself, placing my sandwich gently inside, and then hand another to Adam.

"There are a few more snacks I want to find," I tell him. "Why don't you look around and I'll meet you at the register near where we came in?"

He shrugs. "Sounds good."

I get to the registers just as Adam is unloading his basket to cash out.

"How much are you buying?" I exclaim when I see the pile of food and merchandise in front of him.

He reaches up and rubs the back of his neck with his hand. "I don't know. Just what I needed. This place is amazing."

I grin as he sets a black T-shirt adorned with the cartoonish face of Buc-ee the Beaver on the counter. He adds fudge, chips, and beef jerky to the stack. The next item really catches my attention.

"What are those?" I squeal gleefully.

Adam holds up the bag and shakes it. "Sour gummy worms," he says with a shrug.

"I figured you'd pick something practical and nutritious," I tease.

Adam scoffs, "This is a road trip, Nicole. Now is not the time for healthy snacks."

"So much for your rules." I nudge him with my elbow and grin.

"I'm following road trip rules," he says sensibly. "Normal-life rules don't apply on the road." He winks.

Oh my gosh. I feel like a character in one of those old sitcoms when I suddenly want to chime, "Who are you, and what have you done with Adam?" But I can't stop grinning. This is fun. Adam is fun.

Adam fills up the gas tank while I sit in the passenger seat and inhale my sandwich. So good. Oh, Buc-ee's sliced brisket, I've missed you.

Adam is still finishing up at the pump, so I get out and circle the car toward him.

"Do you want me to drive for a while?"

Adam rests the nozzle back in its holster and closes the gas flap on his car. Then, he lifts his head and squints toward me, shading his eyes with his hand to avoid the glare from the sun behind my head.

"You don't have to," he says.

"I know, but you haven't eaten yet. I could drive a bit while you eat your lunch." Adam hesitates, so I rush to add, "I mean, if you're comfortable with someone else ... with me driving your car. It's fine if you're not."

"You know, that would be great," Adam says with a smile. "I could use a break from driving for a while."

He ducks around the back of the car toward the passenger side while I slide into the driver's seat. I adjust the seat and mirrors before turning the key that's already in the ignition. Before shifting out of park, I reach for my bag of white cheddar nuggees, pop it open, and set it on the center console for easy access. Nuggees are Buc-ee's brand of cheese puffs, except the pieces are smaller, so they maybe fall somewhere between a cheese ball and a cheese puff. Anyway, the white cheddar ones are my favorite.

We're pulling back onto the highway when Adam unwraps his sandwich and takes a bite. I glance at him quickly before shifting my eyes back to the road.

"Well?" I ask.

Adam moans through a mouthful of beef and sauce. He takes a minute to chew and swallow and then answers me. "This is delicious. Seriously. We're definitely stopping at Buc-ee's again on the way home."

"I have zero problems with that," I respond, my heart squeezing in my chest. I don't know why, but Adam's newfound enthusiasm for Buc-ee's makes me ridiculously happy. It's early yet on this trip, but I already feel like Adam and I are cementing our friendship—learning more about each other, establishing shared experiences, exploring how we get along outside of work.

I've had a difficult time making friends since I graduated from college. For a while there, I was fully focused on my master's program and my disintegrating relationship with Steven. Then, I moved to a different state, and while I've tried to put myself out there to meet people other than the ones I work with, it's been hard to connect with anyone. Tasha is great to talk to while we're working, but she's a student and my sense of propriety tells me it's not okay to hang out with her and her other student friends at college parties. Not that college parties sound fun to me, anyway. My blossoming friendship with Ashley feels promising, but she's also busy planning her wedding. I have my sisters, of course, but we're so spread out now.

I'm excited I get to see Molly this weekend; it's a nice coincidence that the conference is being held where she lives. It can be hard to pry her out of her lab, even on weekends, so I'm grateful she can make time for me. She's coming to our presentation on Sunday, and then we're going out to dinner together.

I'm lost in thought as I drive. I glance to the passenger seat and see that Adam has fallen asleep, the back of his head leaning against the headrest and his mouth hanging open slightly. A sense of contentment washes over me, and I smile.

Getting to know Adam has been unexpected. Before we started working on the graphic novel project together, when I thought of him, if I thought of him at all, I assumed he was socially awkward and serious. Now, I'm starting to think that there are two Adams: Work Adam and Fun Adam. Whenever we've interacted outside of the library, he's been thoughtful and funny. Who knew he was funny? And interesting. His hobbies are different from mine, but are similarly centered around learning, similarly nerdy.

Just then, a pickup truck in the lane to the left of me catches my attention in the side mirror. It's zooming up quickly and as it pulls up alongside me, it's forced to slow down to avoid the car in front of it. I slow Adam's car as well, keeping an eye on the truck. I notice the bed is loaded down with stuff—random tools and scrap metal—and the tailgate is down. The truck speeds up and then hits the brakes, slowing long enough to allow some space to build up between it and the car in front of it. Then, it speeds up again to erase the space, braking again just before reaching the front car. It does this several more times, and I slow down even more, trying to stay far enough back to avoid the drama.

Suddenly, the truck jerks to the right, jumping in front of me and hitting the gas to speed forward. A piece of scrap metal tumbles out of the truck bed so quickly that I don't register it right away. It hits the road right in front of me and without thinking, I swerve to avoid it, but I'm too late; my reflexes are too slow. A loud THA-WUMP sounds as I run over the scrap metal. I hold my breath, and for a few seconds, nothing happens. Maybe the tire is fine. Then, I hear the *wub-wub-wub* noise of a flat tire hitting the road, and I know I didn't get lucky. The steering wheel vibrates, and I strain my arm muscles steering the car onto the shoulder.

At some point, Adam jolted up in his seat, and now he's regarding me with wide eyes. My hands shake and adrenaline takes over.

Chapter Twenty-One

Adam

I don't even remember falling asleep, but I'm definitely awake now.

Nicole quickly guides the car to the right shoulder of the highway. When she turns off the engine, I jump out of the car to check the damage. Hands on my hips, I survey the front of the car. Everything looks okay except for the front driver side tire. It's totally shredded. What in the world happened? I survey the highway behind us and see a chunk of metal in the road.

My eyes dart to Nicole, still sitting in the driver's seat. She's gripping the steering wheel, knuckles white. Her eyes have a glazed look. I rush back to the open passenger side door and bend down to peer inside, my hands anchored on the roof of the car.

"What happened?" I wince at the bark in my words. I take a breath and try again. "Are you okay?"

Nicole's hands drop from the steering wheel and onto her lap. They're shaking violently. She closes her eyes and leans her head back on the headrest.

"Nicole," I say gently.

Her eyes open and turn toward me with a jerk. Her pupils are dilated, and I get the sense that though she's looking at me, she can't really see me. I take another deep breath, trying to slow my racing heart. I need to stay calm here. I slide into the passenger seat and lean toward Nicole.

"Nicole," I say softly. "Are you hurt?" She doesn't respond and I'm silently freaking out. "I'm going to check to see if you're injured," I tell her. It doesn't make sense that she would be, though. It's a flat tire—nothing would have happened to us inside the car. Even so, I gently turn her head, looking for anything amiss. I lean over her and check over her left side, down to her legs and feet. Everything looks okay.

Then, she speaks. "I'm sorry, I'm sorry," she says so haltingly and quietly that I strain to hear her. Her voice is tight, and I get the impression that getting these words out is difficult for her.

"No, you're fine, Nicole. You don't need to be sorry," I reassure her.

A light bulb goes off in my head, and I lean forward, pulling out my phone. I surreptitiously google "how to help someone having a panic attack" and skim the results. First advice is to stay calm. Okay, I'm trying.

Provide reassuring words. "Hey, Nicole," I say softly. "You're okay. We're okay. I'm here with you. I won't leave you."

Encourage them to use grounding techniques. Um, okay. I keep reading to see what *that* means: *Hold their hand or provide other reassuring touch.* Yeah, I can do that. I gently reach forward and hold her hands between mine. She's still trembling, but not as strongly as before. I rub circles on her hand with my thumb and keep up the reassuring words. "You're safe," I say. "I won't leave you."

Slowly, she leans forward, moving until her head rests against my chest. She still has her seat belt fastened, and it stretches as she shifts. I keep one hand connected to hers, wedged between our bodies, and the other I move to her back, caressing up and down.

We sit this way for several minutes. I breathe in and out slowly and steadily. Her breath starts out ragged, but soon syncs up with mine. Her pulse slows, too, back to a healthy tempo.

The circumstances suck but having her in my arms is everything. Protecting her. Helping her feel safe. My heart aches with the need to be there for her like this, be this person for her, always.

Finally, she sits up. "Thank you," she says, not meeting my eyes. Her face is pale, her exhaustion clear. I brush a strand of hair from her forehead.

"Are you feeling better?" I ask gently.

She nods hesitantly, and I wait. She clears her throat. "It was a panic attack."

"Have you had them before?"

She nods again, but I don't press. Then, "I'm so sorry, Adam." She finally meets my eyes, tears welling in hers. "Is your car okay?"

"Hey," I say softly. "It's fine. Just a flat tire." I smile at her. "A really, really flat tire." She smiles timidly back, and I ask, "Are *you* okay?"

"I'm embarrassed," she admits. "You let me drive your car, and I messed it up. Then I had a panic attack in front of my coworker..." She trails off, looking away again.

I use my thumb to gently nudge her face back toward mine. "Maybe," I say, "you didn't have a panic attack in front of your coworker. Maybe you had a panic attack in front of your friend."

She stares at me, her green eyes watery. "Yeah," she whispers. "I think I did. My friend." Her mouth tips up in a miniature smile.

Even this small concession, this small victory, thrills me. The elation spurs me to action.

"Alright, enough of this," I say. "I need to find the closest tire place and put on the spare."

Nicole grimaces, guilt flashing across her face. "How can I help?"

"You can help by resting." I consider a minute. "But not in the car. I don't want the jack to fall. Wait here."

I pull the keys from the ignition and hop out of the car, circling around to the trunk. I open it and shuffle the suitcases around until I find what I need: a beach towel—clean, not sandy, because it's been a while since I've been to the beach, but of course it's in here anyway because, yuh know, Florida, where having a beach towel in your car at all times is practically the law—and a folded up beach chair. I walk closer to the line of trees bordering the shoulder and set up the chair. Then, I throw the towel over my shoulder and approach the open passenger side door, planting my palms against the roof of the car and bending to lean in.

"Can you slide over the console to get out this door?" I ask Nicole.

Before her panic attack started, she did pull the car a pretty safe distance away from the highway traffic speeding past, but I'd rather not take the chance. She nods, unbuckling her seatbelt, and lifts her hips up over the center console and into the passenger seat. I step back and take her hand to pull her the rest of the way out. I drape the towel over her shoulders and lead her to the chair. It's not cold out, not really, but I'm hoping the towel will imitate the warm comfort of a blanket for her.

"This isn't necessary," she protests. "I can help you."

I shake my head. "Rest, please. I'll feel better."

Nicole peers up at me, then silently nods and sits back against the chair.

I pull out my phone and search for service stations nearby. I have a tire plan with one of the national chains, but it's too much to hope we're close to one of their locations. But ... huh. First result. It's off the next exit, only about five miles away. Okay, then. I call them to check that they'll honor my plan and to see if they have the tire my car needs in stock. Nicole watches me as I give a friendly mechanic named Jordan the information.

"Great!" I say. "We're just a few miles east of you on the highway here, but I'll change the tire, and we can drive over. Probably thirty minutes? Yeah, perfect. Thank you."

I hang up and turn to Nicole. "Good news. They have the tire in stock, so it'll be quick and easy for them to get us back on the road."

In a small voice, she says, "I can pay for the new tire. It was my fault–"

"There's no need," I quickly interrupt. "It won't cost anything. I bought a nationwide tire plan with them a while back, so it's covered."

I change the tire as quickly as I can, but the bolts are on pretty tightly, so it takes me a few tries to get them loose. Finally, about thirty-five minutes later, the spare tire is on. I pack everything back up in the car and get Nicole settled in the passenger seat. I drive us to the next exit and then down the road to the tire shop. Pulling into a parking spot, I ask Nicole to wait in the car, at least until we know what's up.

A bell jingles as I push through the front door. I note a small waiting area with plastic chairs, a water dispenser with those little cone-shaped paper cups and crinkled hot rod magazines. It's empty. Behind the desk at the other end of the small lobby, a large man stands at a computer. He looks up and greets me as I walk toward him.

"Uh, hi," I start. "I called a little bit ago. I need a tire replaced on my Impala?"

The man introduces himself as Jordan, who I spoke with on the phone. He confirms that they have the tire my car needs in stock, and they can fit me in right away.

I walk back out to the car to get Nicole. We grab our snacks and water bottles. As we settle into the plastic chairs in the waiting area, I tell Nicole, "He said it will take about two hours. We should get to New Orleans by nine. Not soon enough to go to the welcome reception, but still, not too far behind schedule."

She nods in response. "Again, Adam, I'm really sorry."

"Again," I smile. "It's really not your fault."

Nicole stares at the wall behind me, a faraway look in her eyes.

I quietly prompt, "Do you want to talk about it? Friend to friend?" I give her a gentle smile and my heart feels tight when she smiles back.

"I, um, I have pretty severe anxiety," she says. I'm surprised, but I don't interrupt her. "I've been anxious my whole life. Once when I was maybe four, I was backstage after a ballet recital. I let one of the teachers lead me all around searching for my bag—I even described it to her—because I just didn't know how to tell her that I didn't even bring a bag." She shrugs. "Another time, I was maybe seven? There was this babysitter who took me and my sisters to the mall to get ice cream. The ice cream shop was upstairs, and we were going to have to go on an escalator to get there. I just couldn't go on that escalator; I was too afraid. She spent like fifteen minutes trying to convince me it was fine and then got frustrated and we left. Molly was so mad at me. It was my fault we couldn't get ice cream. When Mom found out, she was mad, too, at the babysitter. Never hired her again. The next day Mom bought all the fixings for ice cream sundaes—chocolate sauce, caramel, sprinkles, whipped cream. We had so much fun. Molly forgave me.

"Around middle school, I started having symptoms of depression too. All the hormones and everything. I was a pretty morose teenager. Angsty with no reason to be. A little emo, a little goth, but without ear gauges or anything. I could never stand how those looked. I usually wore all black."

Again, I'm surprised, but I want her to continue, so I say nothing. Instead, I reach for her hand, tucking it inside my own.

"It got pretty bad. I had a lot of dark thoughts. Dark emotions. My parents took me to the doctor, and I started taking medication. Things were much better after that. I felt more like myself. Even with the medication, I'll always feel a little anxious, especially when I'm stressed. But the depression has only come back once. After I graduated from college during my first semester in library school."

Nicole stops talking for so long that I wonder if she's done.

I clear my throat. "What happened?" I ask. "I mean, did something trigger it?"

She looks up at me, her eyes glassy. I'm about to tell her that she doesn't need to say, doesn't need to talk about it anymore, when she drops her head and continues.

"My, uh, boyfriend at the time," she starts. Her eyes flick up to mine for a tiny moment. "We went to college together and dated for over three years. After we graduated, we both stayed local. I was in library school, and he was, well, mostly couch surfing and looking for a job. He ran hot and cold. Either I was the love of his life and he couldn't get enough of me, or he couldn't stand to be near me and froze me out. Sometimes within the same week. I, um, I took it very personally. I was in love with him. My anxiety was through the roof because I never knew where I stood with him. I second-guessed everything I did around him, everything I said. I would lie in bed after hanging out with him and dissect every word, convinced that if I had only worded things this way or didn't talk about whatever, he would love me better." She puffs out a long breath. "Obviously things were pretty toxic, but I didn't realize it at the time. When he finally broke up with me, I started seeing a therapist more often, in addition to the medication."

She stops now and meets my eyes, flashing me a sheepish smile. As if *she's* ashamed. As if she's the one who was in the wrong. My hands are bunched into fists, knuckles pressing into my thighs. I don't remember ever being as mad as I am right now. I'm not an angry person. I remind myself that anger is not going to help Nicole right now. I breathe a deep breath through my nose and release the air through my mouth.

"Nicole," I start, but my voice sounds scratchy. I clear my throat and try again. "I'm honored you trust me enough to share that with me. I wouldn't have guessed."

"I'm in such a better place now," she rushes to say. "Really, I am. Like I said, though, the anxiety never really goes away, and every once in a while, I have a panic attack, like the one today."

She pauses and her eyebrows pinch together, as if she's trying to solve a riddle. "I've never before come out of an attack as quickly as I did today," she says slowly.

The intense green of her eyes captures me and I can't look away. Not that I want to. She's holding me in place with just her gaze, and I can hardly breathe. Before I can say or do anything to act on the impulse to reach for her and crush her against my chest, to shield her from tough emotions and jerk ex-boyfriends, she exhales a long breath, shaking her head quickly back and forth.

"Anyway," she smiles. "You were awesome today."

The quick transition is enough to give me whiplash. Nicole's saying she's done talking about it. Message received.

I force a smile. "Nah," I say.

She pushes on. "You really were! Changing the tire. And the fact that you happened to have a chair in your trunk. You are prepared." She pauses, then smirks. "You were a boy scout, weren't you?"

I feel the tops of my ears warm. "I made Eagle," I admit.

After just under two hours of sharing our Buc-ee's snacks, laughing, and joking together, we're on the road again.

Chapter Twenty-Two

Nicole

F riday morning on the first full day of the conference, I'm still feeling drained from the emotional exertion of the day before. Adam did a pretty good job of talking me out of feeling embarrassed, instead helping me feel safe in my vulnerability, but the aftereffects of the panic attack are still lingering in my nervous system. I'm on edge, but I'm also determined to make the most of this conference I've been looking forward to for weeks.

I spend the morning in various workshops and conference sessions, jotting down pages of notes: AI tools being built into databases, strategies for working well with faculty, the newest trends in pedagogy for library instruction. I stand in line for what feels like an hour to buy an overpriced, wilted sandwich from the food stand inside the convention center.

That afternoon, I carve out some time to visit the exhibit hall. I
follow the NLA conference signs at the convention center until I
reach a stairway. Stepping aside, I stop and look over the half wall
onto the exhibit hall floor below. I gasp. It's like a village. Hundreds
of thousands of square feet of temporary walls, elaborate displays,
large signs, and even stages. I recognize the names of many of the
library vendors, but there are some I've never heard of, too. This
isn't my first NLA conference—I went to one back when I was in
my master's program—but I didn't spend much time in the exhibit
hall when I was here before. Today, I don't have any real goals in the
exhibit hall. I'm not in charge of purchasing so I don't need to meet
with vendors. Instead, I want to get a sense of it, to experience it.
I saw in the directory that there's a graphic novel and gaming stage,
surrounded by booths for comics vendors. I know I want to see that.

I head down the steps, my right arm bent upward for my hand to
grasp the straps of the official NLA conference tote bag I received
when I checked in this morning. It doesn't have much in it, just a
few loose pieces of paper and a pen. I stopped by my room before
coming to the exhibit hall to drop off my computer bag. I kept the
mostly empty tote in case there's any vendor swag I want to pick up.

At the bottom of the stairs, I start making my way through the
rows of vendors, grouped together by type—the database companies
here, the website and catalog vendors there. I walk toward the back
left of the room, where I saw the signs for the graphic novel stage. As
I do, I pass through the aisles housing the book publisher booths.

Booth is a bit of a misnomer here. The large publishers don't have
simple "booths", but rather large hallways of displays with shelving,

tables, life-size cutouts of new characters, and more. Some even laid down their own plush carpeting. Lining these hallways are literal towers of books—ARCs, or advance reader copies, of the publisher's forthcoming releases in any genre you can imagine. ARCs are paperbacks that often lack the final cover art and all the final edits of the official version of a book. Each stack I see holds multiple copies of the same title. Some of the stacks come up as high as my chest, built in a rounded column with each layer of books laid brick wall style, slightly overlapping with each of the two books below it.

These books, believe it or not, are free for the taking. Publishers love putting their forthcoming books in front of the librarians who make purchasing decisions and recommendations. Even though that's not *my* role, the publishers don't really care and don't actually check. A few ask to scan my badge, but for the most part, I just walk through the aisles, picking up books that appeal to me and putting them in my conference tote bag. Often, I just look at the covers and titles (despite the edict not to judge books by their covers), but sometimes I'll skim the summary first before deciding to slip it into my bag. Speaking of which, my tote bag is getting full. I decide that when it runs out of room, I'll leave the publisher section and find that graphic novel stage.

I turn the corner into the realm of a new publisher and a voice to my right says, "Tote bag?" One of the publisher reps is handing me a cute canvas tote with rope handles that says, "When life gives you lemonade, read in the shade."

Um, yes please. Since I now have another bag, I guess I can pick up some more books. I walk through this publisher's area and tuck new books into my new bag. And then, it happens a couple more times: I can't possibly hold another book and am about to continue on, when someone else hands me another tote bag and then I load that tote bag with more free books. Before I know it, I'm carrying around four tote bags bursting with paperbacks—two bags slung over each shoulder. The handles are digging into my skin. My load is not only weighing me down, but also making it difficult to walk through the aisles now that I'm wider and taking up more space. Yeah, I'm starting to think this was not the best idea.

I give up on trying to get to the graphic novel and comics area, and instead make my way toward the perimeter of the room to get my bearings. I need to go back to my hotel and drop off these bags. Oh, shoot. My hotel is a quarter mile away. I'll have to carry all this all that way. Though the exhibit hall is air conditioned, the exertion from carrying the heavy bags is making me overly warm. I lament the cardigan sweater I'm wearing, trapped in place under eight heavy tote bag straps. I can feel the sweat beading on my forehead and the back of my neck behind the cascade of my hair.

After some pivoting, I reach a side wall of the exhibit hall space and dump the bags on the floor so I can rest my shoulders, pull myself together, and make a plan. I start removing my sweater even as I'm trying to remember if I have a hair tie with me. In my peripheral vision, I see someone approaching, and I whirl around.

"Uhh, hey Nicole." Adam eyes me with amusement. "Whatcha got there?"

"I got a little carried away with the ARCs," I explain, one arm still half stuck in my cardigan. I'm a sweaty, rumpled mess. Gah, this is embarrassing.

"I can see that. Need help?" He's smiling as he surveys the situation, his eyes twinkling.

I haven't seen Adam all day. It's a big conference and the sessions we're attending don't really align because our job responsibilities are so different. He's back in his work attire today: black chinos and a red, collared short sleeved shirt. He's carrying a tan, suede messenger bag about the right size to hold a laptop computer. He looks calm and collected, as usual, making me feel even more self-conscious about the state I'm in.

"You don't really want to play my rescuer again, do you?" I half-tease, trying to gauge what he thinks of all this.

The smile drops from his face. "Always," he answers seriously. "Anytime."

My heart skips a beat and the heat in my face intensifies.

"I need to get these all back to my room," I admit. "I'd love some help."

Adam turns his attention to the pile of bags on the floor. He considers a moment, then says, "If you carry my computer bag, I can get all four of your bags."

I start to protest, but Adam is already handing me his messenger bag. He hoists one bag, then another, onto his right shoulder, angling one onto his back and the other on his right side. He repeats that for the other two bags, but on his left side. He pauses a minute to adjust everything, then grins at me.

"Ready when you are," he says.

I quickly sling his (light and comfortable) bag across my chest and lead the way to the stairs. When we get to the street and start toward the hotel, I end up walking a bit behind him, so we don't take up too much space on the sidewalk. After a few minutes, his breath gets heavier, and he shifts the bags with a roll of his shoulders. He moves his right hand to hold the straps on his left side to support the weight better. The movement causes his sleeve on the arm closest to me to ride up, uncovering his biceps and a hint of his tattoo. Under the strain of the weight, they're flexing attractively. I swallow thickly.

Adam looks over his shoulder and I realize I'm staring. "What?" he asks.

I shake my head, clearing my thoughts.

I smile at him sweetly. "You look ridiculous," I say.

He raises his eyebrows over the frame of his glasses and refocuses on the space in front of him as we walk. "Bold words from the person who filled all these bags to begin with," he says, but the corners of his mouth are turned up in a teasing grin.

By the time we get to the bank of elevators in the hotel lobby, Adam is, if not huffing and puffing, definitely feeling the effects of carrying fifty pounds of books over three blocks. As I'm pushing the button inside the elevator for my floor, my stomach swirls with a mixture of embarrassment, gratitude, and something else I'm not ready to identify yet.

"Do you want to set them down until we get to our floor?" I ask him.

"Uh, nah. Honestly, I think it will be harder to put them down and then pick them back up again than just to keep carrying them." The strands of hair framing his forehead are damp and his cheeks are red. He runs a hand through his hair, ruffling it.

When we get to my door, I quickly unlock it and make way for him to go inside. "You can set them here." I gesture to a square of empty floor next to the dresser. He dumps the bags, shaking out his arms and rolling his shoulders to loosen them.

"Well, thank you," I say.

Turning toward me, with a sly smile I've not seen from him before, he asks, "Don't I even get to see the booty?"

"W-what?" I gasp.

Adam laughs. "I carried the bags all the way here. Don't I at least get to see what's in them?"

I roll my eyes. "Oh my gosh. I'm not sure I even remember. Let's take inventory."

We sit on the floor and start emptying the bags, stacking the books in several piles. Adam surveys the loot.

"Nicole, there have to be at least fifty books here!"

I blush. "I already said I got carried away."

He shakes his head, clearly enjoying the situation. He pulls a novel called *The Secret of Hangar 57* off the top of a pile. Skimming the summary, he says, "This one is about an evil scientist whose experiment goes wrong and creates a giant slime monster that terrorizes a small, local airport." Adam lifts his eyebrows at me in question.

"So?"

"So ... how high up on your TBR list is that going to be?"

I laugh. "I liked the cover, okay?"

"Okay..." He grins.

"Hey, they can't all be winners, alright? There are some that sound really good in here too."

He laughs deeply and picks up another book. "I'll grant you that."

As we're sitting on the floor of my hotel room, sorting through the stacks of books, laughing, and talking, I don't realize how much time has passed until my stomach grumbles hungrily. I look at my phone and see it's already 5:30.

"Oh!" I say. "I hope you weren't looking forward to any sessions this afternoon, because I think you've already missed them."

"Nah, it's fine. This is more fun."

I smile at him shyly. "It is," I say. "Want to grab some dinner?"

"Sure! Burnt all my calories on the way here," he says with a smile.

Chapter Twenty-Three

Nicole

"Molly!" I squeal when my sister walks into the hotel lobby. Leaving Adam in the coffee line, I run to give her a hug. She squeezes me back, and I'm once again grateful that this conference is happening in the very city where my big sister lives. I'm also grateful she's willing to come watch my presentation and celebrate with me over dinner afterward. Molly is practically a genius—a scientist who spends most of her time in the lab working on, I don't know, saving the world or something. She's been interested in my work when we've talked about it before, but I also know it's hard for her to change up her normal routine, so it means a lot that she ditched whatever she usually does on a Sunday afternoon and evening to be with me today.

Adam approaches us with a cup in each hand. "Your matcha latte," he says, handing me one of the cups. Turning to Molly, he says, "I don't know what you like, or I would have gotten you one too. This is an Americano, if you want it."

"No, I'm good. But thank you," Molly responds then looks at me expectantly.

"Oh! Sorry. Adam, this is my sister, Molly. Molly, this is Adam, my, um, coworker I told you about."

Adam's eyes snap to mine briefly, and then he smiles slowly. Turning to Molly, he says, "Nice to meet you."

"You too," Molly says.

Adam shifts his gaze back on me. "So," he teases, "you've been talking to your sister about me?"

My face warms and I quickly stutter, "Well, I mean that we're presenting together. Molly's coming to the presentation, so I was telling her about the presentation and how you'll be at the presentation because it's also your presentation..." I trail off lamely.

Molly watches my face with interest, but luckily, she doesn't say anything. Our younger sister, Olivia, would not be as kind.

"Right," Adam says smoothly. "The presentation." He glances at his phone. "Speaking of which, I'm going to head over to the conference center. I'll leave you to catch up. See you in a bit?"

I nod as he walks away. The presentation isn't for another couple of hours, but I know he's nervous about it. Interesting how the tables have turned. Adam, who's calm and collected in most situations, dreads this presentation. And while I worry incessantly about almost everything in my life, I feel confident about the presentation. I know my stuff and that people will find it valuable.

And dressing to impress helps a lot. I'm wearing black and white plaid, tweed-style dress pants that fit me like a glove without being uncomfortable (elastic waistband for the win!). My shirt is a rose gold-colored V-neck with a Swiss dot pattern and ruffle sleeves. On my feet are my favorite silver ballet flats. I feel confident in this outfit—it's professional, but feminine, and comfortable so I won't be fiddling with my clothes instead of focusing on the presentation. I look good.

I wonder if Adam noticed, the unhelpful voice in my head asks. As usual, I ignore it.

When Adam is outside the automatic doors, Molly turns to me, and we walk toward one of the couches in the lobby. "So…" she says, and I brace myself.

"So…" I echo as we sit.

"You never mentioned how handsome Adam is. As a matter of fact, I believe you actually texted that he is *not* cute." She smirks at me knowingly.

Did I? I try to remember as I take a sip of my latte. Was there a time when I didn't appreciate the way his hair falls across his forehead, no matter how hard he tries to keep it combed back? When I didn't look into his honey brown eyes and find myself drowning a little? Or notice the lean strength of his arms? No, he's definitely attractive. A fact I can ignore less and less the more I spend time with him and the more I get to know him.

I shrug. "So, he's cute," I say defensively. "So what?"

"So, seems like there's more to him than just cute. What happened on the drive over here? You texted about car troubles." She nudges my hand for a sip of my latte, so I hand her the cup.

I tell Molly everything about the drive to New Orleans. She's jealous about the Buc-ee's—there aren't any in Louisiana. She gasps when I describe hitting the piece of metal and hugs me as I confess to the panic attack. The look in her eyes shifts from concern to interest when I tell her how much I shared with Adam at the auto shop. I even tell her about the time he and I have been spending together at the conference—how he carried my books and how we've been eating every meal together.

"Oh my gosh, Nicole, this is the cutest falling in love story I've ever heard." Molly gushes when I've finished.

"Pssh," I protest. "No, we're just coworkers." Molly looks at me with her eyebrows raised. "Friends," I amend. "Work friends. Work friend type people. That's all."

"Why do you insist on friend-zoning this man? Because all I see are green flags."

"I'm not friend-zoning him, it's just friendly is all I feel toward him."

Molly arches her eyebrow. I huff out a breath. "Okay," I say. "So, it's the kind of opposite gender friendship that would make our significant others uncomfortable if we had them, but still just friendship."

Molly clicks her tongue in disbelief. "Friendship is *not* all he feels for you, I can tell you that right now. Everything you've told me? He's showing you he wants more."

I sigh. "And that's a problem. Look, I can't like Adam, because he likes me, which means I don't like him."

"Um, what?" Her eyebrows pinch together above her round glasses.

"I've made some pretty bad choices in the past with men," I say. Molly's face softens. "And they all started when a guy I would have never really considered said he was interested in me. I need to be into a man because of who he is, not because he was into me first."

Molly takes my hand. "I hear you, and I know Steven really hurt you. I can understand how that experience would make you hesitant to trust your heart to someone new. But those were his issues, not yours. Nicole, are you sure what you're feeling is just because he likes you? I mean, can you list things about Adam that you like, things that make him a good man and would make him a great partner?"

Of course I can. Easily. It would be a long list. But I can't let my brain go there. I just don't trust myself. I shake my head.

Molly bites her lip and haltingly says, "Are you sure ... you're not taking advantage of Adam?"

My eyes jump up to hers. "What?" I croak out.

"You know he likes you. Despite what you *say*, you like him, too, and I have to wonder if you're maybe sending him nonverbal signals that might be confusing if you don't actually want to date him?" Molly's eyes are soft, but her words hit my heart like an *Oxford English Dictionary* to the toe.

"Am I?" I whisper. My unfocused gaze blurs all the more as I internally reel through my interactions with Adam over the last few months.

"I don't know, Nicole, but if you truly don't want to date Adam, you need to have a frank conversation with him about it. It's not fair to string him along."

Have I been stringing Adam along? I haven't meant to. I shake my head. "Mol, let's just forget it, okay? Let's talk about something else."

She hesitates. Then she nods. "Sure," she says with a tight-lipped smile. "Tell me more about your presentation."

Molly and I arrive at the conference center with time to spare before the presentation. The session before ours in the room we've been assigned seems to have finished early. I peek through the door to see Adam at the front of the room getting a laptop situated and connected to the display screen. I step forward to help him, but Molly pulls me back.

"What do you think about asking Adam to join us for dinner?" she asks.

"That'd be great, if you don't mind," I say. "We're celebrating the presentation, and he's part of that." I shrug. "Only seems fair."

"Agreed. Plus, I'd like to talk to him more. It's my job as your big sister." She grins.

I roll my eyes. "I already told you it's not like that," I say. "But listen, can you ask him? I don't want to seem ... whatever."

She nods, and we head into the room. Adam sees us walking up the aisle and waves weakly. "How are you holding up?" I ask him as we approach.

Adam lets out a long breath. "I'm nervous," he admits. "I'm used to being the behind-the-scenes guy, not the guy everyone's looking at."

"Hey," I say, placing my hand on his arm and waiting until he meets my eyes. "You'll do great. We practiced a bunch, and we'll work together. Don't worry, I won't leave you hanging."

His face relaxes and the corners of his mouth tip up. "Thanks, Nicole," he says quietly. "That means a lot."

Molly clears her throat. "Hey, Adam. We were wondering..." I glare at her. "I was wondering," she amends, "if you'd like to join Nicole and me for dinner after this. To celebrate your presentation."

"I don't want to intrude on your time together," Adam protests.

"No, you wouldn't be," Molly reassures him.

Adam looks at me, a question in his eyes.

"Please, Adam," I say, holding his gaze. "I want you to come."

Adam smiles shyly. "In that case," he says. "Of course I'll come."

"Awesome!" Molly says, thrusting out her hands in a double thumbs-up. "I'll leave you two to finish setting up." She moves to the back of the room and takes a seat.

As our presentation's start time inches closer, the room fills up. And then overflows. When the room moderator calls everyone to attention, the audience is standing room only, with a few people still trickling in and settling against the side walls of the room.

The moderator introduces us, and I speak first, giving the background and purpose of the graphic novel collection.

"Welcome everyone, and thanks for being here. Today, we'll walk you through the processes we followed to start a graphic novel collection in our liberal arts college library," I begin in a clear, confident voice.

Despite our practice and training, Adam's nerves show through during the presentation. His hands are visibly shaking, so he shoves them into his pockets. His voice is a bit shaky, too, nothing like his cool, assured timbre when we're talking one-on-one. But the content is spot on, and I jump in on his parts when it looks like he needs help. Overall, I think it's going great, especially judging by the profusion of questions and comments at the end.

Our session is in the last time slot of the day, and with no one coming in behind us, we hang out for close to fifteen extra minutes answering additional questions and sharing experiences with the other librarians in attendance.

I'm riding the high of accomplishment, of being good at my chosen career. What I'm doing at work is making a difference in people's lives. I'm meaningfully contributing to my profession. After the hard work Adam and I have put into the graphic novel collection project over the last six months, it's validating to know that our ideas are well-received and appreciated by our peers. It strikes me again what a big deal it is to present at NLA; how this room was overflowing with colleagues interested in hearing what I had to say. Contentment washes over me, calming me internally in a way I can't remember feeling in years.

Chapter Twenty-Four

Adam

Well, at least it's over. And I didn't vomit. That has to count for something.

The presentation was a blur. I guess I talked about the stuff I was supposed to talk about? Nicole bailed me out a couple of times, smoothly continuing my train of thought without flustering me further.

I steal a glance at Nicole, and she's in her element—talking to several audience members who approached her when the session ended. She's so good at this.

Ever since Nicole opened up to me the other day in the auto shop, my brain has been busy arranging and rearranging what I know about her, filling in the gaps that existed before, and creating a fuller picture of the woman she is. Understanding her strength and what she's overcome only serves to cement my awe.

I value Dr. Parker's advice, and now that I have a better under-standing of what Nicole's ex put her through, I can see that being a constant in her life while still giving her the space to sort through her own feelings, has been the right call. She's lonely, but afraid to be vulnerable. I can relate.

I'm a patient man, but these last few days with Nicole are testing me unlike anything else. My yearning for her has become a physical ache radiating out from my chest through my entire body. To be around her and not touch her, not take her in my arms and taste her lips, is the most exquisite torture. The tension between us is building, ratcheting up with each flirtatious comment and stolen glance. I know she feels it too. She must.

As most of the attendees file out of the room, I start closing out the windows on the presentation laptop. I glance over at Nicole again, who is smiling and talking with her sister. A cold hand touches my arm, and I turn to see a woman around my age, with curly red hair and glasses. I paste a closed mouth smile on my face and raise my eyebrows.

"Hi," she says shyly, her cheeks pink.

"Hello," I respond.

"Um, I really enjoyed your presentation. I love graphic novels."

"Thank you."

"Do you have much information yet on which titles are most popular among your students? Which have been checked out the most?"

"Oh, well, we really just started circulating them a couple months ago."

"Well, what graphic novels are *your* favorites? My name is Gloria, by the way." Her eyes glimmer, and I realize her hand is still on my arm.

"Ah, I don't actually read them myself. My colleague, Nicole, is really the one with passion for the project."

That's not *quite* true; I have read some graphic novels over the last few months, ones Nicole recommended. I gesture behind me to where Nicole is standing with her sister. I glance toward her and see that she is several feet closer than when I looked last. She's no longer talking to her sister, and her eyes are locked on the red-haired woman, on me. Her fingers are curled against Molly's arm, her grip tightening. The expression on Nicole's face is tight, as if she's barely controlling her emotions.

"Ouch," I hear Molly grumble. "Nicole, let go."

Nicole drops her hand, flexing her fingers, but her eyes stay on me.

Is Nicole ... jealous? Delight fills my body. A laugh bubbles up my throat, but I swallow it down and smother my grin as I turn back toward the red-haired woman.

"This project is just so fascinating to me," the woman coos. "Oh! Maybe we could have a drink together to talk about it more? The conference sessions are done for today."

I feel heat at my back as Nicole stalks closer, no doubt hearing the invitation. She lays her hand on my shoulder, and I instinctively lean into it. I turn and catch her saccharine smile, Nicole's eyes on the red-haired woman, but directing her words to me. "Adam, are you ready to go?" she asks pointedly.

I shift my eyes back to the red-haired woman, focusing on the center of her face, not making eye contact. I clear my throat awkwardly, still fighting a gleeful grin. "I have plans now, but thank you," I manage to say.

"That's too bad," the woman's lips turn pouty, and she shifts her gaze between me and Nicole. "Can I have your card?" she asks. "You know, in case I have questions later about your presentation?"

As I fumble in my messenger bag for my business card, Nicole snaps hers forward toward the woman.

"Here's mine," Nicole says, still smiling that forced, unnatural smile. "I'd be happy to answer any questions you have related to our presentation."

"Oh!" The woman sputters, taking the card from Nicole's hand. "Thank you." She looks over at me and finally slides her hand off my arm. She turns and walks away, looking back over her shoulder once.

My grin bursts free as I finish closing out the laptop, eyeing Nicole's red face as Molly yanks her toward the door.

Chapter Twenty-Five

Nicole

Molly grips my arm and whispers, "What was that?"

I meet her eyes and, seeing a twinkle of I-told-you-so, quickly glance away.

"What was what?" I feign innocence. I press my fingers to my cheeks, trying to cool them. What *was* that? That reaction. I'm not sure I can even explain it. I saw that woman with her smug smile, her hand on Adam's arm, and suddenly I couldn't focus on anything else. She asked him out? Would he have said yes? Yeah, we've been connecting lately, flirting a bit even, but it's not like Adam and I are dating. I have no claim on him. So why, in that moment of Adam talking to another woman, did my heart beat steadily with the refrain "Mine. Mine. Mine"?

I frantically catch my sister's eye, mouthing, "Do I *like* Adam?"

Molly rolls her eyes. "Obviously," she whispers. "That's what Olivia and I have been trying to tell you for months now."

But ... I think I like Adam not because he likes me. I think I like him because he's smart and funny and supportive and interesting and attractive. I think I would like him even if he wasn't interested in me.

Just then, Adam joins us in the hallway. "Are we ready for dinner?" he asks, his eyes bright.

Molly glances at me quickly, then says, "Absolutely. I know the place. We can walk there from here."

Adam smiles. "Perfect,"

The three of us walk to a nearby restaurant. I'm quiet, my brain still reeling over my revelation. Adam's my coworker, my ... friend. I look toward him as he chats with Molly. A lock of his hair falls across his forehead, and he lifts his hand to brush it away. The corners of his eyes crinkle as he laughs at something she says. I think about the photo he hung in my office, his sour gummy worms, the daily memes, how his steadying presence kept me on track throughout the graphic novel project. He's deep and layered; serious and calm on the surface, but with these hidden charms that make me like him more and more as I discover each one.

He looks at me and smiles. My heart thunks in my chest, and I smile softly back at him. We hold each other's gazes over Molly's head for several seconds.

Then, I hear Molly call, "Um, guys?"

I shake my head, breaking eye contact, and realize that Molly has stopped while Adam and I kept walking. I turn back and blink at my sister, who gestures with her right hand.

"We're here," she says.

I take in the two-story stone structure in front of us, a wrought iron balcony stretching across the top floor. We enter through the open door, and inside it's crowded and loud, tables pushed together with hardly enough space to walk between them. Even though we have a roof over our heads, it feels like we're still outside—the walls being mostly windows and those windows being mostly open without screens to block the flow to the street. The floors are rough cobblestone, and a heavy oak bar fills the back wall, dozens of bottles lined up behind it.

"This pub has the best po'boys," Molly tells us. "The other food is good, too. And," her eyes catch mine as she smirks, "they have really good tater tots."

That gets my attention. I grin at her. "What are we waiting for? Let's eat some tots!"

There's a short wait, but we're seated quickly. As we order, my eyes wander again and again to Adam. Half the time when I glance at him, he's already looking at me. I smile shyly. My thoughts bang around inside my head as I try to make sense of my new realization, and what might come next.

I shake my head and focus my attention on Molly. We don't get to see each other too often, so I want to make the most of this time.

"How's work going?" I ask her.

"Fine..." She grimaces.

"What's up?"

"Nothing, it's just they added a new researcher to my team. Jonathan." She makes a face.

"You don't like Jonathan?" Adam asks.

"We just ... tend to always be competing for the same grants, same positions. I've known him for a couple of years now. And he's ... smug."

"Well, there's no way he's as brilliant as you," I say confidently. "You'll show him who's boss."

"Maybe." Molly looks unsure.

"And how's Beaker?" I change the subject, figuring she'd rather talk about her cat. Molly brightens and starts going on about the cute things Beaker has been doing.

"I admit Beaker is cute," I say. "But I just don't get the appeal of cats in general."

Molly mockingly gasps. "Really, Nicole. You're a librarian. You're like legally required to be a cat person!"

"Well." I grin. "I've always been a bit of a rebel."

"I do know this about you." Molly smiles.

"Seriously, though. Dogs are so much better. I wish I could get one, but I'm in the apartment right now, and it just doesn't make sense. Someday..." I trail off. "Oh! Adam has the sweetest dog!"

I feel the weight of Adam's eyes on me as I say this, but I keep my focus on Molly, who's smirking.

"Oh," she says. "You've met Adam's dog?"

I ignore her and turn to Adam. "How old is Joan?" I ask.

Adam tells us about Joan and the conversation flows from there. I'm surprised how much Adam contributes. This is the most I've seen him talk outside of a one-on-one conversation. He makes us laugh with his wry observations.

Our food arrives, and the loaded tater tots I ordered are so good. I've been doing a lot of walking while here at the conference, so I splurge a bit on my food.

As we finish up, Molly pulls out her phone to grab a rideshare back to her apartment. Adam and I wait with her outside the restaurant, but it's only a few minutes before the car pulls up. I give her a hug. As she gets in the car and it drives away, I wave goofily after her, seeing her shake her head at me through the window. Adam watches me with an amused look on his face. When the car is out of sight, I drop my hand, turn toward Adam, and we start walking together back in the direction of the hotel.

Though we're both quiet, it's not awkward. It's comfortable. Companionable. There's an undercurrent of ... something as we walk. A subtext hearkening back to my feelings after the presentation, before dinner. My shoulder bumps his arm. Gently, Adam grasps my hand with his, weaving our fingers together. My heart thumps in my chest, the warmth of his skin setting me on fire. People bustle all around us, heading to the bars and clubs on this Saturday night. Cars rev their engines; a group of women celebrating a bachelorette party, decked out in sparkly tiaras and pink feather boas, laugh loudly as they pass us on the sidewalk; music spills into the street from several directions. But we're in our own bubble, Adam and I, insulated from the noise, locked into this serene moment, walking hand in hand down the streets of New Orleans. Silently. Both knowing that this seemingly inconsequential stroll is a turning point in our relationship, changing everything.

In the elevator ride up to our rooms, Adam studies me. We still don't speak. His brown eyes darken, almost blending in with his pupils in the muted light, but they're soft, deep. He walks me to my door, where he drops my hand, and I finally break the silence.

"You keep surprising me," I say softly.

"Good," he whispers huskily, tucking a strand of hair behind my ear. "Good night, Nicole."

"Good n-night," I stutter, unlocking the door.

I enter my room, and the door thunks closed behind me. I peer through the peephole, watching Adam walk down the hall toward his own room. In a daze, I get ready for bed. I lie in the dark, my head spinning, until I finally fall asleep with a smile on my lips.

Chapter Twenty-Six

Adam

Yeah, no way I can get to sleep after that. Once in my hotel room, I change into basketball shorts and get ready for bed, even though I feel jittery, like I just drank three cups of coffee. Is it weird to be celebrating something as innocent as holding hands? It doesn't feel innocent. It feels ... monumental. It feels like the most important thing that's ever happened to me. The start, I hope, of something amazing.

I wonder how Nicole is feeling. Is she overthinking tonight, second-guessing even this small step? Personally, I could have blown through at least two more steps tonight, but I don't want to push her too much, too soon. But I'm second-guessing, too. Should I have kissed her? A kiss good night would have been a logical progression, but it feels like it would have been forward, almost, to do so when, despite all the time we've spent together, all the little moments, we've never been on a proper date.

But I felt a shift between us tonight. The air changed around us, the energy between us. Maybe she's starting to think of me the way I think of her, the way I've thought of her since the first moment we met. An incredulous laugh bursts out of me. I shake my head, amazed that it could be true.

As has often happened in the last five years, this experience of high emotion brings my father to mind. To think of the many emotions and experiences he's already missed, and the ones yet to come in my life that he will miss, is almost unbearable.

Grief is sneaky. Once the first few months of numbing pain passed, I continue to think of my dad every day. But in the hubbub and structure of the day to day, the thoughts don't hurt. I remember he's gone, of course, but it's a dull remembrance, a phantasm off in the distance. When I sit in the memories, though, dwell on the holes in my life he used to fill, the pain returns, fresh as the moment my mom first called me to break the news.

I was in my mid-twenties at the time, a full-grown adult by any account, but with so much still to experience in life that I will need my dad to help me navigate. Love. Parenting. Aging. It was a heart attack, sudden and unexpected, so it wasn't like he could have written me letters with words of advice in envelopes marked with specific occasions in my life. *On the day of your wedding. On the birth of your first child.* What I wouldn't give for his thoughts, encouragement, and advice documented like that for me to read and reread whenever I want. I try to scrabble together as much as I can remember from things he told me while he was alive, but I'm afraid I tuned him out much too often.

My brain hooks onto an old memory and calls it forward. I was maybe fourteen and my dad took me out on the Gulf for deep sea fishing. This trip wasn't our first or our last, just one deep sea fishing trip in the many we took together. It was summer—the best time of year for fishing in the Gulf of Mexico and also convenient since I didn't have school. My dad's buddy, Cliff, had a forty-foot power catamaran, and we'd tag along with him on days he went out. We went so often that we had our own fishing gear, and then we'd pack a cooler with food, water, and sodas, staying on the water all day.

This particular trip, we were anchored in, bottom fishing, but not doing much catching. Cliff and Dad didn't mind much; they were enjoying being outside on the water and "shooting the breeze" as they would say. But I was restless and kept reeling in my line and then casting it out again, just to keep busy.

"You won't catch anything doing that!" Dad called over to me from across the boat.

"We're not catching anything now," I grumbled.

Cliff laughed. "Patience!" he said.

And sure enough, soon Dad and Cliff's lines were pulling taut, and they started reeling in some decent-sized snapper. Once I stopped fooling around, I caught a couple too, in rapid succession.

Then Cliff, with his eyes trained on the water, shouted, "Bob! Chicken dolphins!"

I turned to look and saw the flashes of neon blue and green that were the telltale sign that a school of mahi mahi was swimming up.

Cliff grabbed some sardines and dropped them along the chum line, giving the mahi mahi incentive to stick around. Then, he pulled his line from the water and replaced his live bait with a gotcha plug.

I watched Cliff drop his line again and almost immediately get a hit. He fought for several minutes to reel it in, his brown skin damp with sweat and glinting in the summer sun. When he had the fish above the water, we shouted when we saw a mahi mahi that looked to be at least fifteen pounds. Cliff dropped him back in the water, still on the line.

When he saw my questioning gaze, he explained, "If we keep him on the line, the rest of the school will stay nearby, and maybe we can catch a couple more."

"Do you want to try?" my dad asked me.

I agreed eagerly. We fixed my line up with a banana jig, and I dropped it in the water. Dad did the same with his line on the other side of the boat.

Soon, Dad was wrestling with a chicken dolphin on the end of his line, tugging and reeling as the fish jumped out of the water and then crashed back down. Finally, he got it in, and we left this second mahi mahi on the line in the water while Cliff brought in his original one.

Finally, a few minutes later, my line pulled, the rod bending sharply toward the water. With Dad and Cliff cheering me on, I fought the mahi for fifteen grueling minutes. The fish yanked my wiry teenage body forward and backward as I reeled with all my strength. When it jumped out of the water, I saw it was huge! At least twenty pounds. The rod dipped down, and I pulled it back up, over and over. Suddenly, I tumbled back onto the floor of the boat, bruising my elbows. The line had snapped and the mahi mahi got away.

In the flood of my disappointment, I forgot how to breathe. I fought back tears, determined not to cry in front of my dad and Cliff. As Cliff steered us home, my dad sat next to me on the bench. Lifting his arm to casually rest across my shoulders, he slowly asked, "You know why I like fishing?"

"Why?" I asked. At the moment, I was pretty sure I hated fishing. Would never go again if I could help it.

"I always learn about life."

"What do you mean?"

"Like fishing, accomplishing anything worthwhile in life requires patience, persistence, and a willingness to face uncertainty." He smiles. "Like in love and relationships. You may not care too much about that now, but someday you will. With fishing, you might wait hours for a catch, just like in life it may take time, more than you'd hoped, to find the right person, or once you find them, for a relationship to develop.

"Both love and fishing involve moments of disappointment and frustration, but also the thrill of a big catch or a meaningful connection. They both require dedication and commitment. But most of all, you need to understand that it's the experience itself that holds value, no matter how it turns out."

He was right that, at the time, I didn't much care for his advice about life and love. And it definitely didn't make me feel better about losing the mahi, but I'm glad the memory has stuck with me. It's bittersweet to pull his words back now from the recesses of my mind. Thinking back on the last six months, his advice seems more relevant than ever.

Not that I'm "catching" Nicole. Trying to be a meaningful part of her life is taking all my emotional strength, but at the same time, building it up and heightening my resilience. For sure, walking with her tonight, hand in hand, was the thrill of my life.

I prop the pillows up against the headboard and sit on the bed, reclining back. I close my eyes and heave out a sigh. Nope, still not tired. Between the leftover nervous energy from the presentation this afternoon, the excitement of my evening with Nicole, and the slow ache of remembering my father, I'm not sure how I'll settle down enough to fall asleep.

I swing my legs around to climb out of bed. Setting up my laptop on the little hotel desk, I launch a computer game. All the stress of the day, both good and bad, drops out of focus as I take turn after turn in the game and get lost in the fictional world. I don't emerge until the early hours of the morning, when I finally crawl into bed and spend the few hours that remain in a soft, dreamless sleep.

Chapter Twenty-Seven

Nicole

Molly:

Nicole! What happened after I left last night? We need the deets!

Olivia:

deets? wow mol are you 40?

Molly:

What should I say?

Olivia:

spill the tea

Olivia:

but wut happened

Nicole:

Nothing dramatic. But...

Molly:

...

Olivia:

...

Nicole:

We held hands

Olivia:

lame

Molly:

Is that all?

Nicole:

Yes. But I'm finally ready for more, if he still wants it

Molly:

Of course he does

Olivia:

of course he does

Nicole:

Oookay. Well we're driving back to fl today so wish me luck

Molly:

I pack my suitcase the next morning, and shift around my books to condense them into fewer bags, if possible. It's a really good thing we didn't end up flying.

Adam texts to meet him in the hotel lobby at eight. He also texts a meme that says:

"Last night, I had a nightmare that disco music was making a comeback. At first, I was afraid. I was petrified!"

It's funny, but I maybe expected something, I don't know … flirtier after last night. A meme that acknowledges the shift between us, that signals that he wants to pursue a relationship with me and see where this goes. But maybe that's asking too much of a meme.

I run down to the lobby to get a luggage cart—there's no way I'm going to be able to carry everything on my own. I load up the cart and steer it precariously out my hotel room door, down the hall, and into the elevator. When I arrive in the lobby, Adam's already waiting for me. He sees me pushing the cart, and leaving his suitcase, rushes over to take it from me.

"I forgot about your bags of books," he says as he approaches. "I'm sorry. I would have met you at your room to help."

I wave a hand. "No need. I have it all under control." Of course, the cart takes that moment to decide to zig when I'm clearly telling it to zag, and I crash it into a trashcan.

"I can see that." He grins and moves to stand in front of me. Tucking a strand of hair behind my ear, he murmurs, "Good morning."

Butterflies erupt in my stomach, and for once, I let them stay. I smile up at Adam. "Good morning to you."

"Full disclosure: I didn't get very much sleep last night."

"Oh," I say, as my brain starts to spin with a thousand scenarios. "Did you go out again?" Maybe he ended up meeting with that redhead after all. Maybe he wanted to go explore Bourbon Street.

Adam looks surprised. "Of course not. I was just restless and then I started thinking about my dad, and I ended up playing a computer game until much too late."

I relax my shoulders. "You couldn't sleep?"

He shakes his head. "Do you mind driving? At least for the first little while?"

I shuffle back a step. "Really?" I gape, grabbing his arm. "You actually trust me to drive your car again after what happened?"

He shrugs. "Of course." He drops his voice. "That flat tire could have happened to anyone, Nicole. It wasn't your fault."

I nod and blink back a few tears. The flat tire really *feels* like my fault. But Adam still trusts me. "I'll still be extra careful," I promise.

He hands me the keys. "If you go get the car and pull it around out front, I'll get all the luggage loaded."

"Deal."

Adam falls asleep quickly after we start driving. True to my word, I focus on the road but steal a few glances at the passenger seat when I can. Adam's head rests against the back of the seat, his face turned toward me. His glasses are off, grasped loosely in his right hand. Without them, his face looks younger, almost boyish, despite the stubble that shows he didn't shave this morning. His eye lashes are long, laying delicately against his cheek. His mouth hangs open just a little. His positioning doesn't suggest he would feel comfortable, but he hasn't stirred, so the seat must be relaxing enough.

I pass the time while driving by listening to an audiobook. I have it on my phone, which I connect to Bluetooth in Adam's car so it plays through the speakers. Rather than subject Adam to any ill-timed spicy scenes if he wakes up, and subject myself to the ensuing embarrassment, the book I turn on is more women's fiction than romance. I think about the term "women's fiction" and wonder why there isn't a genre called "men's fiction." Is it because men are presumed to not read fiction? Or because books written about men are considered to apply to everyone, but books about women must only interest other women?

Unfortunately, my thought tangent causes me to miss hearing the details of how the main character's boyfriend dies while ... walking the dog or something? I skip back and let it play again. Ohhhh.

I've been driving, and Adam's been sleeping, for about four hours when I see a Buc-ee's sign. The gas gauge is getting low and I'm getting hungry, so I pull off. It's a different Buc-ee's than where we stopped on the way to New Orleans, a little further west. I park and, leaving Adam still asleep in the car, I head inside. Picking out my own lunch is easy: sliced brisket sandwich and white cheddar nuggees. But I browse around to find lunch for Adam, too. He liked the sliced brisket sandwich the other day, so that's a safe bet. I pick up a bag of sour gummy worms, and finally a fresh fruit cup. Then, I grab two bottles of water and cash out.

When I return to the car, my plan is to move it around to the gas pumps and fill the tank, but I see the passenger side door open, with Adam sitting sideways with his feet on the ground. As I approach, he grins at me.

"Hey there, sleepyhead," I tease.

"Sorry," he says. "I'm not very good company today. And it looks like I missed a Buc-ee's run?"

"Don't worry," I reassure him, handing him the bag with his food. "I've got you."

He peeks into the bag and then looks up at me in awe. "You got me lunch?"

I shrug. "Of course. I think you'll like what I got, but if I missed anything, I guess you can go in yourself now that you're awake."

He opens the bag again. "No, this is perfect. Thank you." He chuckles. "You even got me sour gummy worms."

I nod. "And I was about to get gas since we're running low."

He stands, stretching his legs as he does. "I can take over driving again now. I'm feeling much better."

I laugh, handing him the keys. "Well, sure. After your four-hour nap."

After eating my lunch, I end up falling asleep for a while, too. I thought I would feel too self-conscious to fall asleep in front of Adam, but as the car rolls along, the hum of the tires against the road has my eyelids turning heavy. I don't try to fight it. I feel cozy and secure in the front seat of his car, so I let sleep take me.

Before I know it, the light outside has faded, and we're exiting the highway toward St. Anastasia.

Adam pulls up outside my apartment just as the last few rays of the light from the sun are swallowed in the inky night sky.

He puts the car in park and unbuckles his seatbelt. "I'll help you carry everything in," he offers.

I nod and wait outside the car while he opens the trunk and shuffles around inside for my bags. I take two of the bags of books, the straps hoisted up on my shoulders, and he manages my suitcase and the rest of the books. I dig through my bag for my house keys as we walk up the stairs. When we reach the top, I have them ready, unlocking the door.

With the memory of my embarrassment after Soapbox lifting to the top of my mind, I ask Adam to set the bags just inside the doorway and I don't invite him any further inside. He doesn't seem to notice or mind. Instead, he stands on the landing outside my front door, fiddling with his car keys and looking nervous.

I search for the right words to say and finally blurt, "Thank you for volunteering your car for this trip. And doing most of the driving. I'm sorry again about the tire."

He lifts his eyes to mine. "Don't mention it," he says.

We're quiet for another awkward minute. He hasn't brought up last night at all today. Maybe I'm reading too much into it. I should forget it happened, go inside, and Adam and I can return to our work-type friends sort of relationship. To be fair, holding hands is decidedly not a big deal, really just the smallest step toward anything romantic. But it feels like a monumental risk to me, an action I hadn't considered taking with anyone else since Steven. Even now, my hand twitches, wanting to touch him. He's so close, right in front of me. I could just lift my hand and place it on his arm or his shoulder. What would he think? I feel my eyebrows pulling together—those worry lines down my forehead are going to be deep in a couple of decades.

Breaking the spiraling train of my thoughts, Adam slowly reaches toward me and runs his index finger across my forehead, nestling into that space between my eyebrows, smoothing it out.

"Are you okay?" he asks in a husky voice.

I swallow. "Yep. Yes. Of course," I say too brightly.

His hand moves down my face until he's cupping it, his thumb moving slowly across the skin at the top of my cheek. I close my eyes, reveling in the sensation.

"Can I take you to dinner this week?" Adam asks softly.

"I'd like that," I answer, covering his hand with my own.

He gazes into my eyes for a beat, a smile spreading slowly across his face. "Friday?"

I nod. My throat feels thick, and I'm not sure my voice will work if I try to answer in words.

"Good." He hesitates. "I'm off the next few days, driving down to visit my mom. I'll be back Thursday night, though. I can meet you here at six and then we'll walk, if that's okay?"

Oh. He's going on another trip? We just got back from the conference. I try to hide my disappointment as I clear my throat and say, "Of course. I'll see you then, I guess."

"See you Friday. Good night, Nicole."

With that, he turns and descends the stairs. Just before he rounds the front of the car on his way to the driver's seat, he looks up at me. I can't see the expression on his face in the dusky evening light, but I wave. He lifts his hand back at me before he disappears into the car.

The next morning, Adam texts me a meme that shows two characters from *The Simpsons*, Lisa and Ralph, walking together. At the top it says:

"When you're socially awkward but you still give it a shot."

And in the picture, Ralph is asking Lisa,

"...do you like stuff?"

Okay, so this meme doesn't say everything, but at least it's flirtier than the disco meme. He's saying he's giving this a shot, right? Us a shot? Maybe I'm reading too much into the memes, but my brain craves certainty, and all I'm feeling is unsure. When I add up all the signals, they seem to imply that Friday is a date, but he didn't use the word date. I sigh to myself as I walk out the door to work. It's going to be a long week.

Chapter Twenty-Eight

Adam

I had this trip to Naples to see my mom planned before our NLA presentation proposal was accepted. She had a minor outpatient procedure scheduled, and I wanted to be there to drive her back and forth and make sure she was okay. But now, as I'm driving up I-75 back toward St. Anastasia on Thursday afternoon, I worry it was a mistake to leave Nicole hanging like that. We had a moment—a whole series of moments really—in New Orleans. I was so tired on the drive home that I feel like I basically ignored her. She agreed to dinner tomorrow night, but I fear I've lost momentum somehow. I can picture her replaying the New Orleans trip over and over in her mind and worrying about our interactions, questioning what it meant to me. My asking for a date should have been a straightforward indication of my romantic interest, but knowing Nicole, she'll find a way to rationalize it into being less significant than it is.

I get back to town late, so it's not until Friday morning that I stop by the pet resort to pick up Joan, who's overjoyed to see me. She wags her tail so hard I wonder if it's going to fall off.

My thoughts stay on Nicole all day. We texted while I was gone. Just casual things. I sent her memes, of course, but leveled them up. I'm sending her flirty memes now, or at least what I construe to be flirty, given that I am not, by nature, a flirtatious person. The one I sent this morning said:

"How do introverts flirt? Eye contact."

I included my own message about how I'm excited to "see" her tonight. That's funny, right? Flirty? I inwardly groan. Imagine getting this far and then letting my awkwardness ruin it all. But I've been myself all along with Nicole, and she seems to like it. Like me.

Okay, self-doubt neutralized. For now. My next challenge is wardrobe. I want to look nice, but not like I look at work. Honestly, I care very little about clothing. I wear dress pants and shirts to work, and I wear what makes me feel comfortable when I'm at home. Clothes to wear on a date is an alien concept. I do an embarrassing amount of googling "men's casual date outfits" as I decide. Plus, as the calendar creeps closer to May, Florida forgets all about spring and jumps right into the arms of summer, meaning it's too warm for jeans. Cargo shorts feel too schlubby. Finally, I settle on casual navy-blue shorts that hit right above my knees, and a button down short-sleeved shirt—white with a subtle dot and cross pattern. I leave it untucked, with the top two collar buttons undone.

I'm exhausted before I even leave the house. I'm also buzzing a little with nerves but a lot with excitement.

I park in front of Nicole's apartment at six and walk up the steps to her door. She answers my knock quickly, and I'm too stunned to greet her. Her face looks fresh—less done up than what she typically wears for work. Her lavender hair, which has grown out a bit, is pulled off her forehead in a tiny half ponytail near the back of her head. She wears a white tank top that's tight against her skin, tucked impossibly neatly into black shorts with a red and white floral print and black lace trim. The shorts make her legs look remarkably long, stretching down to her white Vans.

"Wow," I finally stammer.

She smirks at me. "That sounds like a good 'wow.'"

"Uh, yeah." I swallow thickly. "Definitely a good wow." Meeting her eyes, I add, "You look beautiful."

She blushes and smiles. "Thank you." Then, she takes her time perusing from my white tennis shoes all the way up to my face. When she meets my eyes again, hers are dark. "You look really nice, too."

If I make it to the end of this night before kissing her, it will be a miracle.

I push away that thought—for now—and take her hand instead. "We're walking tonight, if that's okay," I say. "Staying downtown."

She nods.

We walk a couple of blocks to an upscale casual restaurant with rooftop seating that overlooks the intercoastal waterway. We're up high enough that a cool breeze cuts the humidity a little.

"This is gorgeous!" Nicole exclaims, looking down at the streets below from our table. We order and wait for our food, the conversation veering toward stilted. She seems anxious. When the server sets our food in front of us, Nicole's expression is one of relief.

"Hey," I say gently, tapping the top of her hand across the table. "What's going on?"

"Well, it's just..." she hesitates and then blurts, "this is a date, right?"

"Yes," I say firmly. "This is absolutely a date."

"Okay, because it's just I wasn't totally sure, and I know we held hands in New Orleans and my sisters were like definitely it's a date, but maybe I was reading too much into things?" She looks down at her plate.

This tentative, unsure version of Nicole kills me. At work, she's the picture of confidence and strength. Never hesitating to speak up in meetings. I would never have known, had she not told me, the way she agonizes over each conversation after the fact, obsessing over her choice of words and the reactions of others in the room. It strikes me then that knowing this about Nicole, knowing the parts of her that she keeps hidden, is a privilege. I'm honored by her trust. And though she fears that sharing these parts of herself will drive people away, for me, I've never wanted to be closer to her more than I do now. She's no longer the Nicole I saw in my early infatuation, pretty, but two-dimensional, hazy at the edges. She's in focus now, a full person with depth and weakness and joyful beauty. A person who loves tater tots but doesn't think she ought to eat too many. Who makes bold choices, and then overthinks the risks when it's already too late to turn back. Who charms the whole room but allows few people to see who she is beneath the sparkling personality and fearful of rejection.

"Nicole," I say, wanting her full attention. "Look at me." She raises her eyes, and I hate the uncertainty I see on her face. I reach across the table and take her hand in mine. "You're not reading too much into this. To any of it. I like you. I like you a lot, actually. I want to date you."

"You do?" she whispers.

"I've never wanted anything more." The truth of that statement hits me in the chest as I say it. She's it for me. I knew it the minute I saw her standing in the doorway of my office.

She slowly smiles then, her lips curving up shyly. "Okay," she says softly.

She picks her fork up and takes a bite of her braised short rib. My eyes track the movement up to her mouth. "So delicious," she sighs.

My whole body heats, and I let myself imagine, just for a moment, what her lips would taste like.

She looks up at me then and blushes at whatever she sees on my face.

"What?"

I clear my throat. "Nothing," I say.

The moment passes, and we fill the rest of the time eating and chatting with our typical ease. She catches me up on the library gossip from the week, and I recount my trip to Naples.

"Do you want to get dessert?" I ask as we finish our meals.

Nicole groans and rubs her stomach, then brightens. "Can we get ice cream?" she asks. "Somewhere else?"

"Anything you want," I say. "Do you want to walk a bit first?"

Nicole shrugs. "Sure.".

After I pay the check, we leave the restaurant and start walking. I take her hand right away and guide our steps to the waterfront. We walk all the way down the sidewalk by the water, and then back, holding hands and talking about everything and nothing.

We turn down Cannon Street, a narrow pedestrian thoroughfare lined with restaurants and shops. We stop at a shop known for its chocolates, but that also has amazing ice cream. We both order waffle cones—she chooses chocolate chip cookie dough and laughs at my order: Superman swirl.

"No, nuh-uh," she laughs. "You are not ordering Superman ice cream."

"Sure I am," I shrug. "I like the fruit flavors."

She rolls her eyes as we step outside the shop and find an empty bench. "This is like the sour gummy worms all over again," she sighs.

I sit first on one end of the concrete bench backed up against the smooth stucco wall of the candy shop. My pulse ratchets up when Nicole sits directly next to me, our thighs touching.

She's still teasing me as we start eating our ice cream. "That's the ice cream Mr. July is going to order? Really?" Her eyes sparkle.

I groan. "You're never going to forget that story, are you?"

She leans toward me, her shoulder only just brushing against my arm. I instinctively angle closer, and I'm staring into her eyes, our lips inches apart. "Never ever," she hums, before tilting her body away again. I catch my breath as she focuses on her ice cream.

I look up to see Nicole watching me over her cone. "Can I ask you a question?"

I grin. "You just did."

She rolls her eyes. "Can I ask you multiple questions?"

I laugh. "You can ask me whatever questions you want."

"How long have you been interested in me?"

Oh boy. Moment of truth, I guess. "Since the first time I saw you, standing with Herb in my office doorway the day you came to interview," I answer honestly.

Her eyes widen. "Really? All that time? Why didn't you say anything before?"

I shrug and smile. "I have no game."

She laughs. "But I like that about you," she says. "I don't like games. My ex played far too many, and I never knew where I stood with him. I was always on edge."

What a jerk. I will never understand men who feel the need to keep women guessing. It speaks to their own insecurities.

She blushes and looks away. "Sorry. I guess it's bad form to talk about an ex on a first date."

"I don't mind," I say. "I want to know everything about you. Truly. Besides, this doesn't really feel like a first date, does it?"

She's quiet for a moment. "No," she says with surprise in her voice. "It really doesn't."

I grin. "Must be because we've already spent so much time together. The whole romance trope of work colleagues to friends to lovers..." I feel my face burning as I trail off. I can't believe I just said that.

She bursts out laughing. "Let's not jump ahead," she teases.

I feel heat all the way up to the tips of my ears, not only from embarrassment, but now I *am* jumping ahead, in my brain at least. *Shut it down, Adam*, I order myself as I picture my palms sliding over Nicole's curves, fingers tangling in soft, lavender hair. Maybe it's my imagination, considering my current train of thought, but Nicole's eyes look darker, her cheeks flushing as she bites her lip.

I clear my throat. "Anyway," I say.

"Anyway," she echoes. We stare at each other for a beat.

"*Now* it kind of feels like a first date," she says, her eyes twinkling.

"Yeah, I made things awkward. My superpower," I say dryly.

Nicole laughs. "Everyone has to be good at something," she quips, and we're grinning at each other.

I hold her gaze, and the grin on her face dips. She leans closer, holding eye contact. My heart drums in my chest, and I'm getting that jittery feeling again. I'm hypnotized in this moment, standing at the precipice of the desire that has been fizzing inside me since I sat captivated in Nicole's interview presentation almost two years ago. We've been locked in a back and forth these last several months, me pushing forward, scraping for any morsel of progress, and her flitting away again even when I think she'll linger. And I let her go every time, hoping she'd flutter back to me, that she'd recognize me as a safe place to land.

I survey her now, tendrils of pastel hair loose and wild around her face. Emerald eyes dilated and deep, like the most verdant jungle. Smooth skin tinted red on the apples of her cheeks, just under a cluster of delicate freckles. Pink lips supple and pinched between her teeth. Glowing. Ethereal. Ephemeral.

Before I can overthink it, I'm drifting forward. I slide my free hand onto the back of her neck and my eyes drop closed. Nicole gasps softly just as my lips brush against hers, gently, tentatively inquiring. She answers me back with an assurance that steals my breath. Her hand moves to rest on my thigh, gripping the fabric of my shorts, and I angle my head closer, pressing harder, tasting the chocolate on her mouth. I inhale through my nose and smell the thick, sugary ice cream and the ginger zest of her skin. The heat that has been simmering between us all night, for months now, really, finally boils over as we come together, no longer a back and forth, but a union, a blending of sensibilities and fervor.

Her teeth scrape against my bottom lip, and I suppress a moan. Distracted, I let her take the lead as she parts my lips with her tongue. I trail a hand down her spine as I push her closer into me.

Suddenly, I'm jolted out of the best kiss of my life by a shocking cold sensation. I'm utterly confused at first, my brain not making connections between the sensations I'm feeling and the nerve endings where they're occurring. A glance at Nicole's face tells me she's just as perplexed as to what might have happened, why I pulled away. Finally, I look at my elbow and see Nicole's half eaten ice cream cone, still grasped in her hand, pressing against my forearm.

"Oh," I say. I look up at Nicole, and her cheeks are flushed.

"I ... I forgot I was holding it," she manages.

I laugh and kiss her quickly on the lips. God, she's adorable. As I emerge from my Nicole-induced haze, more details take shape. For one, the ice cream cone in my left hand is dripping messily onto my shoes.

"I guess we both got a little carried away." I smile sheepishly.

"I didn't mind," Nicole says boldly, holding my gaze.

"Me neither," I murmur. "But maybe let's get some napkins."

After I get cleaned up, we walk slowly back to her apartment, stealing kisses every few yards. In late spring in St. Anastasia, the jasmine vines blossom with delicate white flowers exploding onto greenery across the city. The heavy, sweet aroma of the jasmine blossoms wafts into the streets. It's a heady combination: Nicole's lips and the fragrant, sultry smell of jasmine. It's a scent I know I'll forevermore associate with this night, with this woman, and with this start of a dream come true.

Chapter Twenty-Nine

Nicole

I 'm grinning. I'm grinning and I can't stop. And I don't care. I've never felt so swept away. I reflect on every romance book I've read, the phase when the heroine is so enamored with her paramour that she can't focus and can't concentrate on anything else. To be honest, it always sounded like a bunch of rubbish to me. None of my personal experiences with romance up to this point have ever felt like this—so light, so hopeful, so full of promise.

Adam and I text all through the weekend. Memes, of course, but just idle chatter, too. He sends me a meme that says:

Good Flirts: I'm enjoying getting to know you and don't want it to stop.

Better Flirts: I'm trying so hard not to kiss you right now.

Me Flirting: Did you know, according to NASA, 1993's Jurassic Park is the 7th most scientifically accurate film ever made?

I answer with a laughing emoji and then a kissy face emoji and the words "Obviously your brand of flirting works for me."

I know. We're disgusting. And I don't care.

You know when you're down about something, a breakup maybe, and you just wallow in your cruddy emotions? Eating your feelings and bumming around watching comfort movies? My Saturday is the opposite of that. Instead of wallowing, I'm luxuriating in my giddy emotions. Forgetting to eat and sighing dreamily through my romance books, my heart jumping every time my phone pings.

On Sunday, Adam has my favorite sandwich delivered to my door. With a side of tater tots.

I call him after the delivery guy leaves. When he answers, I just say, "You sure know the way to a woman's heart."

"Yeah?" he asks, and I can hear the smile in his voice.

"Yeah," I reply. "Tater tots."

His rich laugh echoes over the phone line. "I'm glad you like them," he says. "But listen, can I come over for a couple of hours this afternoon? I want to talk to you."

With his change in tone from flirty to serious, my stomach clenches. "That doesn't sound great," I say.

"No, Nicole, I promise. Nothing like that. But if you're free..." He trails off.

"Yeah, sure," I say, trying to sound breezy.

"Okay. About two o'clock?"

"Sure," I answer.

"But, seriously, Nicole," he says softly. "I know this is the exact wrong thing to say to you, but please don't worry."

"Worry is my default setting," I joke weakly.

"I know," he murmurs. "But you don't need to with me. Ever. You'll see."

Over the next couple of hours, I try "not worrying" as Adam requested, but I'm going a little stir crazy. I'm writing a mental list of anything and everything this talk might be about. I think I'm up to one hundred items. Maybe he likes me, but like, doesn't think he has time to date right now. Or maybe after spending more time with me, he doesn't like me as much as he thought he would and figures it will be easier to break things off now. Oh, maybe he's moving. I gasp aloud. Maybe he's dying!

Promptly at two o'clock, a knock sounds on my door. I open it to reveal Adam, looking delicious in basketball shorts and a white T-shirt that's tight across his chest and arms. He hasn't shaved, and the scruff covering his jawline makes my fingers ache to scratch against his chin. He's holding a small bouquet of flowers and several leaves of paper. He holds out the flowers and I take them as he kisses me softly on the cheek, his stubble scraping against my face.

"Hi," he says in my ear. He takes a step back, closing the door behind him. "I brought the flowers as a romantic gesture," he explains, "because I recognize that the main reason for my visit today is very, uh..." he grimaces, "not romantic."

"Oo-kaay," I respond.

As we move further into the living room, I realize this is the first time he's really been inside my apartment. He looks around the space curiously, drifting over to the bookcase and skimming the titles on the spines.

"You read romance?" he asks.

"Yeah, some," I downplay.

"Hmm," he vocalizes with a tilt of his head.

"What?"

He locks eyes with me. "Just a lot of pressure," he teases with a grin.

I roll my eyes and gesture for him to sit on the couch.

I curl one leg underneath myself as I sit on the cushion opposite Adam. "Your not-romantic reason for visiting?" I prompt.

"Ah, right." He frowns and squints his eyes. "I'm not sure how to say this so I'm going to just say it." He thrusts the papers toward me and as I take them from his hand, he blurts, "We need to fill out this paperwork for HR."

Um. Okay, not even on the top one hundred list of what I was expecting. I study the papers and see that they are, indeed, official-looking forms labeled with the heading "Amorous Relationship Disclosure." I stare at the forms. Then, I lift my head and stare at Adam.

I huff out an incredulous laugh. "Is this for real?"

Adam rubs the back of his neck, his ears red. "Yeah," he says. "Harkness HR allows um, you know, 'amorous relationships' among employees, even in the same department, as long as there's no conflict of interest relating to, uh, reporting structure. And as long as the employees submit the proper paperwork."

I'm biting back a smile now, but I keep the stern expression on my face.

"How long have you been sitting on these forms?" I ask.

He shrugs, dipping his chin down to look at his hands clasped in his lap. "A couple of months? Just in case." He flinches.

I can't keep holding it in; I burst out laughing. I let my shoulders fall against the back of the couch and pull both legs up toward my chest as I convulse in a fit of giggles. Adam watches me cautiously, his expression moving from dubious to bemused.

Finally, I compose myself, and wiping the water from my eyes, startle Adam even more by climbing onto his lap. When he recovers, he shifts his arms to loop around my back, pulling my body into his. Cupping my hands around both sides of his face, I gaze into his eyes and say, "In your own, very Adam-like way, this is actually incredibly romantic. Get me a pen and I will sign your forms, sir." I punctuate this decree with a peck on the tip of his nose.

"Thank you," he says dryly. Then, he clears his throat and shifts underneath me. "But there's more."

"Uh huh," I say warily, transferring back to my own couch cushion. "Tell me."

"Well," he starts, then hesitates. "I know our jobs are important to both of us. And I know, for me, that means that there's a certain level of professionalism I expect of myself when I'm at work. So, even though it's not strictly against the rules at Harkness, I would like to request that you and I, um, refrain from ... anything ... unprofessional while we're on campus."

I arch an eyebrow. "Meaning?"

His face flushes. "No PDA at work," he clarifies.

"Are you serious?" I blink at him.

He grimaces. "Yes?"

"So, what if I kiss you at work? You'll push me away? You'll be like 'Ew, gross, don't kiss me'?"

"Nicole, please just don't kiss me at work," he pleads.

I fold my arms across my chest. "Listen, I'm a very affectionate person. I don't know if that's going to work for me."

He swallows. "Trust me, I appreciate that about you very, very much, but I'm just saying *at work*."

"I don't understand why it's a big deal," I argue.

Adam heaves out an exasperated breath. "I'm concerned about the perception, Nicole. We have coworkers who might not take us as seriously if we're going around the library being ... 'affectionate' with each other. I don't want anyone to think I'm some kind of office floozy, or worse, that *you* are."

"Office floozy?" I totally lose it again. Like, tears streaming down my cheeks, stitch-in-my-side laughing fit. "Oh my gosh, Adam!"

His eyes narrow. "You're making fun of me," he says flatly. "Can you please be serious about this?"

"How am I supposed to be serious?" I ask between howls of laughter. "When my new boyfriend brings paperwork to my house and says we have to do some sort of relationship agreement and lectures me about PDA at work? I'm going to start calling you Sheldon. Sheldon Cooper!"

"In my defense," Adam sighs, "if we didn't work in the same place, I would never..." He trails off as a smile spreads slowly across his face. "Wait a minute. Back up a second. What did you say? Your new what?"

That sobers me up. "Uhhh," I stall. "Boyfriend?" I ask questioningly and then rush ahead. "Unless you think it's too soon, but I kind of thought that's the direction you were going with this whole paperwork thing."

"It's not too soon for me," Adam says and leans in to kiss me.

I back away. "No sir," I say, shaking my head and smirking. "No kissing. We agreed."

Adam rolls his eyes. "That's just at the school, like while we're working. As long as we're not on the Harkness campus, I'll kiss you wherever and however you want."

I tsk. "Big promises," I tease.

His eyes darken and glitter. "And I mean them."

"Guess what my new boyfriend had me do this afternoon," I text my sisters after Adam goes home.

Olivia:

eww nobody needs to think about that

Nicole:

Get your mind out of the gutter, Liv [eye roll emoji]

Molly:

Wait. New boyfriend? Does that mean…

Molly:

You and Adam? [heart eye emoji]

Molly:

I just squealed so loud you probably heard me all the way in Florida

Molly:

Which isn't great since I'm at the lab…

Nicole:

You're at the lab? On a Sunday evening? By yourself?

Molly:

No, Jonathan is here for some unknown reason

Molly:

Oh, he heard me squeal

Molly:

He's coming over here. Hold on a sec

Molly:

Okay, I'm back. God, he's so annoying

Olivia:

anyway

Molly:

Anyway. What did your NEW BOYFRIEND have you do this afternoon?

Nicole:

HR paperwork about our relationship status [laughing emoji]

Olivia:

omg

Molly:

Practical and responsible. I like it

Nicole:

You would

Molly:

But how are *you* feeling about everything?

Nicole:

Really good. Peaceful and happy

Molly:

[heart emoji]

Olivia:

i'm really happy for you sis [heart emoji]

Chapter Thirty

Nicole

The next morning, Adam insists that we personally inform Herb of our relationship. Doing so is not an HR requirement—after filing the paperwork, which Adam did last night, HR reviews it and notifies the supervisor—but Adam sees it as a necessary courtesy. I feel ten kinds of awkward about it, but I have to begrudgingly admit that because we're a small, close-knit team at Parker Library, it makes sense to get it out in the open.

We go together to knock on Herb's open door. He gestures for us to come in.

"What can I do for you?" Herb asks.

Thinking about Adam's bumbling awkwardness talking to *me* about all this yesterday, I can only imagine how he plans to handle Herb. So, I rip off the band-aid.

"Adam and I are dating," I announce.

Adam's mouth drops open and Herb freezes. Both men are staring at me.

"We submitted the paperwork stuff to HR," I continue. "But we wanted to let you know personally."

"Oh, uh, sure, of course. Thank you," Herb stammers.

"We promise to remain professional on the job," I persist, deftly pinching Adam's arm. "But if you notice any problems, please let us know."

"Uh, yes, naturally," Herb fiddles with some folders on his desk. "Anything else?"

"Nope. Thank you for your time."

Backing out into the hallway, I whisper to Adam, "Close your mouth." He blinks at me, and I grin.

"Well," I smile. "That's taken care of." I salute in his direction. "Have a productive workday, sir."

He closes his eyes and shakes his head as I turn toward my own office.

In the middle of the afternoon, I text Adam a meme, just to mess with him. It says:

"dating me is easy u just have to kiss me every 3 minutes."

He texts back, "After work. Stop distracting me," with a wink-face emoji.

A few minutes later, he saunters past my office door, then doubles back and casually leans against the doorframe.

"Hey," he says.

"Hello, work colleague," I quip.

"Stop being a brat," he chides, lips quirking.

"Stop leaning seductively in my doorway," I counter.

He straightens, his smile growing. "Come over after work," he says earnestly. "I'll cook dinner. We can watch a movie or something."

I grin. "Only if Joan will be there."

Adam drives me to my apartment after work so I can change before we head to his house. He loiters in the living room, poking around, while I change clothes in my room. After wasting too much time debating the options, I finally put on leggings and a cropped T-shirt. I emerge to find Adam studying the framed photos of my family on the end tables of the couch. He looks up when I come out.

"I've met Molly," he says. "This is the rest of your family?"

"Yes." I point to a photo in an obnoxiously pink, sparkly frame. "Me, of course, Molly, and then the blonde is our younger sister, Olivia."

"You have blonde hair in this picture, too," he notes.

"Oh. Yeah. That's my natural hair color. We took that picture about three years ago."

"You didn't dye your hair then?"

"No, I did, when I could. I started dyeing my hair in high school, mostly black." I cringe when I think of my style back then. It works for some people, and I'm all for doing what you love, but it wasn't really me. I remember that Adam knows a bit about my backstory here. I can't believe I told him not only about my darker high school days, but about Steven, too. And it didn't scare him off. "I got into the more colorful shades starting in college. I was a little broke when that picture was taken." I laugh. "A few months later, I had some extra funds and actually did a mermaid balayage."

Adam nods. "I have no idea what that means."

"Balayage is when you have different colors that all kind of blend one into another. Mermaid style is a mixture of greens, blues, and purples. It was expensive because they have to hand paint the different colors. I saved up a while for it. Hence the natural hair in that picture."

Adam's cheeks flush slightly. "You're beautiful with every hair color I've seen you have."

I chuckle. "That's cheesy." But my insides go all warm and mooshy.

"Still true."

I step closer and wrap my arms around his waist. "Thank you," I amend. "You haven't seen my hair that many colors, though, have you?"

He thinks a minute. "Brick red when you interviewed, then a cotton candy pink, but only for a few months."

"Yeah, I didn't like the pink as much as I thought I would," I interject.

Adam continues, "Then like this teal color for a while, and now the lavender. Plus, your blonde hair in the picture."

My eyes widen, my face buried in his chest. "Wow, you really have been obsessed with me for a while, haven't you?"

Instead of blushing or hiding, he uses the side of his index finger to tip up my chin, so we're face to face. "Let's just say I noticed you from the beginning and could never look away."

The mooshy feeling is back. I lift myself onto my toes and skim my lips against the underside of his chin. He lowers his head and meets my mouth. After a few minutes, I push my hand against his chest and break away.

"Joan is waiting for us," I remind him.

We're quiet in the car, each of us lost in our thoughts. Then I say, "Isn't it interesting how someone can be totally obsessed with another person, and if the other person feels the same way, it's sweet, but if they don't, it's stalking?"

Adam barks out a laugh. "What?"

"I mean, if Herb had never stuck you on the graphic novel project with me or you never worked up the courage to, you know, actually pursue me, how long until the status quo would have become creepy?"

He snorts. "Are you calling me a stalker?"

I shrug. "I mean, not *exactly*, but..."

He shakes his head and glances at me briefly before turning his eyes back to the road. "Yes, I think that whether the attention is welcome is an important boundary line between romantic intentions and stalking. Did you ever feel uncomfortable around me? Honestly."

I consider the question, recalling our interactions throughout the last six months and before. "No," I admit. "Even after I realized you had a crush on me, I always thought you were respectful, if a bit obvious." I smirk.

Adam purses his lips, then reaches across the center console and takes my hand. "You know," he hums, "sometimes in the two years since I met you, I would look at you while you were lost in thought, in your own little world, and wonder, 'What goes on in her head? What is she like when her guard is down, and she feels safe to be herself?'"

"Aww," I coo. "And now you know."

He squeezes my hand. "Now I know," he agrees. His tone turns playful. "And I regret it just a little bit."

I gasp and push his hand away while he laughs. "Back at you, buddy," I mutter sardonically, but I pull his hand back and press a kiss to his palm. He closes his fingers around it and grazes his knuckles across my thigh.

"I don't regret it at all," he concedes. "And I'm looking forward to learning everything else."

The conversation reminds me of something Molly said in New Orleans. I clear my throat.

"Adam," I start, heart thumping in my chest. "Did I ever take advantage of your feelings for me?"

"No," he says quickly.

"Really?" I ask, peering over at him, my eyebrows raised. "I know I must have sent you a lot of mixed signals. I actually hadn't been to therapy since I moved here. The hassle of finding somebody new and intake appointments and everything. But I had my first appointment with a new therapist last week after we got back from the conference while you were visiting your mom. I think ... I think my brain was trying to protect me. After everything with my ex, my brain labeled all romantic relationships as a threat. I think I was literally in the clinical definition of denial. I'm sorry I hurt you."

"Hey," he says softly, squeezing my hand, "it doesn't matter. We're together now."

I shake my head. "But it does matter," I protest. "*You* matter. I promise I'll do better."

My relationship with Steven shattered me; I placed my trust in him when he never deserved it, and it made me question my own judgment—how I could have read the situation so wrong. Adam has been showing me for months now that he's trustworthy, that he cares about me, and that my feelings matter. Even while I was outwardly keeping him at arm's length, my subconscious recognized Adam as a refuge—his predictability and steadiness are a balm to my anxious brain, especially compared to what I went through with Steven. More than a refuge, really, because I don't want to use Adam to hide away from the world, I want us to confront the world together. Now that I've finally recognized, in spite of my anxiety brain, that I want to be with him, I'm not holding back. I know I can fall for him easily—I think I'm more than halfway there already.

Adam cooks us a chicken dish with vegetables and some kind of delicious sauce that probably contains magic. I don't ask because I don't want to know too much and spoil the illusion.

Joan is almost as excited to see me as I am to see her, and while Adam cooks, Joan and I cuddle on the couch.

After dinner, I take advantage of our new relationship status to choose what we watch. I know he'll yield to whatever I want. I suggest my comfort show, *Gilmore Girls*. I'm surprised that Adam's never seen it, not even one episode. So, we start at season one, episode one in Luke's Diner with Lorelai begging for coffee.

After the second episode, I stand. "It's getting late," I say. "Are you about ready to drive me home?"

Adam's eyes dart from me to the screen. His eyebrows pull together. "But," he protests, reading the synopsis for the next episode, "Rory and Richard are about to go golfing."

I laugh. "Oh my gosh! You love *Gilmore Girls* now."

Adam sets his jaw. "Yeah, fine. I can admit it. It's a cute show. They probably need to cut down on the caffeine and sugar though."

"Fine." I smirk, plopping onto his lap. "If you want to watch one more episode instead of driving me home and saying goodnight, we can." I loop my arms around his neck. "It will just mean less time for saying goodnight."

Adam raises his eyebrows. "Ah, on second thought. Let me grab my keys."

Chapter Thirty-One

Adam

Nicole and I fall into a satisfying pattern over the next few weeks. By early May, spring classes are finishing up at Harkness and in the library, we're prepping for the busyness of finals, including the de-stress events we hold for the frazzled students. This semester, Nicole is planning an activity around the graphic novel collection. She had a professor in the art department create a few illustrated how-to pages showing the process for drawing panels in comics. She'll laminate them and put them out on a table near the graphic novel shelf with paper, colored pencils, and other supplies so students can draw their own short comics. So, yeah, my girlfriend is brilliant.

We spend evenings at each other's places several times a week, and on the weekends neither of us work, we go out. So far, we've been miniature golfing, to the movies, and on a ghost tour with Ashley and Paul. Plus, ice cream. Always ice cream. And kissing whenever possible, except, of course, at work.

I'm in awe of the amount of time we spend together now, how easily she talks to me and shares with me. I spent so much time on the outside of her life hoping to get in, and then months on the doorstep trying to capture glances through the half-open doorway, that now that she's invited me inside, I'm desperate to see everything and cherish it all. I'm falling fast—if I wasn't already gone for her months ago.

This week, I work on the weekend, so I'm off on Thursday and Friday. After spending the day with Joan while Nicole's at work, I leave her on her own and bring takeout to Nicole's apartment. I think we're on date eight or nine.

After eating outside on the balcony, we stretch out on the couch, me on one end and her on the other, angled sideways with her feet in my lap. I'm flipping through one of the graphic novels Nicole had recommended. While I'm still not as enthused about graphic novels as she is, I've come to appreciate them. I just don't feel as immersed as I do when I read a novel, or even a nonfiction book. Nicole's reading an e-book, a romance novel, I think. I breathe in and realize how content I feel. Being here with Nicole, each doing our own thing but together, feels comfortable, companionable. Natural. Like something I wouldn't mind doing the rest of my life.

Just then, Nicole breathes a wispy sigh that makes my stomach flip and my heart rate tick up. I raise my eyes to see her, and she's totally focused on the screen in front of her. I'm not sure she even realizes she made the noise. As I watch, she moves her hand on top of her heart. Her mouth hangs open slightly. Suddenly, she flips over the tablet and drops it to her lap, leaning back against the armrest of the couch and closing her eyes.

"Everything okay?" I ask.

"Oh my gosh." She blushes now as she meets my eyes. "I just read the swooniest first kiss scene. Behind a waterfall. Easily in my top five fantasy spots."

This gets my attention. She has an actual, thought-out list of fantasy make out spots? Yeah, I'm going to need more information about that immediately.

I quirk up my eyebrows. "Really?" I say as casually as I can muster. "What, uh, what else is on this top five list?"

Her face is beet red now from her cheeks all the way to the tips of her ears. She looks absolutely adorable. "Well, no, not like a formal list or anything."

"But it's something you've thought about?" I can tell she has. I can also tell that she now thoroughly regrets mentioning it.

"A little," she admits reluctantly.

"And what's the number one, top spot you want to be kissed?"

Still blushing, now she drops her gaze, studying her hands. "It's silly," she says.

"I promise you that silly is the last thing I'll think it is." Probably I'll think it's thrilling, perfect, sexy, no matter what it is.

Nicole meets my eyes again, a renewed boldness in her expression. "A library," she says. "Against a bookcase."

I imagine pushing her backward, pinning her between the stacks and my body, gripping the back of her neck with my hand. My throat goes completely dry, and my heart pounds in my ears. She notices my reaction and a self-satisfied smile settles on her lips. Without another word, she picks up her tablet and switches it back on, settling back to read some more.

I, on the other hand, feel a bit ... distracted. I check my watch. It's late on a Thursday night. Normally Parker Library would be closed by now, but it's finals week so we're open late for students who are cramming. At the same time, it's late enough that none of the librarians or full-time staff will be there anymore. Just a couple of student workers and a security guard periodically on their rounds. I rub my chin. Am I seriously considering this? We're just a couple of blocks away. If we're caught, not only would it be fully embarrassing, but there could also be repercussions for our jobs. What I'm contemplating is the exact opposite of professional behavior. I push the thoughts away. I couldn't.

My eyes dart over to Nicole, who has stumbled back into her novel, immersed and oblivious to my inner conflict. She holds the tablet with one hand, the other hand curled into a fist, propped under her chin. The dreamy look in her emerald eyes as they flick across the screen are my undoing. She's turned my world upside down. I've been driving down a serene country road all my life, but now, suddenly, I'm in the middle of a city intersection—lights flashing around me, unpredictable and wild. The pulse of the traffic terrifies and energizes me at the same time.

I take a deep breath and ask myself, "What do I *want* to do? Ignoring what I *should* do, ignoring the rules, what do I want?" The answer is easy once I clear away the doubts. I'll do anything to make her happy. I want to kiss my girlfriend, this amazing, sexy woman I'm falling in love with, against a shelf full of books.

I nod my head decisively, stand up from the couch, and extend my hand to Nicole.

"Come on," I say.

Chapter Thirty-Two

Nicole

I peer up at Adam standing over me next to the couch.

"Come on, Nicole," he repeats, holding out his hand, a determined glint in his eyes.

Dropping my tablet, I take his hand, and he hauls me to my feet.

"What are we doing?" I ask as he pulls me toward the front door.

"You'll see," he says.

Is Adam being ... spontaneous? My stomach flutters, and I turn myself over to him, ready to follow wherever he's leading.

We slip on our shoes, pausing at the threshold long enough for me to lock the door. It's late, and the streets are mostly quiet as Adam practically bounds down the steps of my apartment, tugging me behind him. I'm wearing black joggers and an oversized T-shirt. Up to now, it has been a simple night at home. I hadn't planned to go anywhere or see anyone other than Adam. The night air is warm and sticky against my arms, my heart racing as quickly as my feet. Adam turns a corner headed toward campus, and both my heart and my feet stutter to a near stop.

"Adam!" I eek out, half confusion, half glee, pulling back against his hand. He turns to me, a deadly smirk on his lips. His eyes glitter as he pulls me closer, ducking his head until his mouth is right up against my ear. "Come on," he whispers thickly.

I'm grinning like an idiot, side by side with Adam now as we rush through the streets. When we reach the front steps of Parker Library, Adam drops my hand. Out of the corner of his mouth and without making eye contact, he instructs, "Be cool."

I immediately start cracking up. Already out of breath from our race over here, I bend over and put my hands on my knees as I try to collect myself enough to go inside. Adam takes a couple steps away, eyeing me warily.

I take a deep breath and stand. "I'm cool, I'm cool," I say, which unleashes another bout of laughter, tears leaking out of the corners of my eyes. Finally, I steady my breathing, wipe my eyes, and school my expression into a mask of seriousness.

"I'm sorry," I say solemnly. "I'm ready now."

"You better be," Adam grumbles as he takes his Parker Library badge out of his pocket and taps it against the scanner by the front entrance. The leftmost door makes a *thunking* sound as it unlocks. Adam pulls it open, motioning me to step inside ahead of him.

We walk quietly and calmly through the main lobby. Two bored-looking student workers sit at the circulation desk, hardly glancing at us as we pass. At the top of the stairs, Adam gently takes my hand again. The second floor is nearly deserted. I see a few students at the study carrels around the perimeter, but it's eerily quiet. We pass through the stacks and finally duck into a row buffeted on either side by empty carrels. I glance around at the books on the shelves. The PN 1000s. Poetry. Seems fitting.

Adam hesitates. Now that he's gotten me here, he looks unsure of what to do with me. Facing him, our bodies parallel with the shelves, I place one of my hands onto his shoulder and the other on his chest. My eyes locked with his, I inch forward. He steps back. I step forward again, and he steps back. Slowly, we continue this dance across the narrow aisle, until Adam's broad shoulders bump against the shelves, making a distinct but hollow *clunk* sound. The books on the top shelf wobble a bit. Strung out on the high of this night, these zany circumstances, I nearly start laughing again, until I'm quickly sobered by the heated look in Adam's eyes. He reaches his arms around my waist and pulls my body flush against his. As he lifts one of his hands up to tangle in my hair, his mouth covers mine.

I shift my arms, moving my hands behind Adam's neck. He tips his head to one side, breaking away from my lips to trail hot kisses up my jawline to the tender skin below my ear. I shiver as his mouth catches on my earlobe. I swallow a moan, but he feels the vibration in my throat, and his lips are back on mine, needy and intense. I part my lips and his tongue sweeps through my mouth. Reaching my hand higher to bury my fingers in the hair above his collar, I gently scratch my nails against his scalp. He growls, and moving both hands to grip the backs of my thighs, lifts me up and wraps my legs around his torso. He moves forward until my back is against the shelves on the other side of the aisle. The scent of old paper and dust spreads around me, mixing with the smell of sweat on our skin. When he finally slides me back down to the ground, we're both breathless. Adam quietly kisses my forehead, and then the top of my head, running his hands up and down my arms.

"Let's go," he murmurs next to my ear. He nudges me forward, giving me a warning look and touching his index finger to my lips. As we get to the end of the aisle, he drops his hands to his side, and we walk back down the stairs and through the lobby without touching.

Once we're outside, he bumps me with his shoulder. "Well?" he asks with a smirk.

"Well, what?"

"How was it?" He motions toward the library building.

Grinning, I place my hand on his cheek and say, "Easily in the top five hottest moments of my life."

His mouth drops open. "In the top five?" he sputters.

I laugh and dart away from him down the steps. I feel him on my heels as I turn the corner. He grabs me around the waist and spins me to face him. I push against his chest playfully. Laughing, I say, "Okay! Okay! Number one top spot to you, sir."

He smiles and pulls me against his chest. "Hottest moment of your life?" he murmurs into my hair.

I pull back and meet his eyes. "Without question," I answer.

He grins and kisses my forehead softly. "Me, too."

The next week, finals are officially over and we're all transitioning into our summer projects. I'm in my office, checking each of my online subject guides and making a list of which need to be updated before the fall term.

Herb pops his head through the doorway. "Nicole, can you come meet with me for a moment, please?"

Nervously, I follow him down the hall. When we enter his office, I see Adam already sitting at the small table there.

"If this is about Thursday..." I trail off when Adam subtly shakes his head at me, a glint of panic in his eyes.

"What happened Thursday?" Herb asks.

"Never mind," I answer and take the chair across from Adam as Herb sits between us.

"What's going on, Herb?" Adam asks.

"I just heard from one of our friends on the board of trustees," he says. "It seems that high-ranking members of the Harkness leadership, namely Dr. Clifton and his cronies, have been making a fuss about the graphic novel collection." Dr. Clifton is the college provost.

I'm immediately on alert. I sit up straighter. "What kind of fuss?"

Herb clears his throat. "The kind where Dr. Clifton doesn't think the content of the graphic novels is appropriate for the library."

"What content?" I demand.

"To be honest, Nicole, I don't think that Dr. Clifton has any idea what graphic novels we even have in our collection, let alone their content. I think he has a problem with us having graphic novels at all."

"But that's not fair!" I object. "The graphic novels we bought are wholly appropriate for the degree programs at Harkness. Faculty members are already using them in their classes to teach students."

Herb holds up his hand, as if to ward off my protests. "Right now, they just want more information. A list of the titles, their synopses, that kind of thing."

Adam glances at me quickly, then says, "I have a spreadsheet of all the titles that lists how much they cost, which academic department they match up with, and their Library of Congress subject headings."

"That's perfect," says Herb.

"Herb," I warn, "if they start digging into these titles, they are going to find themes they don't like. But they're the same themes that students in English classes read in their assigned works of literature, and that students in art history study in great paintings, and students in history classes learn about throughout all human history. It's nothing they won't find in the rest of our library's collection."

Herb sighs. "I know," he says. "Right now, they're only asking for more information. We'll see what happens next."

My brain starts whirling with the possibilities of all the things that might "happen next." I'm not afraid of a little controversy, and I am prepared to stand up for this project. I believe in it. But Adam. He was dragged into the project. He didn't choose this. I don't want to put him in the position of fighting this battle, too. He may not even want to.

"Herb," I say resolutely, "the graphic novel collection is my project. I introduced it. I pushed for it. So, I'm the one who should be held accountable for it to the leadership. I understand that because you approved it as the director of the library, you're implicated here as well, but Adam doesn't need to be involved—"

"No," Adam interjects, but I talk over him.

"The graphic novel collection is not his responsibility. Can we leave him out of it?" I finish.

I hazard a quick glance at Adam, and his jaw is tight.

"I don't want to be left out," Adam bites out. "This is my project, too. And I stand behind the work I did on it."

Herb's eyes bob between me and Adam as he considers our words. "I agree with Adam," he finally says. "You will both do any work the leadership needs done for them to feel comfortable with the graphic novel collection being part of our library." He shifts to look at me directly. "It's a good project, and it was done well. Neither of you should doubt that."

As we step into the hallway, I start, "Adam—"

He cuts me off quickly. "Let's talk in your office."

I nod, and we walk down the hall.

When we're settled with the door closed, I jump in before Adam can say anything. "I know you're upset," I begin, "but I was just thinking of you. You're Mr. Rules, and this could lead to a confrontation with the leadership of the college, literally a nightmare scenario for you. You don't want to do that."

When he speaks, Adam's voice is controlled, his words clipped. "I do like the structure of rules, but we didn't break any in doing this project. I worked hard to make sure the title choices were academically vetted and supported. I have confidence in my work, and

I am a man who takes responsibility for my actions, even when it's uncomfortable."

A rock lodges in the pit of my stomach. Words and intentions and feelings have gotten mixed up somehow and they're all swirling into a tornado. And I think it's my fault. I look at Adam again, and it's no longer anger I see in his eyes, but hurt.

"I would have thought," Adam continues, his voice shifting now, cracking, "that you would know me well enough by now to know that I would never let someone else take the fall for me. Especially you. Is that really what you think of me? That I'm, what, too weak, to stand up for what's right?"

"No, of course not," I say softly. I try to take his hand, but he pulls away. I feel panic inching up my throat as my heart hammers in my chest. I have the sudden sense that I'm losing everything and that nothing I can do will stop it.

A thought comes from the back of my mind, like a pinprick of light in the fog. *Breathe*, it says. *Breathe*. I close my eyes and inhale deeply, holding it for seven seconds before exhaling gently through my mouth. Once I do, the panic slowly recedes, and I'm left feeling solid and strong.

I take Adam's hand again, softly rubbing my thumb against his palm. This time, he lets me.

"I would never ask you to fight my battles for me," I tell him.

His expression changes again, to remorse as the brown of his eyes sharpens into amber.

"And I would never let you fight alone," he rejoins, his voice gruff.

"I know." I look him straight in the eye so he can see my sincerity and my trust in him. "I'm sorry."

He sighs. "I'm sorry, too. I overreacted."

I smile slowly and squeeze his hand. "Was that our first fight?"

"Yeah, I think it was," he answers, but he sounds tired.

Fluttering my eye lashes, I grin and tease, "Too bad we can't make up, since we're at work and all."

He finally smiles, and my relief at seeing him back at ease with me is palpable. He squeezes my hand. "Later," he promises.

Chapter Thirty-Three

Adam

I email Herb my spreadsheet of the graphic novels and we wait. Two weeks go by, and we don't hear anything else, but Nicole's nervous energy is ramping up, and I'm on edge. Not really because of the graphic novel controversy and not really because of Nicole, but because my daily routine is no longer as consistent as it was. I've been stretching and growing my comfort zone on a weekly basis, or so it feels.

I remember my mom's questions back around Christmas. *Is she the type that will get you out of the house? Who won't let you miss out on life?* I'm now out of my house a lot more, much to Joan's consternation, and life is coming at me so fast, I'd have to be blind to miss it. Apparently, I am now the type of person who makes out with a woman in the library where he works. I'm the type of person involved in defending against book banning plots. I'm a person who buys junk food, not that I really eat it, mind you, but buys junk food just to see Nicole's shoulders scrunch up, her eyes squeeze shut, and that closed-lipped, satisfied smile spread across her face. I'm the first to admit that I'm happier than I remember being ever, but I'm also tense more often. I've traded my loneliness for, like, the entire spectrum of human emotion and it's throwing me for a loop.

Ever since my overreaction after our meeting with Herb, Nicole watches me more closely as if trying to tune into my emotions and get in front of them. Her anxiety about how I'm feeling adds another emotion to my mix: guilt.

Soon after Nicole shared her depression and anxiety struggles with me, while I was in Naples with my mom, in fact, I started researching. I learned more about the conditions, and found lists of ways I can support her.

I want her to feel secure with me. I want her to rest in my presence, not worry. I want her to want me as much as I want her. I want her to be successful in everything she does at work. I want her to be all of her and feel confident in that. And all the wanting is leaving me exhausted.

Nicole notices. One evening, we're at my house, lounging on the couch after eating the dinner I cooked for us. Joan is snuggling against one of my sides, and Nicole's laying back against the armrest on the other, her thighs and knees across my lap. We're binging *Gilmore Girls*, which I unabashedly love, thank you very much, and don't feel emasculated for it at all.

In between episodes, we pause to decide whether to watch one more or call it a night. Nicole sits up, and linking her arm through mine, lays her head on my shoulder. She was not kidding about being affectionate. Other than at work, she always has her hand on my arm, or my shoulder, or wrapped in mine. And I was not kidding about appreciating her affection. When we're touching, I feel balanced, like she's the ballast that holds my body steady.

"Adam," she starts, and I hear the hesitation in her voice. "Is everything okay? Are you still feeling good about us?"

The worry in her tone crushes me, and I recommit then and there to be as transparent as possible with this woman, to communicate with her so she doesn't have to wonder or worry. She still will, I recognize, but I can at least make sure she knows how I'm feeling.

I kiss the top of her head. "I feel amazing about us. You're literally my dream woman, Nicole."

She tilts her head up to look at my face. "But something is bothering you." It's not a question.

I sigh. "It's just uncomfortable being out of my comfort zone," I admit. "You've turned my world upside down, and I needed it, but it's just a lot."

She frowns. "I'm a lot?"

I lean forward and kiss her lips gently, leaning my forehead against hers. "No, you're not a lot. You're the perfect amount. But just all of this living life instead of just existing in it is a lot to adjust to. But well worth it, mostly because of you."

With her so close next to me, I feel her shoulders loosen, the tension easing. "Because I'm a good kisser?" she teases.

My lips curl into a smile. "Because you're a good everything," I answer.

We spend the next few minutes locked to each other, communicating with our mouths, but not using words. When we finally break apart, I think we both feel more settled, though I still sense an uneasiness in her.

"How about you?" I ask. "Everything okay?"

She makes a humming sound in her throat. "You need to know, Adam, to understand me, that in my brain, everything is never okay. I always have some worry or another floating around, though I mostly keep them contained." She's quiet for a minute, as if assessing the contents of her mind. "Right now, the biggest runaway worry is the graphic novel stuff. I don't like not knowing what's going to happen, so my brain is making plans for multiple possible outcomes, most of those worst-case scenarios."

I frown. "How can I help?"

"Being with you does help. But as true as that is, I need you to understand that it's not your job to make sure I don't worry."

"I know," I say, but I'm already thinking of how to help her feel better.

"No," she says. She lays her hands on either side of my face and holds my head in place, her eyes locked on mine. "Listen. It's not your job to make sure I don't worry. I want to be able to talk to you about what's going on in my head and to share my feelings, and hear about yours, but you have to know that I'm not asking you to fix it To fix me."

I feel a pang in my chest. "You're not broken," I say.

"I know," she says, and the confidence in her dazzling smile has my stomach in a flurry.

The next week, Herb calls us into his office again. Nicole and I arrive at his door at the same time, and before we go in, I reach over and give her hand a small squeeze. She squeezes back and smiles weakly at me.

As soon as we see Herb's face, we know it's not good news. Hopefully he *wasn't* in the CIA, because the man has no poker face.

"Take a seat," he says quietly. Once we do, he spreads his hands, palms up, and shrugs. "Well, I wish I could be talking to you under better circumstances, but Dr. Clifton has called a meeting with college leadership, including the board of trustees."

"What kind of meeting?" Nicole asks.

"Sort of a hearing. The leadership and board will listen to us present about the graphic novel collection and then vote to decide if it belongs in the library."

Nicole's face falls, but I focus on the positive news in Herb's words. They're willing to listen to us.

"When's the meeting?" I ask. "And what do we need to do?"

"It's in two weeks." Herb gives a date in early June. "We need to put together information about the collection, how it's good for the college, and how it contributes to student learning. Nicole," Herb turns to her, "I'd like you to speak on behalf of the librarians. I'll talk a bit, too, but you're such a talented speaker and your passion for the project will come through."

I nod. Nicole speaking makes sense in every way. Plus, I'm pretty sure that means I won't have to.

Herb continues, "Adam, of course, will be in the meeting as well. And all three of us will work together to prepare our evidence."

Nicole glances between me and Herb, and then nods. "Okay."

"Take the rest of the day today to absorb the news and start thinking about the presentation. Tomorrow, we'll meet and start brainstorming together. Susan will send meeting invites to your email."

"Thanks, Herb," I say as we stand to leave.

"Yes," Nicole echoes. "Thank you."

I walk Nicole to her office and at the door, she stops and turns to me.

"I need to sit for a while and think about this by myself," she tells me.

My first instinct is to protest, to insist on sitting in her office with her to make sure she's okay, but I stop myself. I remember she doesn't want me to fix problems for her. I remind myself that it's not my job. "Okay," I nod. "Can I walk you home later, though?"

"That would be great."

"Good. If you want to talk before then, I'll be in my office."

She places her hand on my chest, her eyes soft with gratitude. "I know where to find you," she says with a smile.

I meet Nicole back at her office when the workday is over. My car is in the library parking lot, but the walk to Nicole's apartment is so short, I figure I can easily come back for my car later when I go home. I can't stay too long, anyway, since Joan is waiting for me.

Nicole is quiet as we walk. Finally, I squeeze her hand and ask, "What are you thinking about?"

"The hearing," she admits.

"Yeah," I say. "What about it?"

"What it will be like. What we need to present. How Dr. Clifton will react."

"So, everything?"

"Pretty much," she answers with a sad chuckle. "But anyway, how was the rest of your day?"

I stop walking and turn her toward me, placing my hands on her upper arms. She's shutting me out again, just like almost every time we come close to having a deeper conversation about her anxiety. "Please don't," I say urgently. "Don't shut down and change the subject. Trust me, please. I'm here for you. Not to fix anything, but to listen. You said you wanted to be able to talk to me about what's going on in your head, so talk to me."

She searches my face and then nods once. "You're right," she says. "I know you have to get home to Joan, but if you have like thirty minutes? We can talk at my apartment."

I release a breath. "That sounds good," I agree. "Joan can wait a little longer."

When we get to her apartment and go inside, we settle on the couch.

"So…" I prompt.

Nicole takes a deep breath. "Okay," she says with a subdued grin. "Remember, you asked for this. I've been thinking about the hearing all day, and I realize that's going to be my downfall here."

"What do you mean?"

"Well, if I were sitting somewhere, in a meeting or something, and someone said they don't think graphic novels belong in the library, I would immediately start defending our program. I wouldn't stop to think or gather my thoughts, I would just argue." She shrugs.

"The extemporaneous speaking thing."

"Yeah. But with this hearing, I have two weeks to basically over-think everything: ruminate on what they could say and what I would say back and just exhaust myself really with all the possible out-comes. I'm … I'm imagining worst-case scenarios."

"Okay." I pause. "What's the worst-case scenario?"

She looks at me, and then hides her face in her hands. In a muffled voice, she manages, "I get fired." She drops her hands and tears gather in her eyes as she continues. "And don't tell me that getting fired is unlikely. I *know* that. But I'm having trouble *feeling* that."

I sit for a moment absorbing her words. I pull her closer and rub her back in small, soothing strokes. When I speak again, I choose my words carefully. "And what would happen if you get fired?"

"I'll have to find a new job, and it won't be around here, and I'll have to move away…" She sobs against me. "…and we'll break up, and I'll be alone forever."

I don't say anything—*not* trying to fix it—but I do move her so she's directly in my lap. I hold my arms around her tightly.

"I can't leave!" she says wetly into my chest. "I like it here. You're here." The misery in her voice guts me, but at the same time, my heart swells.

"You don't need to worry about me," I say. And then, singing a little, I add, "If you leave, I will follow. Anywhere that you tell me to."

It's part of the theme song for *Gilmore Girls*, and I'm hoping it makes her laugh, but instead her body stills in my arms, and she pulls her head back enough to look up into my face. The skin around her eyes is puffy from crying, her cheeks wet and her nose dripping, but her vulnerability is beautiful to me. Again, I'm struck with a feeling of awe. Nicole trusts me enough to fall apart in front of me. I get to be the one who holds and comforts her. My heart expands in my chest and suddenly, I'm fighting back tears of my own.

"You would leave your job to follow me?" she asks, her eyes wide and dazed.

My instinct is to joke again, something about the two-body problem maybe, but I quash it. I know she needs my certainty right now, something she can hold on to. She has to know where she stands with me. She's first. Always.

"Yes," I say simply, looking into her eyes, the emerald color drowning in tears.

She ducks her head, wiping her face with the back of her hand. She looks at the floor.

"Why?" she asks in the smallest murmur of a voice.

I put my index finger under Nicole's chin and gently lift her face toward mine. When I'm sure she's focused on me, I say quietly, "I love you, Nicole. You're it for me. I understand if you're not there yet, but I've wanted this for so long, wanted you for so long, there's no way I'd give you up now."

Her eyes fill with tears again, but the smile on her lips steadies the thumping of my heart.

"Adam ... I *am* there. I do ... I love you, too."

I lean down to kiss her—a slow, soft kiss I feel all the way down to my toes. Lifting my head, I grin at her.

"So, we're agreed? Whatever happens, no matter what happens, we're in this together. Partners?"

She lets out a giant breath of relief, her eyes shining. "That sounds perfect," she whispers. Then, with a teasing expression, she adds, "You know the lyric is 'where you lead' not 'if you leave'?"

I shrug. "Yeah, but my version fits better."

We spend the next two weeks preparing for the hearing. I write up all my data as talking points. Nicole contacts faculty members who incorporated the graphic novels into their spring term courses or ones she's already been talking to about their fall term classes. Amazingly, despite many of them being out of the office for the summer, five instructors offer to attend the hearing to speak about how the graphic novels are helping their students learn.

With a week until the meeting, Nicole, Herb, and I all sit in Herb's office, each working on a different piece of the presentation before we discuss fitting them together. I'm collating spreadsheets, humming quietly as I work.

But not as quietly as I thought because Herb glances up with a puzzled expression and asks, "Are you humming 'Eye of the Tiger'?"

"No," I lie, my face flushing.

Herb chuckles and shakes his head before turning back to his computer screen.

Listen, preparing for this hearing is as close as I'm ever going to come to a *Rocky Three* moment, and if I need to hum "Eye of the Tiger" to get pumped up, that's what I'm going to do. Just maybe only when I'm in my office by myself.

Herb looks up from the computer again. "I do feel a bit like Rocky, though," he says with a sheepish grin. "Training on the beach with Apollo Creed."

Nicole stops what she's doing and stares at him. Then she glances at me and frowns. "Who's Rocky?"

I groan and remind myself that though Nicole is only a few years younger than me, her parents are an entire generation younger than my parents.

"It's a movie," I tell her. "A movie series really. About a boxer. We'll watch it."

Nicole grimaces. "We don't have to."

"Uh-uh," I retort. "If I have to watch *Gilmore Girls*, you have to watch *Rocky*."

"You love *Gilmore Girls*," she returns, smirking.

Herb laughs and Nicole's eyes go wide. She forgot he was here. I did, too, to be honest.

"Sorry," we say at the same time.

Nicole clears her throat and takes a long drink from her water bottle. Herb looks at her sharply. "Are you okay?" he asks.

"Yeah, fine. My throat's just been a little dry."

By the end of that week, we have our talking points ready to go. I play the role of the board as Herb and Nicole rehearse a few times. Nicole's voice sounds a little scratchy from all the talking, but otherwise she's amazing. There's no way she doesn't convince the board and leadership of the value of the graphic novel collection.

I work the weekend and head home on Sunday evening feeling confident and optimistic. That feeling goes right out the window when Nicole texts me.

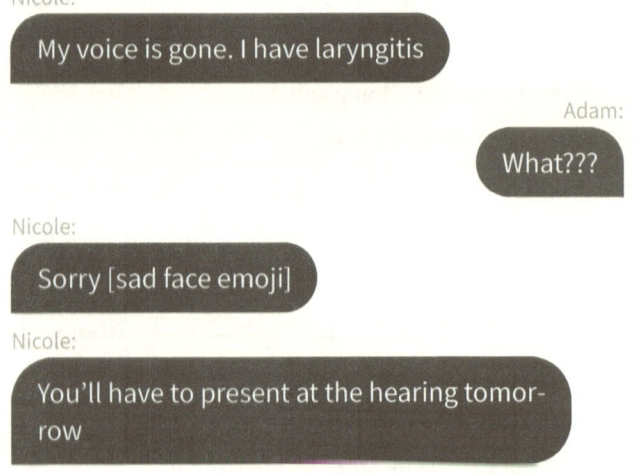

Nicole:
My voice is gone. I have laryngitis

Adam:
What???

Nicole:
Sorry [sad face emoji]

Nicole:
You'll have to present at the hearing tomorrow

Chapter Thirty-Four

Nicole

I sit on top of the desk in Adam's office as he paces the floor in front of me. Stupid throat. Of all the times to lose my voice, the day before a hearing with the college leadership about the future of my passion project is the worst possible. I'm not even sick! I had a cold a little over a week ago, so I guess my body's having a delayed reaction.

Adam's a mess. Even though he helped put together the talking points and watched me present them about half a dozen times, he hasn't had much opportunity to practice for himself. He's gone through the script twice, with me there each time to silently remind him about the breathing and grounding techniques I taught him before NLA. I'm pretty sure he's also puked twice, ducking out of the room pale and clammy and returning a while later looking even worse.

I can't even give him a pep talk because, you know, no voice. Herb tried to encourage Adam a little bit ago, came in and told him not to be nervous, that our data stood for itself. But the effect was pretty much ruined when Herb grimaced at me and held up both hands with his fingers crossed before leaving the room. So, Adam continues pacing, talking while he moves.

"I know what you're thinking," he says. "I got through the NLA presentation just fine, so why am I freaking out so much about this?" He pauses as if waiting for me to respond, and then remembers I can't. "I'll tell you why. The NLA presentation was low stakes. Yes, it was in front of a lot more people, but they were friendly people. People who wanted me to do well and were interested in what I had to say. But that won't happen today. These people will want to pick everything apart. They want me to fail, and they just might get their wish."

I wave my hand to get his attention. When he stops walking and looks at me, I sweep my hands toward myself while demonstrating a deep breath. Then, breathing out again, I move my hands away from my body in a sweeping motion.

"Breathe. Yeah, I need to breathe." He takes a deep breath in and out. I watch as his face relaxes just slightly. Then, he looks up at me again. "Ugh, but I really hate disappointing you. You're so incredible and I love you so much and the graphic novels mean so much to you. I don't want to be the one who messes it up."

I have a revelation then. I'm *not* worried about the graphic novel collection. I'm worried about Adam. Whatever happens after the hearing today, whether the graphic novels stay or go, whether *I* stay or go, I'll be fine. I've been through hard circumstances before, and I survived. When life throws challenges my way again, I'll survive those, too. But the thought is crystal clear in my mind: I want Adam by my side through all of it, all life's ups and downs.

I search across his desk and see his legal pad. I flip to a new page and, finding a pen, write him a note. I tear out the page, fold it into a paper airplane, and send it flying. The plane hits Adam right on the shoulder before bouncing to the ground. He gapes at me, then bends to pick it up. I mouth the words as he reads my rushed penmanship.

All that matters is that I love you and I believe in you. I don't care about the graphic novels; I care about you, and I know you can do it. Not for me or Herb or the library, but for yourself.

His body relaxes as he reads. I know when he gets to the end because he lifts his head and locks eyes with me. I can't speak with words, but I try my hardest to imbue all I'm feeling into the expression on my face. Adam reflects it all back to me, and for the first time all day, his lips kick up into a genuine smile. I stand and step forward to wrap my arms around his waist. His hands land against my back and cling to me.

"Thank you," he whispers into my ear. "I love you."

For good measure, I search up half a dozen encouraging memes and text them to Adam one by one until it's time for the hearing. The best one shows a skeptical-looking Jon Stewart with the caption, "I believe in you. But, I also believe in Bigfoot. So, don't get too excited." I know when Adam sees it while he, Herb, and I are walking across campus to the executive meeting room because he pulls his phone from his pocket, glances at the screen, and snorts out a laugh. His eyes are sparkling when they meet mine.

As the meeting is being called to order, I sneak a glance at Adam across the table. His face is pale, and he fidgets around in his chair, as if he can't get comfortable. As he's shifting, we make eye contact. He holds my gaze; my eyes are a waterfall and he's standing in the deluge. I soften my expression, letting down the walls of professionalism to let him see my love for him, my faith in him. Bit by bit, his body stills and relaxes. Color returns to his face. He looks into my eyes, absorbing my confidence, until Herb begins to speak.

The executive conference room is on the second floor of Harkness' historic main building. One wall is all glass windows showcasing the beautiful old-world streets and architecture of St. Anastasia. Most of the space in the room is filled with a massive oak conference table with high-back chairs on wheels surrounding it. The table seats twenty and every chair is occupied. In addition to the three of us from the library, I count six members of the board of trustees, including Dr. Wright who is a known library champion, five individuals from the college leadership team, including the provost Dr. Clifton, and the five faculty members who agreed to come speak in support of the library. In the corner sits another man who looks familiar, but I can't place him. I tune back into the meeting, turning my attention to my boss.

Herb introduces himself and gives a little background on the graphic novel project. He notes that it's a pilot, but a successful one so far.

"The two employees in charge of this project, Mr. Burgess and Ms. Delaney, are professional librarians who presented me with a well-thought out and researched proposal that I approved," Herb emphasizes. "Research in the literature and expert opinion maintain that graphic novels support critical thinking, engage students, and expand their worldviews."

I hide a smile. That line is directly from our project proposal, where I included references to back up the information.

Herb winds down and then it's Adam's turn. I hold my breath, even as I watch him release his. He pulls air in deeply through his nose, and then quietly blows it out through his mouth.

After a quick glance in my direction, he smiles and begins to talk.

"Mr. Wallen mentioned that our graphic novel collection has been successful, so I want to share some stats to show what he means. On the first day the collection became available in February, ten of the fifty titles were checked out right away, and since then, forty-five of the fifty have been checked out, some multiple times." Adam looks around the room and makes eye contact with the audience as he speaks. "So, clearly the collection is popular, but it's also an academic pursuit. Just a couple of months ago, Ms. Delaney and I presented this project at the National Library Association Annual Conference, which is the largest conference for librarians and in-formation professionals in the country. The organization accepted our presentation proposal out of the thousands they received. The audience during the presentation itself was standing room only."

Adam's voice is strong and steady. He commands the room, and his confidence is stupidly sexy. Before the meeting, he changed into a shirt and tie, leaving on his black chinos. The crisp white shirt clings to his arms and chest, and the burgundy skinny tie complements the honey brown of his eyes.

"Every book in this collection is owned by libraries at other colleges or universities," Adam continues. "Prestigious colleges and universities that we aspire to be like. This is something I checked on myself before we bought the titles. We've also assigned Library of Congress academic subject headings to each book, showing how they fit into the academic record. We currently have partnerships with courses being taught in the art department, the English department, the history department, and even the education department. In the last two months of the spring term, we had ten requests to expand the collection so that students have more options to choose from for their course projects. Faculty members from those courses are here today to support the collection."

Adam pauses and then invites each of the five faculty members in turn to speak about how the graphic novel collection has impacted learning in their courses, or how they plan to use the collection in the fall term. Dr. Calder from the art department even brought a selection of artwork from her students showing the influence of the graphic novels.

Several of the college leaders and board members are nodding, which I take as a good sign. A few even look impressed, which is an even better sign.

Then, Dr. Clifton speaks. "I just don't see how superhero comic books have anything to do with the learning we're trying to foster here at our institution. They're juvenile entertainment for children." He shifts in his seat. "Plus, the content of some of these cartoons is questionable. They don't align with the values of the college."

Childish entertainment? Questionable content? I catch myself gritting my teeth, and for all I know, literal steam may be rising from my head at this very moment. Laryngitis or not, I swallow to moisten my throat and prepare to take him down in my scratchy, barely audible voice.

Before I can say a word, a deep voice speaks calmly from the corner. "Robert, last I checked, you weren't an expert in which educational mediums have value."

Every head turns toward the sound. I now recognize the man as Dr. Henry Parker, the founder of Harkness College. From what I've heard, he's minimally involved in the running of the college as an advisor of sorts. Despite his official role, however, I know his opinions are still taken seriously at Harkness. I've seen him around, but I've never met him in person.

He continues, "My stance is that we've hired professionally-trained librarians to run the library, so let's trust them to do it."

The room is conspicuously silent for a few beats.

Then, Dr. Wright clears her throat. "Hear, hear," she says. "This meeting is a waste of time. I move that we drop this discussion and leave the matter up to the library to handle as they see fit."

"Second," says another board member.

"Fine," says the chairperson. "The motion on the floor is that this meeting be called to a close and that the library handle the graphic novel collection as they see fit. Any discussion?"

No one says anything, though I notice Dr. Clifton's nostrils flaring and the death grip he has on the arms of his chair.

"Hearing none, all in favor of the motion before us, please say 'aye'," the chairperson requests.

Of the six board of trustee members in attendance, nearly all resound with "aye."

"Any opposed?" the chairperson asks.

A lone Dr. Clifton crony on the board lifts his voice to say, "Nay."

"The motion passes. This meeting is adjourned."

I pump my fist under the table as everyone starts talking at once in side conversations with their neighbors. Some of the attendees stand to leave the room or approach colleagues sitting on the other side of the table.

I push back my chair and, shaking hands with the faculty members on either side of me, mouthing my thanks, stand. I slowly pick my way across the room to Adam. When I reach him, I fling my arms around his neck and whisper raspily in his ear, "You were amazing. And you look very handsome."

Adam's neck flushes red as he murmurs, "Thank you."

Breaking out of his arms, I make a beeline toward Dr. Parker to thank him. Adam follows me. When we reach him, I put out my hand and say in my hoarse voice, "Dr. Parker, I'm Nicole Delaney, one of the librarians—"

He smiles. "Oh, I know who you are. I've been hearing a lot about you."

Taken aback, I ask, "From who?"

"From Adam, of course."

I turn my head and see my boyfriend's sheepish expression. I raise my eyebrows in question.

"Well," I say to Dr. Parker. "Thank you for your support today. It really means a lot."

Dr. Parker nods his head decisively. "I'm happy to help." Then, grinning at Adam, he says, "Come see me later this week. I need you to catch me up."

We find Herb next, smiling in his usual affable way. He pats Adam on the back and beams, "I'm proud of you! Excellent work, Adam."

Adam smiles. "Thank you," he says. Then he leans closer to Herb. "I have to know. Is it true? That you were in the CIA?"

Herb leans in, and Adam's face lights up. Herb winks and then whispers, "If I told you, I'd have to kill you."

Adam groans.

After the hearing, there's not much time left in the workday, and neither Adam nor I can focus on anything else anyway. We sit in my office with the door open in case anyone needs to find us, and even though it will surely cost me in the coming days, I risk straining my already-thin voice to rehash the day's events with Adam.

"I can't believe you had an ace up your sleeve the whole time and didn't tell me." I shake my head at Adam in mock offense.

"What do you mean?" he asks.

"Dr. Parker," I say. "Did you know he was going to support us?"

"I didn't realize he'd be at the meeting, but I'm not surprised."

"How do you know him, anyway?"

"Well, we're sort of friends," Adam says tentatively.

"Friends?" I ask dubiously.

"Yeah. We started talking about his dog one day, and now we talk all the time." He shrugs. "He kind of reminds me of my dad."

I raise my eyebrows. "And you talk to him about me?"

Adam smiles, brushing hair off my face. "He's given me some advice along the way."

"Good advice?"

"Very good, based on the outcome." And then, despite his usual no-PDA-at-work rule, Adam leans forward and kisses me softly on the mouth. Testing the boundaries of his good mood, I wrap my arms around his neck, pulling him closer and deepening the kiss. Rather than pull away, which I half expect, his arms encircle my waist and pull me flush against him. Minutes pass that could be hours. Finally, I break the kiss.

Resting my head against his chest, I sigh, "I love you."

"I love you, too," he says.

I reach up to give him another peck and then tease, "Look at you! One victory and you become an office floozy. I never thought I'd see the day."

Adam chuckles and shakes his head. "Your fault," he says. "I'd do pretty much anything for you."

Epilogue

Six Months Later

It's mid-December, and the lights glow once again in the trees and on buildings around downtown St. Anastasia. I have a special date planned for Nicole tonight and though December weather in north Florida can be wildly inconsistent—anywhere from fifty to eighty degrees—I'm pleased that tonight should be on the cool side. Enough to give the air a more Christmassy vibe and allow me to feel cozy rather than sweltering while walking around outside in a sweater.

We spent Thanksgiving in Texas a couple of weeks ago. I met Olivia, the only member of Nicole's family I hadn't yet. Mrs. Delaney—Amy—was so thrilled to have everyone together (including a surprise guest that added quite a bit of drama to the family dynamics, but that's a story for another day) that she had Mr. Delaney—Ben—put the Christmas tree up early, and we all decorated it together. Nicole loved being with her family, and I loved being there with her, seeing where she grew up and teasing her about her untouched childhood bedroom.

Now Parker Library is officially closed for the holidays, and we don't have to be back at work until January. Nicole and I will be driving down to Naples together to spend Christmas with my mom, and then flying to Texas just after Christmas to see her family for a few days. Other than that, we're both staying around town and spending our free time together.

So, to start our winter break off with a bang, we have this special date tonight. I drive to Nicole's apartment and arrive promptly at six o'clock. Before getting out of the car, I wipe my palms against the jeans I'm wearing. Despite the cool air and how comfortable I am in a dark gray shawl collar sweater with a blue T-shirt underneath, my hands are damp. I reach up and fidget with my glasses, and then absently pat my pocket through the jeans.

I bounce up the steps and knock on Nicole's door. As usual, it takes her a minute to open the door, and even then, my view is of the back of her head as she walks away from me toward her bedroom.

"Give me just a couple more minutes," she says. "I'm almost ready to go."

"Wear something nice, but warm," I call after her. "We're going to be outside."

"Got it!" I hear from behind her closed door.

I grin and settle onto the couch. I run through the plan for tonight. Dinner first. Then browsing down Cannon Street, including hot chocolate. And then a walk by the waterfront. Sounds simple, but I'm more nervous about this date than I have probably ever been before about anything. Except public speaking. Still not on my list of favorites. I pat my thigh again, feeling the hard metal of the ring in my pocket.

Nicole steps out of her room just then, and I stand, practically leaving my jaw behind. Nicole's dressed in a deep red, long-sleeved sweater dress that looks like it wraps around her in a complicated way, tied with a sash. The dress hits just above her knees and stretches tight around the curves of her hips. On her feet, she wears dark brown leather boots that stretch all the way up to her knees. In between the boots and dress, I catch the slightest glimpse of black tights. She cut her hair short—she says it's called a pixie cut—just before Thanksgiving in an effort to return it to its natural blonde color, at least for now. I've already seen her scrolling through colorful styles on her phone, so we'll see how long the blonde lasts. Tonight, her hair looks ruffled in a soft way that makes me want to run my fingers through the strands.

My gaze finally lands on her face which is watching me with a smirk.

"Close your mouth," she says.

I snap my jaw closed, and then open it again to say, "You look gorgeous. I mean ... wow."

"Thank you. I could tell you liked the outfit from the way your eyes turned into hearts, and your tongue was hanging out."

"My tongue was not hanging out," I protest. "And I like *you*, not just the outfit."

She laughs. "I know."

She steps forward and wraps her arms around my neck. I run my hands up her arms and, oh my God, this dress is so soft. Seriously, is it made from bunnies? I'll be hard-pressed not to have my hands all over her all night. I move my arms to encircle her waist.

"You look really handsome," she says into my ear.

I think again about the plans I've made for the evening and consider chucking them all to stay here on the couch with her. But no. Tonight is special.

We walk to the rooftop restaurant where we ate on our first date. The host leads us to a reserved table right on the edge, where we have a perfect view of the lights along the water. Even better, we're right under a patio heater so we can enjoy the night air without freezing to death.

"Do you remember the last time we came here?" I ask.

Nicole beams. "Our first date."

I nod. "You changed my life forever that night," I say. "You were everything I wanted, but I never thought I could have you."

Nicole's eyes fill with tears as she leans forward to take my hand over the table. "And you were everything I didn't know I needed." She shakes her head. "How were you so patient with me?"

I chuckle. "Relentless optimism."

We eat our dinner, chatting and laughing. As we finish up, I ask her, "Ready for some more walking?"

She smiles, and we head toward Cannon Street. We pass the candy shop where we got ice cream on our first date. I see her peek inside, so I say, "I figured it's too cold for ice cream tonight, so how about hot chocolate?"

She grins. "It's never too cold for ice cream, but hot chocolate works, too."

Next door to the candy shop is a little café that sells gelato, sandwiches, and some of the best hot chocolate you can have. They call it double truffle hot chocolate and it's rich, creamy, and delicious.

I buy two cups, and we sit outside on our bench. "Do you remember what happened here?" I ask Nicole.

"Adam, sweetie, you know our first date wasn't even a year ago. How bad do you think my memory is?"

I sigh. "Can you please just humor me?" I sweep my hand to punctuate the question and knock Nicole's cup of hot chocolate to the ground. The lid pops off when it hits the concrete and the drink spills into a splotchy brown puddle. I drop my head into my palm and groan.

"Hold that thought," I say. "I'll be right back." I duck into the café to get Nicole a new cup of hot chocolate.

When I sit back down next to her, I ask, "Now, where were we?"

Her mouth forms a cheeky smile. "I was humoring you."

I rub the back of my neck. "Right," I say. "Then can you, please?"

She smiles at me sweetly. "Yes, of course I remember this bench. This is where we had our first kiss."

"That was the most amazing kiss of my life," I start, holding up a hand when she opens her mouth to protest. "Of my life up to that point," I clarify. "Every time I see you, you are more beautiful. And every time I kiss you, I know I'll never be able to stop kissing you for the rest of my life. Kissing you is like coming alive."

She rests her head against my shoulder. "I never realized how safe I could feel being vulnerable with someone else until you," Nicole says. "Kissing you feels like security and freedom all at once."

I kiss her forehead, then trail down to her lips. We share a long, sweet kiss. When we break apart, I nuzzle the side of her face with my nose, and, in a low voice, say "I love you," in her ear.

Then, I stand and pull Nicole to her feet. "More walking," I say. "Grab your cup."

She chuckles. "You really do have a plan, don't you? You are a man on a mission tonight."

I take her hand, and we walk south on Cannon Street to the town square, which is a small green space with tall oak trees decked out in white, twinkling lights. In the center is a giant Christmas tree, ringed at the base with "presents" made of plywood and paint. We stand for a while, sipping our hot chocolate and admiring the lights. At Nicole's insistence, we take a picture in front of the Christmas tree, smiling and holding up our hot chocolate cups.

From there, we cross to the waterfront side of the street near the Fiel Firme Bridge, a drawbridge that connects downtown St. Anastasia to its barrier islands, which also glows with lights. We walk alongside the water away from the bridge on a raised sidewalk. Black metal posts every five feet are connected to each other by heavy iron chains, blocking pedestrians from the edge of the wall that drops down into the water. This time of year, tubes of white lights are woven into the iron chains, creating a luminous effect.

The farther we walk from the bridge, the quieter the sidewalk becomes. We still have groups of other people around us—the holiday light display in St. Anastasia is a major tourist destination November through January—but the night feels stiller and more peaceful.

"Let's sit here," I say to Nicole, nudging her toward a cement bench on the sidewalk overlooking the water, the bridge in the distance. As we sit, a breeze whips past us. Nicole snuggles into my side, and I wrap my arm around her shoulders.

Moment of truth. I rub my sweaty palms against my jeans again. I place a gentle kiss on Nicole's temple, and then slide off the bench, onto one knee in front of her.

After I retrieve the ring from my pocket and hold it hidden in one hand, I take Nicole's hands with my other. She's staring at me, lips slightly parted and a soft expression on her face. She leans forward, rapt.

I clear my throat. "I've been telling you all night how I feel about you." My voice cracks. "How much I love you. So now I only have one thing left to say: Nicole, will you marry me?"

I hold up the ring, which has a white gold band designed to look like vines around the setting, tiny diamonds in the leaves. The stone is a round cut emerald the same color as Nicole's eyes.

Nicole, a glowing smile on her lips and tears rolling down her cheeks, whoops, "Yes!"

I slip the ring onto her finger, and she holds out her hand, admiring it. I stand and pull her up with me, bundling her into my arms. She pulls my head down and finds my lips with hers.

A loud burst of cheering and clapping interrupts our embrace. To my embarrassment, we lift our heads to see about ten people watching us. Several are holding up phones.

"I didn't realize we had an audience," I murmur in her ear.

A few of the onlookers toss out their congratulations. Nicole leaves my arms and approaches the ones with their phones out. I hear her asking to see what they filmed and for them to send it to her. I just shake my head.

Later, as we're walking back to her apartment, I ask, "Were you surprised?"

She glances up at my face and squeaks, "Yes," but she's a terrible liar.

"Really?" I ask with a frown.

She puffs out a laugh, hugging my arm. "Adam, you've been emphasizing all week that tonight is a 'special' date. So, I kind of had a feeling."

Oh. Yeah, now that I think back, I did use the word "special" several times.

Nicole stops walking and turns to me, placing a hand on either side of my face. "Not surprised," she says, a smile as bright as the twinkling lights surrounding us overtaking her face, "but so, so happy."

Bonus Epilogue

Still curious about that calendar photo of Adam that's out there somewhere? Download the bonus epilogue!

https://BookHip.com/TANTVJ
W

Or visit **www.juliemilo.com** and sign up for my newsletter!

Acknowledgements

This book has been a long time coming. Not "a long time coming" in that it took me a long time to get it down from first idea to last page, but a long time coming in that I've wanted to write books my entire life. So for this first book, at least, I need to acknowledge people all along the way in my school and college years who encouraged my love of writing. Teachers mostly. I had one teacher in elementary school who told me that she would look forward to seeing my name on the cover of a book in the book store one day. When I decided to write under my maiden name instead of my married name, that memory was one that came to mind. Of course, my parents were also always supportive and often made sacrifices for me to follow my passions.

In college, I majored in English with a minor in creative writing, and though I learned so many valuable things about literature and writing from those courses, I think they burned me out on creative writing. We read and studied brilliant works of literature that were so emotional—sad, angry, angsty. I came out of it thinking that I could either have a happy life or write good fiction, not both. It was an obvious choice for me. I spent the next fifteen years of my life focusing on building a career I love as an academic librarian, including a lot of scholarly writing, and growing my own family. I'm not exaggerating when I say I wrote almost nothing creative during that time.

And then I started reading sweet romantic comedies and became addicted. I ravenously read everything written by authors like Emma St. Clair, Jenny Proctor, Melanie Jacobson, Julie Christianson, Savannah Scott, Jennifer Peel, Cindy Steel, Katie Bailey, Kate Watson, Kourtney Keisel, Leah Brunner, Laura Langa, Courtney Walsh, Brittany Larsen, Becky Monson, and Jen Atkinson (among others). I was a happier reader than I had been since probably middle school.

Then, one day, I literally woke up with an idea for a sweet romantic comedy of my own. I wrote down what was in my head, and then wrote some more, and then I was shyly telling my husband, "I think I'm writing a book." *Love in the Stacks* is the result, and hopefully just the beginning.

Along the way, I had helpful critique partners in Bonda, Unnichan, and Anastasiia. I met them in a Facebook group for romance writers and they gave me some great feedback on my story. I made quite a few edits based on their suggestions.

Then, I recruited some fantastic beta readers in Rachel, Elaine, Shalene, Andrea, and Camille. They were readers, pure and simple, and that helped me a lot to see some areas of the story where the average reader would be confused or need more information. I made quite a few edits based on their feedback.

In an endeavor like producing a book–there's a lot more to it than just writing!–it really is "who you know," at least it was for me.

For example, when I knew I wanted to incorporate graphic novels into the story, I reached out to a former colleague, Shawn, for their help with what kinds of comics a character like Nicole might read, and what she might recommend to a character like Adam. When I wanted to invest in beautiful, original cover art, I reached out to an artist friend, Sydney, who agreed to stretch a bit beyond her normal comfort zone to create an adorable cover that truly captures how I see Nicole and Adam in my head. And when I realized I needed an author website and sent an SOS out to my Facebook friends, a friend from when I was a teenager, Charlie, offered to help. Fun side note: Charlie and I worked together in high school on *Impressions Teen Magazine*, a creative teen program sponsored by our city's rec department. I wrote for the magazine, and Charlie worked on layout and graphic design. And thank you to Robin, who helped me with a developmental/line edit for this book.

I described a number of real memes and cartoons throughout this book, and while the provenance of specific memes can be difficult to ascertain, I want to acknowledge the people who put in the creative work to bring Adam and Nicole's favorite memes to life. I describe two comic strip style cartoons that absolutely have known creators. The reading-on-a-plane cartoon Adam sends Nicole in Chapter Nine (his first text to her!) is by Mark Parisi at www.offthemark. com. The goldfish cartoon Adam sends Nicole in Chapter Fifteen is by Liz Climo at www.thelittleworldofliz.com.

Finally, the people who keep me going throughout everything I do are my own little family. My son, Gabriel, came up with the idea for the (not real) book *The Secret of Hangar 57*, which Adam teases Nicole about in Chapter Twenty-Two. My daughter, Ana, is one of my biggest fans. She kept asking me for copies of my author business card and, come to find out, she had been giving them to all the teachers at school so they would know about my book! (If you are one of her teachers reading this, I swear she did that on her own. I didn't ask her to!). And my husband, Andy, whose mantra is "whatever you need," at least when it comes to me. I couldn't ask for a better partner.

And thank you to YOU, readers! I hope you enjoyed it. And if you did, I would love it if you would leave a review on Amazon, Goodreads, or another bookish platform. Reviews truly make a huge difference for indie authors, especially debut indie authors like me!

About the Author

Julie Milo spends most of her time reading and writing. When she's not reading and writing scholarly stuff for her day job, she's reading romance, nonfiction, and literary fiction for fun. She writes sweet/kisses only romantic comedies.

Julie was raised, but not born, in Florida where she started dictating stories to her parents before she even knew how to write. By kindergarten she was writing and illustrating picture books and subjecting her classmates to read alouds at school.

Julie currently lives on the Gulf coast of Florida with her thoughtful husband, two amazing children, and two dogs (one delightful pit bull and one very energetic black lab). She loves dessert and hates cold weather.

You can learn more about Julie and her books at www.juliemilo .com.